MW00533062

Tremendous
Cover
Art!
Thanks!

Other books by Jack McGuigan

Agents of Paradox

Dog Walker

Dog Walker II: Shadow Pack

Dog Walker III: Wedding Siege

NANOLAND

JACK McGUIGAN

Gorilla House

CHICAGO

GORILLA HOUSE
GorillaHouseBooks.com
jack@gorillahousebooks.com

Cover Illustration by Juho Huttunen.
artstation.com/northernhermit

Map and Comic Illustration by Manoela Costa.
manoelacosta.com

Edited by Merino Toss.

Special Thanks to Alex Hoffmeyer, Ryan Linich, Mike Pokryfke, and Brian Wessel.

ISBN 978-0-9992982-2-0 (hardcover)
ISBN 978-0-9992982-6-8 (paperback)

For the critters, eventually.

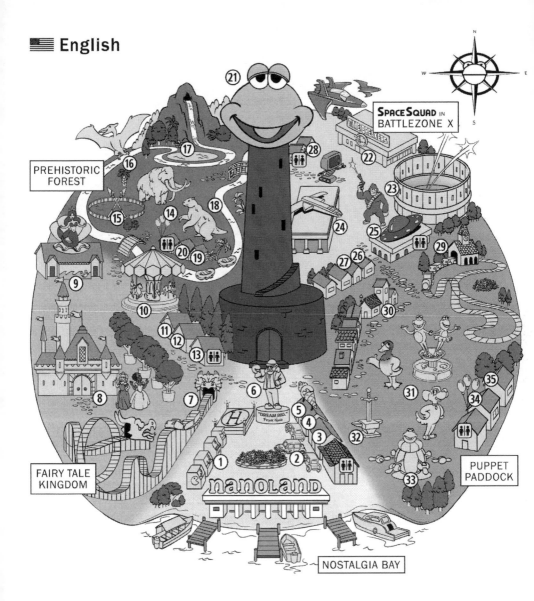

nanoland
2024 GUIDEMAP

NOSTALGIA BAY

1. Nostalgia Bay Arcade ⊘
Your favorite Nano games from the 80s and 90s. *Free-to-play with Nanopass.*

2. Classic CARnival ⊚
Featuring Jungle Jack's "Hot Jalopy" until 9/21. *See Nano Auto Review for news and upcoming vehicles.*

▲ 3. Gift Emporium ⊞
One-Stop Shopping Destination for Nano Character gifts and souvenirs.

4. Nostalgic Theater ⊘
Feature Films throughout the day in glorious 35mm. *Upgraded seats available via Nanopass. Check sign for showtimes.*

⑪ 5. Retro Refreshments
Hand-scooped ice cream, all-beef franks and ice-cold cola. **L S**

6. Frank Nano Statue ⊚
"Dream Big."

FAIRY TALE KINGDOM

7. Danger Dragon ⊘ ▲
⍊ 38"/97cm. Race down the back of a living, breathing dragon. *Expectant mothers should not ride.*

8. Princess Photo Pavilion ⊚
Meet some of your favorite Nano Princesses!

9. Mermaid Cove ⊘ ⊚
Journey below the waves with Monica and all her friends on a musical adventure. *Mermaid tails available via Nanopass.*

10. Fantasy Carousel ⊘
A traditional merry-go-round featuring creatures of myth and legend.

▲ 11. Treasures & Trinkets
On-trend apparel and souvenirs for Nano fans of all ages.

⑪ 12. Winnifred's Royal Tea Party
Character dining with Nano Princesses. *Separately priced experience.* **B L D**

⑪ 13. Enchanted Eats ⊞
Sate thy magical hunger with these medieval treats.
B - Coffee and Pastries
L - Sandwiches, Salads and Soups
D - French-inspired dining

PREHISTORIC FOREST

14. Meet the Mammoths ⊚
Long-lost beasts walk among us!

15. Savage Stunt Show
Closed for Reimagining.

16. Pterosaur Fliers ⊘ ▲
Sail high above the trees on an ancient winged reptile.

17. Plummet Falls ⊘ ▲
⍊ 40"/102cm. Plunge down a real waterfall on this thrilling flume ride.

18. Big Sam Sloth ⊚ ▲
Meet Jungle Jack's best friend, the megatherium known as Sam. *Note: "Ride the Sloth" is a separately priced experience.*

▲ 19. Megafauna Memorabilia
Gifts, apparel and collectables for adventurers.

⑪ 20. Big Sam's Burger Slam ⊞
Burgers, chicken nuggets, salads and kids' meals. *"Jungle Juice" 21+.* **L D S**

FROG TOWER

21. Frankie Frog ⊚
Watch the top of the tower for news and updates from the World's Favorite Frog.

Hey-yah!
Hey-yah!

BATTLEZONE X

22. Time Breakers: The Ride ⊘ ▲
⍊ 40"/102cm. Zoom across eras on the greatest ride of all time.

22. Cosmic Coliseum ⊘ ▲
Slap on your blasters and fight for the fate of the galaxy. *New scores posted daily. Must be 9+ to compete. "Star swords" available via Nanopass.*

24. Sky Wing Racers ⊘ ▲
⍊ 38"/97cm. Fly the fastest ship in the cosmos as you race across the stars. *Upgrades available via Nanopass.*

⑪ 25. Bombadape's Battle Burritos
Fine Mexican cuisine made fresh by the Cosmic Ape. **L D**

▲ 26. The Blast Zone
Toys, gifts and apparel from every galaxy in the nega-quadrant.

▲ 27. Berk's Workshop ⊚
Build-Your-Own cosmic blaster with Berk MacEntyre.

⑪ 28. Celestial Cantina ⊞
Enjoy exotic meals and treats that are out of this world. *"Space Beverages" 21+.*
B L D S

PUPPET PADDOCK

29. Choo Choo Railroad ⊞ ▲
Board a rustic freight train with Frankie as your conductor.

30. Frogville Theater ⊚
The laughs never stop at this all-day puppet theater. *Musical revues on the hour.*

31. Meet the Nano Friends ⊚
Frankie, Dingus and all their friends. See *sign for character times.*

32. King Arthur's Sword ⊚
A new Prince or Princess of Nanoland is crowned each day. *8 and under.*

⑪ 33. Frankie's Froggerflies
Shrink down and soar over the paddock aboard Frankie's favorite treat.

⑪ 34. Frannie's Pizzazzy Pizza ⊞
Fine Italian dining, ice cream, cotton candy and more. *Birthday Room must be reserved in advance.* **L D S**

▲ 35. Mad Mallard's Mad Mart
Bring Frankie and his friends home as toys, souvenirs and apparel.

LEGEND

⊘ Nanopass experience available
▲ Physical Considerations
⍊ Minimum Height Requirement
⊚ Photo Opportunity

⊞ **Restrooms**

▲ **Shopping**

⑪ **Dining**
See Nano Eating Guide for dietary restriction and pricing details.
B - Breakfast   **L** - Lunch
D - Dinner   **S** - Snack

A MESSAGE FROM FRANK

"Dreams are just memories you haven't yet made, and they always come true at Nanoland. So do me a favor and dream big."

- FRANK NANO

Map and Comic Artwork by
Manoela Costa
ManoelaCosta.com

TRANSPORTATION

Ferryboat Service
is available to the Transportation and Ticket Center in Naples, FL.

Personal Watercraft Service
is available to Frankie's Lillypad Resort, StarSquad Galactic Oasis and Nanohaven Royal Suites. See front desk for reservations and availability.

Nostalgia Bay Helipad
is available for approved aircraft via reservation only. Please contact Nano Aerial Operations Department for assistance.

nanoland

FRANK NANO PROUDLY PRESENTS

Frogged Up

Have you ever kissed a frog?

Boy, I sure did.

That's me.

Dee Green. Age 16.

Oldest of six girls.

DEE!

GO CHECK THE TRAPS!

≥sigh≤

All my life, I wanted to be a **princess**.

But I was a **frog catcher** like my parents.

It was never going to happen.

Until...

Greetings! I am Prince Francois Girard, heir to the Grenoillian throne.

A witch has cursed me into this dreadful form, but a **kiss** from a beautiful girl will change me back.

Free me and I will grant your every desire.

Tell you what, frog face.

You make me a **princess** and you've got a deal.

We kissed.

He was slimy. It was gross.

There was a flash of light, and wouldn't you know it...

1

"I became a princess!"

Princess Dee paused for a reaction as her sky-blue dress twinkled under the hot lights. The little girl stared past her, focusing entirely on Princess Winnifred, the blond woman in the pink dress posing with a different girl on the other side of the room. This kid wasn't listening. They never did.

"Alright, baby," Princess Dee pointed the girl at the photographer. She grinned widely, displaying as many perfect white teeth as she could. "Smile for the camera."

A flash of light, and the girl gave Dee a quick one-arm hug before running over and scanning her nanoband against the sensor on the photographer's camera.

The girl tugged her mother's sleeve. "Can I see Winnifred now?"

Dee sighed through her photogenic smile. Her wig tingled. She reached up to poke it before stopping herself. Princess Winnifred gave Dee a sly wink before beckoning the girl over.

The Frog Princess was envisioned as a pixelated remake of one of the more obscure Nano Princess films of the 1970s. Through the latter half of the nineties, the press paid much attention to the fact that Princess Dee would be the first black Nano Princess. The studio brought in respected black thinkers to consult on the script. They paired one of Frank Nano's original team of puppeteers with a young black filmmaker as co-directors. The film was primed and ready to be a big blockbuster summer release. Then the younger director quit.

Then the older director quit.

Three more came and went, and when it was eventually released in 2003, Princess Dee's movie—by then retitled *Frogged Up* in an attempt to appeal to young boys—opened at #8 at the box office, eventually earning two million dollars on a sixty million budget. The film was an enormous bomb. Critics complained of derivative songs and stale romance. Audiences mostly flocked to the big-budget superhero sequel opening that same weekend. At any rate, the film was overshadowed six months later with the release of *Princess Bop*: an even hipper, fresher take on the Nano Princess brand starring the pinker, blonder Princess Winnifred.

In Nanoland, the two characters were always paired together in the meet-and-greet in the Princess Photo Pavilion, with Dee first in line. Since no child on this green Earth had seen *Frogged Up*, Dee usually had to pitch her entire movie to each guest. The higher-ups would surely have phased out the character by now, except that after twenty years, the Frank Nano Company had added exactly zero new black princesses to their stable. Princess Dee filled a quota.

"What the what?!" Princess Winnifred squealed upon seeing the girl's *Princess Bop* t-shirt. "Me on a shirt? Hashtag epic!"

The parents laughed. Dee glanced up at the clock mounted discretely above the entrance. She tapped her wrist.

"Sorry, kids!" Babs, Dee's host, turned to the guests, "The princesses need to take a five-minute break for magical tea time, but they'll be right back, ok?"

"Awww!" groaned dozens of children and several adults.

Every costumed character at Nanoland had a host to deal with guests while allowing the performers to stay in character. That was Babs. She'd been there for decades, and she was awesome.

She guided Dee around the corner of the stage to a dimly lit hallway, a dead end with no doors. The two of them stepped into, then through, a blank wall, slowing down to allow the cold, metallic nanobots time to bio-scan them for employee DNA.

As the pixels parted, they entered a small behind-the-scenes dressing room. There were two mirrors, two vanities, and two stools, as well as a single mini-fridge full of water. The only light was directly above the mirrors. They kept the rest of the room dark so that the glow wouldn't bleed through the pixelated wall.

"Are you ok, Alicia?" Babs said. "You seem off."

"Wig's on the fritz again." Alicia Amandi removed her Princess Dee wig and shook out the dead nanobots. Various sensors glowed on the underside. "I think it's burning my scalp."

"They need to update that thing," Babs said. "Most of the wigs are fully pixelated now."

"Hey, Alicia." Princess Winnifred twirled as she entered the room. Her long blond hair dissolved from her head, drifting in a golden wave before reforming on a mannequin on her vanity. Savannah scratched at her pink crew cut. "I think you slipped out of character for a beat back there. Y'all gotta be careful with that."

Alicia flipped her off without looking. Pasha, the alternate Princess Dee, was at the other vanity, fixing her makeup in a blue dress identical to Alicia's. They all had dresses. The wig was the expensive part.

Pasha's hands shook as she applied her mascara. This was only her second week, and the last few shifts hadn't gone so great. Alicia put her hand on the woman's arm, steadying it. They smiled at each other in the mirror.

Winnifred's host, Greg, was the last to enter. He handed Savannah a vape pen, and she took a long drag. Flavored steam clouded up from her face and into a vent on the ceiling.

She looked around the room. "Where's Britt?"

"She quit this morning," Greg said, yawning as he scrolled on his tablet. "Something about her mom being sick. You've got a double shift."

"Oh," Pasha said. "That's awful."

"Hell no, it ain't." Savannah checked herself in the mirror. "More money for me. We don't get paid enough to get all weepy about people's moms. You know you'd make more bank working at a gas station, right?"

Mild terror flashed across Pasha's face. "Gas station?"

"Hey." Alicia turned Pasha to face her. "Ignore her. Look at me."

Pasha's eyes met hers. Alicia picked up a liner and touched up Pasha's brows.

"Have you ever kissed a frog?" Alicia said.

Pasha nodded. "Boy, I sure did."

"Let me hear the voice."

Pasha repeated it, this time a little higher. "*Boi, ah sure dihd.*"

"You're not British. You're Southern. For some reason. *Boy, ah shoah dayd.* Talk like Savannah."

"Piss off, darlin'," Savannah said.

Pasha closed her eyes and took a breath. She tried again. "*Boy, ah shoah dayd.*"

"*Girl...*" Alicia slid the Princess Dee wig onto Pasha's head and adjusted it into place. "You got this. You were a princess before you got here. All you gotta do is show them. Are you a princess?"

Pasha nodded. "I'm a princess."

"What's that, Dee Green?"

"*Ah'm a preyncess.*"

"Damn right." Alicia turned to her host. "I'm gonna go eat."

"You're back on at two," Babs said. "Bring me a soda, will you?"

Alicia ducked through another invisible door and entered a plain concrete hallway lit with fluorescent lights. She passed a laundry cart and a few members of the stage crew in their green and gray jumpsuits, who all nodded politely.

Here at Nanoland, there were two levels to the backstage area. The theme park guests experienced was one story up from ground level. The top level of the backstage ran inside the facades and fake storefronts, winding around the edges of the property, with lots of hidden windows giving employees an insider's view of the park and its attractions. The bottom level contained all the maintenance equipment, laundry machines, trash removal, and everything else needed to run the most popular theme park on Earth. There were moving sidewalks, so the cast and crew could zip across the island in a hurry. After a week, most people took the bottom floor everywhere, but Alicia still liked to walk upstairs, where she could see all the guests enjoying themselves. She loved Nanoland. What would be the point of working there if she didn't love it?

She stopped at a window in the Photo Pavilion overlooking the Fairy Tale Kingdom. The line was already building up after only five minutes of break. Those five minutes would add thirty minutes of wait times to the queue. There were always more guests, but princesses needed to eat.

Danger Dragon roared past next door, hurling guests at 155 miles per hour along pixel-coated steel tracks that rose and fell rhythmically as the dragon-shaped roller coaster breathed. The steel beast curled its tail in a backward loop to guide the cart back toward its flame-spewing head. Below, the Fantasy Carousel rotated guests riding realistic pegasuses and unicorns in a pleasant, leisurely circle. That was more

Alicia's speed. The coaster made her sick.

"Hey-yah hey-yah, park guests!"

Frog Tower, visible from anywhere in the park, loomed overhead. Four stories of blackened steel, made to look taller with forced perspective, were topped off with an enormous, glowing, semi-transparent puppet head. Frankie Frog, Frank Nano's first puppet and most famous creation, grinned as he spoke, his deep nasal voice echoing across dozens of speakers.

"Shake your tails and shine your scales!" The frog's translucent mouth flapped like a giant hand was inside it. "Head on over to Mermaid Cove to see the latest reimagining of one of the Frank Nano Company's most beloved intellectual properties! Mermaid Monica's getting a makeover! Yaaay!"

Alicia turned. Crowds gathered around Mermaid Cove as it shimmered. The walls of the ride building rippled like water, and the statues and boats surrounding the ride changed ever so slightly, becoming a little more dilapidated and realistically weathered.

Mermaid's Tale came out in the early nineties, part of the second wave of princess movies released in the wake of Frank Nano's unexpected death in 1989. The film had been a big hit for the company, with then-state-of-the-art effects, combining the latest in animatronic puppets and Nano's patented nanobot pixels. But, like every successful property in the back catalog, it had a modern remake coming out, and it was time to update the attraction.

Mermaid Monica herself, a twelve-foot statue outside the ride, also rippled. Silvery mist shifted across her surface like fairy dust. When it cleared, the figure was slightly different. The mermaid's costume had gained a greater level of fine detail, and her face and hair had changed to match the actress from the new movie. This once-in-a-lifetime event had occurred every day for the last month.

Alicia strolled on. The sweeping orchestral film score playing on hidden speakers transitioned to tribal drums and chants as she entered the canopy of the Prehistoric Forest. Trees, vines, glaciers, and various culturally-nonspecific ruins dotted the landscape. Dinosaurs—smaller ones—walked amongst the guests alongside extinct mammals like wooly mammoths and rhinos, as well as lightly anthropomorphized versions of living animals like chimpanzees and tigers. Each of these creatures was an advanced animatronic in a pixelated shell. The pixels handled faces, skin, and any other minute details the robot would

5

struggle with.

Big Sam, a gigantic Pleistocene ground sloth, loped lazily across the grounds with a dozen children on his back. He was always a favorite with guests. Above him, pterodactyls and big bats flapped and soared, also carrying riders.

A mechanical roar reverberated across the jungle as waves rose above the trees. Plummet Falls had just ejected the latest group of guests down its hundred-foot waterfall drop. Water splattered Alicia's window as the small boat came crashing into the landing lagoon. A couple of crew members she didn't recognize giggled as they stood gawking out the window in front of her. A boy and a girl. High school kids. New hires.

"You should see this place at night," Alicia said. "The leaves are all bioluminescent."

"Wow," said the girl. She noticed Alicia's dress, and her eyes lit up. "Are you Princess Dee?"

"Not until my break's over." Alicia pointed. "Watch the elephant."

The kids turned just as the wooly mammoth raised its trunk and sprayed water on everyone surrounding it. The new hires laughed. Alicia continued on.

The background music went from tribal drums to a mix of orchestra and eighties synth as Alicia entered Battlezone X. Neon lights flashed as guests flew past on hovercycles, battling with glowing swords and laser rifles available at kiosks throughout the area. Guests were encouraged to aim for each other's nanobands to score points. An ever-changing scoreboard tallied the day's totals. The top ten were usually lifers, guests with season passes who came here every day to battle in the Cosmic Coliseum.

An unusually sizable crowd had formed in a dark corner of the Battlezone. It seemed like it was mostly older men, and it took Alicia a second to remember what was over there. Tucked in the back of the area was an old-fashioned indoor simulator ride based on *Time Breakers*, Frank Nano's directorial debut. Time Breakers: The Ride was being retired today under orders from the new CEO, who had announced it in a press release weeks earlier. The future depicted in both the movie and the ride had passed by nine years ago. Alicia smiled. She liked that ride, but it was probably time for it to go.

She walked along the interior path behind the gift shops, down toward the Puppet Paddock. There, lifelike recreations of Nano's original puppet characters—Frankie Frog, Frannie Frog, Dingus Dog, and the Mad Mallard—walked and talked among guests. Interacting with people in puppet costumes was only fun for so long, of course, so there were also various pint-sized rides and attractions. A steam train chugged along the back wall, across from Frogville Theater, which was an entire village full of puppet stages. Each window was filled with characters, joking around with each other and the audience.

King Arthur's Sword was right at the border of the paddock and the park entrance, Nostalgia Bay. It had bounced between the Puppet Paddock and Fairy Tale Kingdom for a while before settling in its current spot. *Nano King Arthur* was a fantasy film, after all, but it starred Frankie Frog.

The Mad Mallard stood over the sword, wings raised.

"Let it be known!" quacked the mallard, a medieval bard costume draped over his feathered body. His voice came from a speaker beneath the anvil, not his mouth. The costumed characters weren't allowed to speak. "That they who so draweth the sword from this stone shall be the right born ruler of all Nanoland!"

Alicia watched closely. The sword could only be drawn by children under seven. Initially, there had been a cast member standing nearby with a hidden foot pedal, which would release the sword when a kid sufficiently small and cute enough to please the crowd went for it. Nowadays, the pixels on the sword's handle scanned the kids' nanobands, and the park's AI chose an appropriate winner. The new Prince or Princess of Nanoland got free ice cream and express access to all the rides for the rest of the day.

A young boy—Big curly hair. Space Squad t-shirt. Cute as a button. Alicia thought he had a real shot—stepped up to the anvil and wrapped his tiny fingers around the hilt of the sword. With a grunt of determination, he wrenched the blade free and raised it to the heavens.

"Behold! An heir has been found!" The Mad Mallard took the sword away from the boy before he could stab anyone. "All hail Prince Aiden of Knoxville!"

The crowd's applause was drowned out almost immediately by the booming voice of Frankie Frog. "Hey-yah Hey-yah, park guests!"

Alicia flinched involuntarily. The frog was much louder when you were right underneath him. Everyone around her looked up.

"You're all in for a real treat! A *real* treat! The new Chairman and CEO of the Frank Nano Company, Barclay Bloom, will arrive at the

Nostalgia Bay Helipad in just a few hours! Come on by and take a gander!"

Alicia nodded up at the glowing frog. "I'll be there, Frankie."

•○•

The interior of Frog Tower was only accessible to cast members. The bottom floor was a cafeteria known as the Frog Feed. Open eighteen hours a day, seven days a week, the Frog Feed offered buffet-style dining alongside gift shops filled with discounted merchandise for any cast members that wanted to spend their paychecks on toys. The second level held a fancy restaurant called Anura, which Alicia had only heard about but never seen, which had served various celebrities and dignitaries throughout the years. The two floors above that were for the higher-ups: the suits, the executives, and the major shareholders. There was also something involving white lab coats? To be honest, no one at Alicia's level knew what was up there.

Jimmy Lee sat alone at a two-person table near the back, wearing a full Dingus Dog costume: golden fur, bow tie collar, denim overalls, the works. The head and gloves were propped against the wall to his side. The empty golden retriever head stared at Jimmy's burger with googly-eyed longing as he took a bite.

Alicia kissed his forehead and took a fry off his plate as she sat across from him. They'd been dating for three months. Nothing too serious.

"Look at this," she said, gesturing to her plate. "The healthiest option today is chicken nuggets. They feed us like fourth graders and fire us if we gain two pounds."

A woman in a yellow dress bumped Alicia's shoulder as she walked past before sitting at a table filled with petite women in large ballgowns of various colors, along with several clean-shaven men in crowns, naval uniforms, and shiny shoes.

Jimmy saw her staring. "You can sit with them if you want. I know that's a thing. All the royals hanging out together. I wouldn't be offended."

One of the princesses made a comment, and all the royals glanced at Jimmy and Alicia before snickering amongst themselves. Jimmy raised up to his full height, glaring at them. Dingus Dog had to tower above the other classic puppet characters, so the performer was usually in the 6'5", 6'6" region. Jimmy was Chinese: the first Asian Dingus, but he wasn't the type to brag about that.

"I like sitting with you." Alicia smiled and took another fry off his plate. "Barclay Bloom's gonna be here in two hours, right after my next shift. I'll take some pictures with the kids, put on normal people clothes, and then introduce myself. 'Oh, hello, Mr. Bloom. I saw in Variety that you're working on a *Frogged Up* remake.'" She switched into her Dee voice. "*I've got a teensy l'il bit of experience in that role. How you likin' this Dixie charm, sugah?*"

"Do you really think the CEO will cast you on the spot?" Jimmy said. "Can he even do that?"

"Ninety-nine percent of show business is networking. I just need to be a person he knows." Alicia leaned in closer. "I need to think about the future. You know Emma? She's been the Mermaid Monica in the cove for four years, and they fired her this morning. Monica's black in the new movie."

"Well," Jimmy shrugged. "You're already black."

"I'm almost twenty-nine. I've been here since I was eighteen. Most people leave when they're twenty-two or twenty-three. If they don't cast me in the movie, they'll cast some light-skinned teenager that looks nothing like me, and I am out of here anyway. But they *will* cast me because no one else on Earth has a decade of experience playing this character. I look exactly like the puppet. I can act, I can sing–"

Jimmy took a bite of his burger. Ketchup oozed out the back onto his Dingus suit. Alicia grabbed a wad of napkins and wiped it before it could soak in. The princesses at the other table laughed quietly.

"This is my shot, Jimmy," Alicia said, wiping his chest. "I don't know how many more I'm gonna get."

"I just don't think you have to become a movie star to stay employed. The Big Frog's usually pretty good to people that stick around." Jimmy pointed his thumb toward the food line. "Doris used to play Princess Winnifred."

Across the room, Doris the lunch lady slopped mashed potatoes onto a cast member's plate. A fly buzzed down and landed on the scoop. She glared at it before covering it with another mound of potato. Her eyes flicked toward Jimmy and Alicia, who quickly turned away.

"You might have a point," Jimmy said.

"I gotta get back." Alicia crammed two chicken nuggets in her mouth as she stood. "I took the long way here. You'd better swap that head, babe. It's got three eyes."

9

She gathered up her trash and left. Jimmy picked up the Dingus head and squinted at it. Sure enough, a third, smaller googly eye wobbled beneath the left one.

That wasn't there when he picked the head off the shelf.

Was it?

2

Patricia Najmanovich, née Kaminski, was only seven months pregnant when she started feeling contractions. Her husband, Jacob Allen Najmanovich, was a typesetter at the Chicago Tribune, working late as he often did. After Patricia drove herself to the hospital, the doctors on staff performed an emergency c-section. Jacob Francis Najmanovich was born at 8:45pm on December 11th, 1949.

Gertrude "Gertie" Najmanovich (*sister*)**:** They kept Mom and my brother at the hospital for weeks after he was born. I was ten years old, going to the all-girls' school across the street, so every day, at lunch and after school, I would rush over and just hold him and stare at him. He weighed four pounds. He was *so* small. Dad could hold him in one hand, you know? Right from the start, I knew I would spend my whole life taking care of this kid. I knew he would need his big sister looking out for him.

Judith Oleska (*neighbor*)**:** They were such a lovely family, and they were so happy when they had the baby. Jake and Trish had been trying to have a second child for years. His sister was almost a teenager when he was born. When they came home from the hospital, the entire neighborhood came out, and we hosted this big barbeque in our backyard. Everybody brought food, and all the kids were running around. All the moms took turns holding this tiny, tiny baby. Jake was so proud, shaking hands and passing out cigars. It's a shame what happened.

Gertie: My father had a fatal heart attack in his sleep. He was only forty. My brother was two.

Frank Nano: I don't remember my dad. My mom had a box of his stuff in her closet–just his driver's license, his wedding ring, a watch, a comb...things she couldn't bring herself to throw away. That was all there was. It's fine. You don't know what you're missing when you're a little kid. Everything's normal.

But I think...Some of my earliest memories are of my mom crying out of nowhere. I remember going in the yard to play and my sister was sitting alone on the swing set. Everybody was still in mourning, you know? It's probably how I ended up here. I've spent my whole life trying to cheer people up.

Look, I don't want to talk about that. You want to hear about the puppets?

Judith: He was bright, always very tall, but a shy boy. I don't remember seeing him with the other kids.

Frank: My mom would sign me up for sports at the park district, hoping one would stick. She put me in indoor soccer—which, this was the fifties, that was a new exotic thing—and at the first practice, I opened the door to the gym, and somebody shouted, "Heads up!"

I woke up twenty minutes later in the coach's office with cotton balls stuffed in my nose. Never even made it into the gym. *[laughs]* I'm not an athlete. But that's ok, cause we had a TV.

Gertie: We had to pry him away from that thing with a crowbar. He watched so much TV that Mom used to hide it in the attic. My brother always found it. I guess he probably needed it. Mom was working two jobs, and I was a teenager. I was going out with my friends. He was home with the TV. Him and Chuck Flanagan.

Charles "Chuck" Flanagan (*childhood friend*)**:** We were always picked last for sports and things at school, and we had similar interests, so we ended up hanging out. You kinda find the kids who're at your level. I was small, and I had asthma. I wasn't gonna be the captain of no football team.

Frank: Me and Chuck, we'd go to the newsstand, get comic books and monster mags, and pore over them until the pages started falling out.

Chuck: We would pay sixty cents at The Davis over on Lincoln. Westerns, crime flicks, musicals...it didn't matter. We'd watch anything. We were there so much we got to know the grown-ups working there. I mean, I did. Jakey would just clam up the moment anybody looked at him. You know, it wasn't always easy being friends with him.

Frank: They had these monster movie marathons after midnight on channel nine, so I used to stay up until three or four in the morning. I'd be a zombie at school, just like lurching around. It was the best.

At some point, I saw *Frankenstein*, the original one, and I was so taken with Colin Clive's performance as the doctor that I started asking people to call me "Frank."

Chuck: This is what I'm saying. This kid names himself after Frankenstein in the fifth grade, and I'm just standing next to him, trying not to get my ass kicked.

Frank: My middle name is Francis. People do that! It's fine.

Chuck: And that was *before* he got into puppets.

Gertie: I don't know what he saw that drew him into puppetry. I'm not sure he knows, either. But at some point, there was just yarn, fabric, and ping-pong balls everywhere. He would sew these little creatures out of felt and plastic, and then he would crouch in front of the TV, behind the coffee table, and do these little skits for my mother and me. That was the beginning of Frankie Frog, there in our living room. But, of course, he wasn't a frog yet, just a green sock with googly eyes.

Frank: There's a craft to puppets. It's like a magic trick. You need to keep them moving at all times, bobbing their arms, glancing around at stuff, or else they stop being characters and go back to being felt. You have to hold a conversation with yourself, keep the voices straight, and keep the eye lines right.

I got pretty good at it, and I must have impressed my mom cause she bought me this little Double 8 camera so I could film my shows. She saved up Blue Chip Stamps. Do you remember those? She was a janitor at the high school. That was a lot, you know? It meant a lot to me.

Gertie: She was just amazed to see him talk. It's not like he was doing a lot of performing before that. It was easier for him with puppets. Frankie Frog could say and do things Jakey Najmanovich couldn't.

Frank: Getting that camera was like a bomb going off in my head. It hadn't really occurred to me before then that movies were a thing that people made. They appeared fully formed in glowing boxes. And now I could make my own! I stole fire from the gods.

I got a little obsessed.

Gertie: The puppet shows became puppet films. Frankie Frog left the living room and started going on little adventures.

Frank: I only had twenty-five feet of film per reel, which was a little under a minute, so I would pack as much as I could into that minute. I taught myself to do stop motion, slow motion, matte paintings, all the tricks you can do in-camera.

Chuck: I'm the bartender in the cowboy one. A lot of these are online now. My daughter showed me.

Frank: You couldn't rewatch a movie back then. Once it was out of theaters it was just, like, gone. So, a lot of my movies were me trying to recreate movies I'd seen at home. They do a giant ant, and Frankie Frog meets a giant ant. Pterodactyl destroys Tokyo, pterodactyl destroys Chicago.

Mostly, it was puppets. I could've used some real actors, but convincing my sister to film a fight scene at two in the morning was tough. Frankie was always there for me.

Chuck: Freshman year of high school, there's a talent show. Frank brings a couple of his movies in. Not any I was in, but I wished I were, cause the crowd went *nuts*. Eyes glued to the projector, gasping at the scary parts, laughing at the jokes.

He got a standing ovation. Swear to God.

Frank: I had girls walking up to me in the hall and telling me they liked the movies. Like, actual human women. That didn't happen before that.

Chuck: I think it went to his head a little. He started busting out the frog puppet at school. He'd talk through it at lunch. *[Frankie Frog impression]* "Hey-yah, hey-yah! You got bologna today, huh?"

I know how this looks, alright? I know I'll come across like an asshole in your book. Frank Nano's only friend ditched him in high school. I feel bad about it. But that's kids, man.

Gertie: He was alone a lot. Mom was working, and I was living in this tiny apartment downtown. I came home on Sundays, but... *[pauses]* He stopped going to school, and nobody noticed for a month.

Frank: I wanted to keep making movies, but I was brushing up against the limits of what I could film in my house. This was Chicago in the early sixties. There weren't exactly film studios, but we did have a TV station.

Dean Skilling (*executive producer, WCN Kids Mornings*)**:** I was at WCN at the time, producing the children's programming lineup. Mostly syndicated shows, but we made a few locally. *Captain Cowbell. The Magic Cat. Library Island.* The big hit was, as we all know, *Sweeto the Clown.*

Every morning, after I poured my coffee, I would go down to the *Sweeto* soundstage and see how things were going. And every day, there's this kid, seven feet tall, big mop of hair, leaning against the wall and watching everyone else work. After a week, I'm like, who is this lazy son of a bitch? I go to the key grip. He doesn't know him. Sound doesn't know who he is. The camera crew has no idea.

Turns out, he's fifteen years old. He's been sneaking into the building.

Frank: It wasn't exactly Fort Knox. They had two guards, one daytime and one nighttime. They switched at five AM, so they were both upstairs. There was a window in the back room of the kitchen that had no lock. So, I climbed in there. I found a pass in the locker room and copied it.

Dean: I had security escort him out and chop up his fake ID. Two days later, I pass him in the hall. *[laughs]* It's cute now because of who he is, but I want to be clear to any young people reading your book: Do *not* do this.

Frank: I could tell Dean was the boss, so I brought in some sample movies. I was like, "Before you call the cops, can I show you what I can do? If you hate it, I promise you'll never see me again."

Dean: He showed me these crude little puppet shows he'd filmed at home. Nothing amazing, but I could see some spark in there. He had natural talent, so I gave him a slot: five minutes every weekday after *Sweeto* to do a puppet show. The clown was running a little short. So, I figured, how badly could the kid mess it up?

Frank: He gave me ten bucks an episode, which even then was a very small amount of money, but I dropped out of high school anyway.

Chuck: One day, we never saw him again.

Gertie: Mom was pissed. Of course she was.

Frank: It was a completely different experience, doing a puppet show on actual TV. Just in terms of, like…I could put a monitor on the floor and see what the camera saw while filming it. That's enormously useful when puppeteering.

I used to have to take reels of film to the drugstore. Film the whole thing, bring it in, wait a week, bring it home, feed it into the projector, and *then* I could see what worked and what didn't. By the time I edited the thing, my mom had thrown out all the sets. Now I had instant feedback. It was amazing.

Dean: We got the Nielsen ratings back, and they went up at the end of *Sweeto*. Some kids were tuning in just for the puppets at the end. So, I gave Frankie his own half-hour slot.

Frank: My own show! I called it *Nano Tales*. I called myself Frank Nano. Gentrified my name a little.

Gertie: I started acting as his manager then. Frank was a brilliant artist, he always was, but he had no head for business. He always needed an adult he could trust to speak for him in boardrooms. There are a lot of meetings in TV, even local children's TV. Educators, parents, investors. He could light up a room with the frog on his hand, but the moment they started talking earnings and sponsors and ratings, you could see his eyes glaze over. That's when I would step in.

Frank: It was twenty-six minutes with the commercials every weekday morning, so I had a little over two hours each week. That's a lot of time to fill with puppets. I ran out of material almost immediately, so I started repurposing old fairy tales, Aesop's fables, tall tales, and stuff like that. Anything and everything in the public domain got a Frankie Frog version.

I could do three characters at once by myself, as long as one was just standing there, but quickly, it became clear that I needed another pair of hands.

Bethany Darby (*future wife*): I was eighteen years old, studying theater at Columbia College, when I saw an ad in the paper saying they needed puppeteers for *Nano Tales*. I was familiar with the show, believe it or not, because my little nephew watched it religiously. I knew who Frank Nano was, but I had no idea what he looked like. He was never on TV as himself. I assumed he was eighty years old. That's what you picture on the other end of a puppet. A kindly old man with suspenders and a big mustache.

I go to the audition. I'm in an empty waiting room. This lanky teenage boy was sitting there, quietly painting the backdrop on a tiny stage. He smiled at me. He was very shy, but he was cute, so I asked him if he knew Mr. Nano. What's he like? Is he nice? And he says, "Oh, he's awful. He's so mean. He's always showing up drunk and throwing things."

So now I'm terrified. What did I get myself into? Dean called me into the office, so I went in, but I was standing there shaking, trying to figure out how to get out of this building. And then the boy from the other room walks in. *[holds out hand]* "Hi, I'm Frank."

Dean: Frank wrote all the scripts, but Beth was the better performer. I kept making Frank give her more characters.

Frank: We would do a lot of fairy tales, which are pretty princess-heavy, and Beth had to give each one a distinct voice and personality. I don't know how she did it.

Gertie: Beth did all the princesses, the evil queens, Frannie Frog, all the female puppets. Frank would have the big ideas, but Beth was always funnier. Her characters had genuine honesty to them. She gave them a soul.

Frank: She was a great puppeteer, which was good because I still would've hired her if she sucked. The moment I saw her, I knew I wanted to spend every waking moment with this woman.

Beth: We were crouched behind a table together for hours every day. What's surprising is how long it took for us to hook up.

Frank: Out of that show came Frankie Frog, Frannie Frog, the Mad Mallard, and most of the princesses. We filmed every day for three years. No sick days. No vacations. Back then, at WCN, it was all shot live, and they used to reuse the tapes and record over old TV episodes, so almost none of that exists anymore. It's easier to see my home movies from when I was a little kid.

Beth: I finished college with my Frannie Frog money. They kept giving us raises, because the ratings were so good that we were bringing in big-time advertisers. We were getting evening numbers at nine AM. Every five-year-old in the Chicagoland area was watching.

Dean: End of year three, Frank comes into my office, and I have this deal ready for him. And it was a great deal. I'm already paying him twice what anyone else was making, and this was more than that. He was making more money than Sweeto the Clown. I wouldn't say that if he wasn't dead.

And Frank says, "Dean, I'm done."

He walked away.

Frank: I turned twenty, and...I don't know. I couldn't do it anymore. I was burnt out on puppets, and there wasn't enough time to do anything else.

Gertie: Today, we would call it a quarter-life crisis. Back then, we just thought he was nuts. A high school dropout quitting his cushy TV job.

Beth: Frank always had a ticking clock in his head.

Frank: My dad died when he was forty. His dad died when he was thirty-eight. Both had heart attacks. They dropped dead in their sleep. If I only had twenty years left, I couldn't spend them all doing a local puppet show.

Beth: He wanted to make movies.

Frank: I *had* to make movies, Ethan. What're you reading?

Ethan O'Brien looked up from his phone. The screen went dark the moment his head turned away.

"Huh?"

His dad was staring at him. "I said, what're you reading?"

"I got a biography of Frank Nano," Ethan said. "*Nanolandia.* I just started it. It's good."

"Oh, cool." His dad, Kevin, gestured to their surroundings. "I just thought you might want to enjoy this vacation that I'm spending thousands of dollars per day on."

They were on a small boat, motorized and self-piloting, cruising smoothly across the several miles of ocean between mainland Florida and the entrance to Nanoland. At the moment, the real world was on the edge of disappearing over the horizon. Ethan scanned ahead and thought he could just about make out Frog Tower. Maybe not.

His sister Maddie, five years old, was on their dad's lap, bouncing excitely. She wore a Princess Winnifred Halloween costume, as she had most days for the past year. His sister Hailey, seven, was clutching her stomach and looking a little off. Ethan was twelve, thirteen next April.

The boy pocketed his phone. He yawned. He'd barely slept last night, spending hours in his sleeping bag on the hotel floor—there were only two beds—staring at the ceiling, sick to his stomach with anticipation.

"I don't feel so good," Hailey muttered.

"I told you not to eat those crab cakes," Kevin said. "O'Briens can't mess around with seafood. We're midwestern folk."

"Daddy," Maddie said. "How come Mama didn't come with?"

"Well, Mom likes being alone at a hotel more than rides and parades. Isn't that *weird*?"

"So weird!"

"What do you guys wanna do first? Nostalgia Bay Arcade?"

"That's for old people!" Maddie shouted. "I wanna meet princesses!"

"I'm tall enough for Danger Dragon this year," Hailey said. She immediately went pale at the thought of being on a roller coaster.

"I gotta go on Time Breakers: The Ride," Ethan said. "It's the last day. This is my only chance."

"Yeah, that's too bad." Kevin shrugged. "Why would they close your ride?"

"*Time Breakers* was Frank Nano's first movie. He had to make a deal with another studio to make it, which means the Frank Nano Company doesn't own it outright. They can't do a sequel or a remake without sharing the profits, so they haven't, and now nobody's seen it. It was also Frank's favorite ride, and he had it in his will that they couldn't update it, so they're just closing it instead. It's gonna be another Space Squad thing. Nobody cares about *Time Breakers*, Dad."

Kevin switched Maddie to his other leg. "Except you."

"Except me," Ethan agreed. "I care a lot."

"That's some real inside baseball stuff. You got all that from your book?"

"No. I don't know. I already know it." Ethan felt a little embarrassed. "I gotta go on that ride, Dad."

"You will. I promise. But we gotta do what the little kids want first, right?" Kevin grunted as he stood Maddie in front of him. "That's the deal."

"Princess Winnifred is gonna be so happy to see me!" Maddie announced to no one in particular. "I'm gonna tell her I saw her movie a hundred times, and I watched every episode of the show, and I have her doll and her books and–"

Hailey puked over the side of the boat into the pristine ocean waters. The other two kids recoiled away from her.

Kevin frowned. "Maybe we oughta take you back to the hotel."

"No! Dad! No. Dad…" Hailey sat up, wobbling in her seat, and put her hands on her dad's face, aiming it at hers. She looked him dead in the eyes. "I'm going to Nanoland. It's a magical world of wonder and delights, and I am *going* to it."

Kevin glanced over her shoulder at the miles of open sea between them and the resort. They'd lose multiple non-refundable hours of their day going back and forth. "Are you sure?"

"It's Nanoland," Hailey said.

Orchestral music played from speakers hidden in the boat's interior, building in intensity and grandeur as they grew closer to their destination. Just as the park became visible, a gigantic human head made from swirling silver particles rose from the water. A man's face, with long hair, a bushy beard, a trucker hat, and aviator sunglasses. Frank Nano's trademarked look.

"Welcome, Madeline." Frank's voice spoke through the boat's speakers. His enormous mouth didn't quite line up with the words, and there was a hiss of static, as though this were an old audio clip recorded decades earlier. "Welcome, Hailey. Welcome, Ethan. Welcome, Korvin."

"Korvin?" Kevin shook his nanoband. "Dang it, did I misspell my own name?"

"In a few moments, you'll embark on an unforgettable journey filled with wonder and excitement. What you see in my park may seem like a dream, but dreams are just memories you haven't yet made. Nothing is impossible here. Dreams always come true at Nanoland. So, do me a favor…"

Each of the family's nanobands lit up and beeped. They were inside park property.

The enormous face smiled as the silver sparkles forming it began to glow.

"Dream big."

Frank's head exploded into fireworks.

3

Alicia returned to the dimly lit dressing room a little sweaty and frazzled. She set Babs's Coke on the vanity and popped a breath mint to hide the smell of chicken nuggets as she sat down to fix her makeup. Savannah was already dressed, leaning against the wall and vaping.

"Not even an apple or something?" Alicia said.

Savannah snickered. "Last time I ate in the cafeteria, it took three days to work it off. Not everyone is naturally skinny well into their middle age."

"Uh-huh." Alicia fixed her eyeshadow. "That's me, just good genes, forty minutes of cardio every morning, and—"

Pasha passed through the invisible door with Babs at her side. She ripped her wig off like she'd been thinking about it for hours. "This wig! Jesus!"

Alicia smiled. "How'd it go?"

Pasha handed her the wig. She spoke in her Princess Dee voice. *"Ah spent months workin' on muh accent to portray a character that's plumb forgotten by the populah culchah."*

"Takes the pressure off, right?"

"She did a hundred and sixty," Babs said, sipping her soda. "She did great."

Each Nano princess was expected to meet and greet 172 guests per hour-long shift. It was a general rule. Newbies usually did a little less. On her best day, Alicia banged through 214 photo ops, but at that rate, they weren't getting the complete experience. Just a picture and a wave.

21

She adjusted the wig into place and closed her eyes as the pixelated sensors molded to her scalp. Her ears filled with the chatter of park employees on the encrypted internal audio network. She tapped her jaw twice.

"Testing," she said. "How's it looking, Ron?"

"Light crowd in there, kid." Ron, the Princess Pavilion's security officer, was listening through their wigs and observing the room on four hidden security cameras. "Everybody's either gawking at the new mermaid or the parade."

Ron had started at Nanoland just before Alicia, and he'd called her 'kid' from the beginning, even though he was only a few years older than her. She didn't love it, but he was a decent guy. He and his wife baked cookies for the whole princess team every Christmas.

Babs finished drinking her soda in one gulp. "Twenty seconds, ladies."

Savannah set her vape rig down and patted her dress in the mirror. Greg, her host, entered something into his tablet. She raised her arms, and her wig swirled up from the mannequin, golden particles spiraling around her in streams before settling on her head like birds on a power line.

Alicia stood and gave Pasha a kind nudge with her elbow.

"You got this," Pasha said.

The two princesses passed through the wall and strolled gracefully out onto the guest area, flanked by their hosts. They were greeted by no one at all. All the guests were outside. They relaxed into their natural postures.

A pop remix medley of Nano movie songs reverberated on the walls of the small pavilion. Through the doors beyond the empty velvet-roped queue, they could see dozens of people facing away from them—little kids on their dads' shoulders, strollers blocking the sidewalk. Over the guests' heads, the tops of elaborate floats rolled along, decorated with a mix of human dancers, animatronics with pixelated shells (nanomatronics), and pure nanotech creations. Flying fish danced among mermaids. Puppet animals wailed on jazz instruments.

"Has there ever been *no* line?" Savannah said. "I've never seen this."

"The times are changing." Alicia adjusted her wig beneath her tiara. "Who wants to meet us when they've got the real thing?"

New to the parade this year: the Real Nano Princesses,

nanomatronic versions of the princesses with their designs pulled from the actual movie models. They were kept elevated on their floats, as pixelated faces at a high enough level of detail to trick the human eye ran hot enough to burn skin.

Each princess had her own individual float, where she sang a signature song while dancing. The nanomatronic Winnifred floated past, her impossibly long blond hair held aloft by sky-blue robins as she brushed it, just like in the movie. Her human equivalent huffed in annoyance.

"Have you girls seen the new Night Parade yet?" Babs said. "There's a big neon octopus to tie in with the new *Mermaid's Tale*. It's neat."

Greg didn't look up from his tablet. "Who doesn't love a big octopus?"

A float full of original Nano Tales puppet characters passed. Frankie Frog and Frannie Frog waved to the crowd from their lily pad tower, arm in arm, as Dingus Dog and the Mad Mallard danced their costumed hearts out below them. Dingus had a barely noticeable ketchup stain on his chest. Alicia smiled.

"You still going with Asian Dingus?" Savannah said.

"Don't call him that. His name's Jimmy. You know he's got a master's degree in Mechanical Engineering? He had a six-figure job lined up, and he put it on hold to do this."

Savannah scowled, more confused than impressed. "Why?"

Dingus pointed directly at Alicia, who gave him a practiced curtsy as he went back to punch-dancing. The float drifted out of view.

Alicia shrugged. "Some people gotta dance."

Her face snapped into a broad smile as someone entered the photo pavilion. Princesses had to smile whenever visible to guests, just in case someone took a picture. When she first started, Alicia used to come home with bruise lines on her cheeks.

"Hello, ladies." The man who stepped out of the sunlight and into their pavilion wore a red Hawaiian shirt and tight jeans. He had a duffle bag at his side and a grin on his face. "Am I interrupting?"

"Well, who's this ray of sunshine?" Princess Dee said. "Come on over, sugah."

Something about this guy put her on edge. Grown men taking pictures with princesses alone weren't that unusual, but Alicia'd been here long enough to sense when something was off. She glanced over and saw that Savannah felt it, too, though she'd never let it show on her face.

He reached into his duffle bag, and for a moment, everyone in the room tensed until he revealed the green-and-brown duck puppet. The puppet rubbed its ping-pong ball eyes like it was waking up.

Dee stifled a sigh. *One of these guys.*

"Cracked crackers!" the man said through the duck, in what was actually a good approximation of the Mad Mallard's voice. "Somebody turn a light on in here! I'm straining my little peepers!"

"Mad *Mallard.*" The man watched the princesses expectantly for a reaction. "We're here to take our picture, remember?"

"Did you make the duck talk?!" Princess Winnifred shouted. "Awesomesauce! Epic win!"

"That's wonderful," Dee said. "Say, have you ever kissed a frog?"

"Can't say that I have!" The man laughed as he approached, weaving his way through the red velvet queue, stepping over the ropes whenever they seemed low enough. The duck laughed, too, a staccato quack like a sputtering car engine. The man kept glancing at Dee, smiling like he had something more to say. As he reached the end of the line, the photographer got into position. Babs stopped him.

"Sir," Babs said. "I need to scan your nanoband."

He lifted the bottom of the puppet to reveal a well-worn wristband. An older model. Dee was surprised it still beeped when scanned.

"Boy, I sure kissed one," Dee said. "It all started at my daddy's frog trappin' ranch. There I was: Dee Green, age sixteen. I–"

"Wait a minute." The man searched her face, still smiling. "Alicia? Alicia Amandi?"

Alicia's blood ran cold. The duck looked at the man, then at the princess, up and down, sizing her up. She raised her finger to her jaw.

"It's me, Trent Santiago! We did that monster musical together back in Milwaukee?"

The Mad Mallard nodded enthusiastically.

"I-I'm sure I don't know who you mean," Dee said. She tried to think of the code word. It had been months since she'd used it. "I'm Princess Dee. Can you smile for the camera?"

"Oh, sorry, you probably have to stay in character." Trent didn't turn to face the photographer and instead got closer to Dee. She leaned away. "Listen, since we know each other, I was hoping you could put in a good word? It's not easy getting an audition at this place. If there are any openings in the Puppet Paddock–"

Dee touched his back and guided him gently around until he was facing the doors. "Smile for the nice lady and have a nanomagical day."

There was a soft buzz inside her wig as she said the word *nanomagical*. The photographer's camera flashed, and as Trent blinked, a stocky bald guy in a black polo shirt and cargo shorts emerged from the shadows, seemingly from nowhere. He put his hand on Trent's shoulder.

"Alright, buddy," Ron said. "That's enough pictures for today, ok?"

"Oh, I'm–" The man flinched. "No, it's ok, we're old friends."

"Yeah, you're from the kingdom of Grenoilia? Come on..." he pinned the man's duck arm behind his back and led him toward the exit.

"Ow! Wait!" the man struggled to free himself, to no avail. "Just wait for a second! I didn't meet Winnifred yet!"

"OMG, that duck was so random!" Winnifred smiled apologetically. She waved. "Come back soon, Mister Ducky McDuckerson! Ha ha, did I say that out loud?"

Ron led Trent out of the pavilion and toward the hidden security center near the entrance to the park. Alicia mouthed a "thank you" to Ron as he left. He gave her a nod. Both princesses broke character the moment the two men were out of sight.

Savannah shuddered. "You know him?"

"No." Alicia shook her head. "I was in that play, though. In high school. He's way too old to have been in school with me. That was weird."

"Probably got it off a website," Babs said. "You can't hide anything anymore."

Savannah nodded. "Paige, the Winnifred over on the stage show, had a guy come up to her, claiming to be her real father. Got all her info from her aunt's social media. Just some asshole."

"You handled it well, though," Babs added.

"The moment he said my real name, I'd have ripped his balls off," Savannah said.

Alicia laughed. "Princess Dee wouldn't, sugah."

Outside, the parade continued on. The *Frogged Up* float drifted into view. The nanomatronic Princess Dee twirled gracefully amongst a chorus of frogs as she sang her most famous song, "Hop into your Heart." She looked identical to the Dee from the movie, but something was missing in her oversized, unblinking eyes. As she spun, those eyes locked onto Alicia's, and her head stayed in that place a little too long before it moved with the rest of her body.

"Do you ever feel like the robot princesses don't like us?" she said.

Winnifred looked at her. "You've been here too long."

The float passed, and the crowd dispersed toward it. The parade was ending. Alicia realized she wasn't smiling and turned it back on.

•○•

The performers from the parade—the human ones—trudged into the break room below Frog Tower, down in the backstage area of the park. Everyone was exhausted from twenty-seven minutes of relentless dancing and waving. The animal characters, covered in fur from head-to-toe under the Florida sun, lined up and took turns dumping the sweat out of their helmets into a trough.

Jimmy tilted his Dingus head sideways and poured out two pounds of bodily fluids before setting it on the rack and grabbing a towel. A man with a long gray ponytail in a hairnet leaned against a nearby wall, eating a churro.

"Churro Charlie!" Jimmy said, drying his hair. "How can you still eat those things?"

Charlie smiled. He'd been working the churro stand in Prehistoric Forest since the park had opened, long enough to become a mythical figure among the other cast members. The man ate three churros a day and, despite this, remained thin as a rail. He didn't talk about his many fried-dough-related health problems. Not part of his legend.

"This one's savory." The man pondered the tube of fried dough in his hand. He chewed it a little, his mustache rolling in a wave like a caterpillar. "Cheeseburger flavored."

"Oh, yeah?" Jimmy said. "We sell those?"

"Nah," Churro Charlie said.

Jimmy nodded. He knew from experience that his follow-up questions would only prolong the confusion.

"You see that puddle?" Charlie pointed with his churro at a wet patch in the middle of the floor in front of them. "Air conditioning pipes drip, so there used to be a drain there. Now it's over there."

He used the churro to direct Jimmy's gaze three feet to the left. A small metal drain sat bone dry next to the puddle.

"Weird." Jimmy threw his towel in the bin. "Why would they move it?"

"Nobody moved it. It was there an hour ago."

Charlie pushed himself upright with a loud grunt and strolled over to Jimmy.

"There's been a lot of that lately. Little things are off. Bushes facing the wrong direction. Doors that open the wrong way. Typos in the signs..." The man took another bite and chewed, lost in his own thoughts. "You must've seen it."

Jimmy checked Dingus's head. This one only had two eyes. He'd never thought about where the costumes came from. He assumed there was an entire team of costumers and seamstresses somewhere at Nanoland, but he'd never seen them.

"The park is sick," Charlie said. He bundled up his wrapper and tossed it in the towel bin. "I think it's his fault."

"Who?"

Charlie gestured over his shoulder to the TV mounted in the corner, showing a live news broadcast of the park. All the other cast members and performers in the break room had gathered to watch.

"There he is!" someone shouted.

On the screen, a white dot in the sky slowly grew into a white helicopter, which roared as it did a smooth and dramatic spin maneuver before setting down on the helipad in Nostalgia Bay. The crowd of guests already gathered around the pad moved in closer, pushing against the velvet ropes and cheering as the blades slowed to a stop. The door to the helicopter swung open, and Barclay Bloom stepped out and waved.

He wore a white suit over a sky-blue t-shirt. His longish blond hair fluttered around his tanned face. He removed the dark sunglasses he'd been wearing while flying the helicopter and replaced them with a lighter shade of the same sunglasses. Barclay shook hands with a few executives—Gertie Nano, Frank's sister, was the only one Jimmy recognized—as he stepped up to the podium prepared for him.

"Hey-yah hey-yah," he said into the microphone, smiling at his own half-assed Frankie Frog impression. "Did you all go see the new mermaid? I saw it from the sky. Wowza!"

The crowd laughed politely. Bloom raised his hand to stop them.

"Before he died, my dear friend and mentor, Kenneth Sakai, spent thirty years carrying on Frank Nano's creative legacy. He once said that the hardest part of his job was 'standing in the shadow of greatness.' Now that I'm standing in *his* shadow, I understand what that means. He will be missed."

He paused, allowing the audience a moment to digest how thoughtful that was.

Jimmy said, "I heard he's building a moon colony."

Churro Charlie snorted.

"This is the end of an era, but every ending is a new beginning. We've got a whole slew of exciting projects in development across all our divisions. Movies! Streaming! Television! Publishing! Music! Toys! Games! And, of course: Nanoland!"

Bloom gestured to his surroundings. The crowd cheered.

"But, unfortunately, I can't talk about that yet." He shrugged apologetically. "There'll be more announcements at NanoCon. Now, if you'll excuse me, I haven't been here since I was a kid, and I'm excited to ride some of these rides. I'll see you out there! Thank you! Dream big!"

He waved to the crowd as he turned away, disappearing into a group of suits and security people.

"Shadow of greatness, my ass." Churro Charlie spat in the puddle where the drain used to be. "Hostile takeover the moment Mr. Sakai died, and now he's waving to the masses from his stage like a conquering hero."

"I think he's cool," said one of the younger cast members. "He flew that helicopter himself."

Churro Charlie snorted. "Never trust a man over forty who thinks he's cool."

He turned to leave, but Jimmy stopped him.

"Wait, look." Jimmy pointed at the screen as the camera panned out to show more of the crowd. "My girlfriend's on TV."

4

Alicia pushed her way through the throngs of guests toward Bloom and his entourage, who were exiting the stage and heading into Frog Tower. She'd changed into regular human clothes; she spent so much time at work that she only owned a handful of shirts, but she was wearing her good one. She'd left her princess makeup on to save time, and she hoped it didn't look ridiculous. Alicia had been here for years, doing this, so she'd sort of lost track of how normal people dressed.

A couple of security guards blocked her path, then receded as she passed through the invisible wall. Her low-level employee status was enough to get her this far. She hurried to catch up.

Barclay Bloom walked quickly, his expensive loafers barely touching the tiled floor. To his right, a short, bearded man with a tablet was explaining something technical. Reggie. That was his name. Head software engineer for the park. Dr. Reginald Cundy, everyone called him Reggie. Alicia knew his face, she'd seen him buying snacks in the Frog Feed, but she'd never talked to him. They worked in different worlds.

"The errors in operations are increasing exponentially, Mr. Bloom," Reggie said, struggling to keep up. "We could be headed toward an event."

"An event? Oh, is this the thing from that meeting?" Barclay scanned the tablet as Reggie held it in front of him. "Why is this making it all the way to me? Can't you guys just take care of it?"

Alicia caught up to the back of the entourage and walked along with them. They entered a guarded elevator, and no one batted an eye as she slipped into the front row, right before the doors closed.

"Sir, we might be able to repair the system if we were to shut it down and reboot it, but we'd need you to sign off on that. It's a major fix."

"Why?"

"We've never done it. We'd have to close the park for a few days and run some tests."

Alicia stood on her tiptoes and tapped Gertie Nano on the shoulder. The old woman turned and smiled, but she seemed a little disappointed to see Alicia.

Barclay turned to a man in a suit standing to his left, a thin bald man. "How much would we lose if we closed Nanoland for three days?"

The man shook his head. "You don't want to do that."

"Well," Barclay turned back to Reggie. "Think of something else, bud."

Ding! The elevator doors opened, and all the suits filed out after Barclay. Gertie hung back and stopped Alicia outside the elevator.

Gertie was Frank's only surviving family member, and therefore a multi-millionaire several times over, but she still came in every morning at seven a.m. and stayed late into the evening, doing work far below her station out of pure loyalty to the park. She loved Nanoland. She was especially invested in Fairy Tale Kingdom, having worked most extensively on the original puppet princess films in the 1970s. She was still managing the princesses in a hands-on way when Alicia had started, only slowing a little now that she was in her eighties. Gertie was stern, a perfectionist with high standards, but she was nice. The princesses called her "Grandma Nano". Alicia liked her a lot.

"Alicia!" Gertie whispered once the entourage was out of earshot. "What are you doing here? You're not supposed to be up here."

"I'm networking." Alicia said. "Can you introduce me to Mr. Bloom?"

Alicia suddenly realized they were in the waiting area outside Anura, the fancy restaurant one floor above the lunch room. A gilded pattern of Frankie Frog heads papered the surrounding walls. She knew about this place as a concept, but no one she knew had ever seen it. She resisted the urge to gawk because she was a professional.

Gertie's concern turned to shock. "Why on earth do you want to

30

meet Barclay Bloom?"

"Remember when that cheerleading championship sent forty-eight teams to the park, and I had to work thirty-six hours straight? You said you owed me one."

"Dear," Gertie held Alicia's arms. She spoke patiently. "This is not a good idea."

"You know I wouldn't do this if I didn't need to."

Gertie considered this, then nodded. She brought Alicia over to where Barclay stood, talking with his entourage, and tapped his shoulder. Alicia had enough experience in customer service to recognize Barclay Bloom's face clicking into public persona mode as he turned and saw her. Downstairs, Alicia was a princess. Up here, she was just another guest.

"Barclay, I'd like you to meet Alicia Amandi," Gertie said. "She's been one of our face characters in Fairy Tale Kingdom for over nine years."

"Great," Barclay said, shaking her hand. "That's great. You all do great work out there. Nine years, huh?"

"Mr. Bloom," Alicia said, pulling some sheets of paper from her purse. "I understand you're remaking *Frogged Up* in live action soon."

"We sure are!" He turned to one suit and said softly, "What is that?"

"First black princess," said the suit.

"Black princess!" Barclay said. "The frog one. Fantastic. Is that you? That must be exciting."

"Yes." Alicia nodded, "I wanted to—"

"If you want a sneak peek, I don't think they're filming yet, but we've got some great people—"

"I want to audition to play Princess Dee." Alicia got the words out as fast as possible before he could keep talking.

She held out her resume. The CEO leaned away from it instinctually.

"Ah." was all he said.

"I have almost a decade of experience playing this part. That's more than the voice of the puppet and more than the woman who played Dee on Broadway. Nobody knows Dee better than me."

"She really is outstanding," Gertie added. "We've had people request her specifically when they come to Nanoland."

"That right?" Barclay took the papers and flipped through them.

"I have a master's in performance at the Nano Arts Campus,

including a minor in stage combat. I used to teach the kids using the sword fight choreography from *Frogged Up*. I can sing, I can act. I've written some of my own songs! I know you're probably planning on using the old ones, but–"

"Well, listen," Barclay said, slapping the resume with the back of his hand before handing it back to her. "This all looks great. You seem talented, but I don't make these decisions. I'm sure if you send this to Casting–"

"Sir, with all due respect," Alicia said. "We've all sent our headshots to that address. Nobody's been cast out of the slush pile in nineteen years."

Barclay bit his lip. "Ok. You've been with the company for a long time. You seem like you've done your homework. How are your numbers?"

"Like, the people taking pictures? About two hundred an hour–"

"No." Barclay laughed a little. "How's your social media following? Which ones are you big on?"

"Oh, uh, we have to set everything private." Alicia felt her resume slip out of her hand. She winced as it hit the carpet. "That's a rule here."

Barclay nodded. "These things are a whole big international affair. It costs us half a billion dollars to make one, so we need someone with a built-in audience in a lead role to make our money back. That's just good business."

"Sir." A server came around the corner, menus in hand. "The table is ready."

"Look, you're already a princess," Barclay said. "You're out in the park every day, making people happy. The kids think you're the real thing. That's not nothing, right?"

He turned and headed back over to his entourage. Alicia glanced back at Gertie, who patted her hand. Her foot brushed her resume on the floor, flipping the top page over and revealing her headshot.

Her own face stared up at her expectantly.

"Mr. Bloom!" Alicia spoke forcefully enough that everyone in the room paid attention. Barclay turned back.

"I grew up in a one-bedroom apartment in Wisconsin with four brothers. My single father worked two jobs to keep us fed and in school. I had to save for years to buy a one-way plane ticket to Florida. I spent my first seven months as a Nano princess sleeping in a co-worker's van until I made enough to rent an apartment with four roommates. You want to sell a movie? There's your marketing hook."

She spread her arms and gestured to herself.

"Rags to riches, baby! A real-life Dee Green story. I have given everything to the Frank Nano Company. I believe in this place. You're always telling us to dream big. This is it. I can't dream any bigger than this."

Gertie smiled. Alicia bent down and gathered up her papers.

Barclay stepped toward her. "Is any of that true?"

"I don't have any brothers." Alicia held out her resume again. "Now you know I can act."

The CEO smiled, too, despite himself. He took her headshot and lifted his sunglasses to get a better look at the picture. He exhaled through his nose.

"Tell you what," he handed the papers back to her. "I shouldn't tell you about this, but there's a secret audition in LA."

Alicia gasped. She steadied herself. "An audition?"

"We don't want people just showing up. It's a short list. First Tuesday of next month. If you–"

An electronic alarm jangled out throughout the restaurant, red lights flashing from the corners of the room. Reggie's face glowed red as something changed on his tablet.

He shouted. "Code 2-2-2!"

Several security guards entered the room—not the plain clothes ones from outside. These were the behind-the-scenes guards in their gray-and-blue jumpsuits with nightsticks and tasers.

"This way, Miss Nano." One guard took Gertie's arm and escorted her away. Barclay pointed at Alicia.

"Get her out of here," he said.

Two guards grabbed her by the arms and led her toward the elevator.

"Wait!" Alicia was still holding her resume as they dragged her away. She dropped it. "Where's the audition?! Where should I go?"

"It was nice meeting you!" Barclay waved at her without looking. "Keep smiling out there!"

The guards shoved her into the elevator and entered with her, holding her there.

"Just tell me!" Alicia shouted. "Finish saying the thing!"

The doors closed in her face. After a quick, silent ride down to the first floor, the guards dumped Alicia in the hallway before stepping back into the elevator. The alarm was still ringing in her ears, but she couldn't hear it down here.

She walked down the hall and checked the lunchroom. Everyone was going about their business, getting trays, filling them with food, and eating. She went outside and found park guests milling about, taking pictures, buying popcorn, and pushing strollers. A small boy was pointing at a balloon salesman and crying. Nothing seemed out of the ordinary. Just a typical day at Nanoland.

Alicia gazed up at Frog Tower, squinting in the sunlight as she searched for the floor where she had been. It was hard to tell with the forced perspective. The windows were their usual green, but those probably weren't real windows.

She shook her head. "What the hell was that?"

5

Frank and Bethany Nano were married at the Chicago Civic Center (now the Richard J. Daley Center) on May 7, 1970.

Beth: We'd saved up some money during the run of the show. Not a lot, because we were young, but some. We wanted to move to Los Angeles and break into film, but my parents wouldn't let me go unless we made it official. So, I borrowed a dress from my cousin Cheryl, and we went to the courthouse. Frank's sister came as the witness.

Gertie: It was a beautiful ten-minute ceremony. They were so in love. I took one picture, and of course, I cropped off the top of my brother's big head.

Frank: I'd marry her again right now if I could.

Beth: The next morning, we piled everything we owned into Frank's beat-up old Ford and drove out to California. I had a girlfriend living out there, so we crashed on her couch for about a week until we found the absolute grimiest studio apartment you've ever seen.

Frank: The bed folded into the wall, and it was all rusted underneath. If you flipped it up the wrong way, the springs would snag you in the arm, so we left it down and ate dinner in bed.

Beth: The wallpaper was peeling. The fridge leaked. One of the windows was wedged open at the top, so the rain always came in.

Frank: The bathroom didn't have a door, just one of those bead curtains. Whenever Beth had to, er, "use the facilities," she made me take a walk around the block.

Beth: Every once in a while, to this day, I have a stress dream where the bank revokes my mortgage, and I have to go live in that apartment.

Frank: I had all my best ideas there. There was nothing else to do. So, that was the genesis of *Time Breakers*: me, lying on that stupid bed, in my underwear because it was always ninety degrees, staring at stains on the ceiling and dreaming up science fiction.

Beth: Gertie was making calls for us back in Chicago. She'd just gotten married, too, and she didn't want to make the move, but she was always the best at that stuff.

Gertie: *Nano Tales* had been successful enough as a regional program that I had a few pitch meetings lined up for Frank. General get-to-know-you things.

Beth: That was when he grew the beard and started wearing those sunglasses all the time. He was trying to be hip for the Hollywood people.

Frank: It was the seventies. I was cool.

Gertie: He was so shy. He would've covered his entire face if he could.

Frank: I had three meetings with people you've heard of. I talked about sci-fi pictures the whole time for the first two, but all they wanted was puppets. I had a script, sketches, paintings, and a couple of models I put together. Their eyes glazed over. All they ever wanted was more Frankie Frog. The early seventies were not a great time to sell science fiction. It was seen as embarrassing.

So for the third meeting, I worked out a whole pitch for a *Nano Tales* movie. Frankie Frog goes to the big city and brings his friends along. I had musical numbers and roles that we could fill with celebrity guests. Give them the kiddie picture they all seemed to want. I put everything I had into it. I was selling out, but I was genuinely trying to sell out as best I could.

No callback. Nothing. None of it went anywhere.

Beth: I was working as a waitress to bring in a little cash, and it was only a few months before we were living off of that. It was never quite enough for both food and rent.

Frank: We lost weight. Beth was only yea big to begin with. Things were dire.

Beth: Less than a year later, we were back in Chicago.

Frank: Like nothing had happened. Right back where we started.

Beth: Once we were home, Frank retreated into himself for a while. He would stay up late watching TV and sleep until two or three in the afternoon.

Gertie: He'd never been rejected before. That's what it was. Movies had dumped him. As much as he likes to talk about his rough childhood, with sports and things, he had never failed at anything that mattered to him. Frank was usually very successful at being Frank.

Beth: I don't think I've ever told him this. About a month after we were back in Chicago, I met with Dean Skilling at WCN. I wanted to see if I could get the old show back. We needed the money. I brought Gertie.

Gertie: I went with her. We got dressed up, and we brought a pitch packet, but the meeting lasted all of five minutes. Dean practically threw us out the door.

Dean: We had two other puppet shows on the air by then, with the stars contracted for the next decade. Frank taught me that. Get 'em under contract! You can't just quit and ask for your old television show back a year later. Frank left. We moved on.

Gertie: I wish I could say Frank learned not to burn bridges like that, but...

Frank: My mom, starting when I was about sixteen years old, showed me every ad in the newspaper for a reliable blue-collar union job. Electricians, bus drivers, cops, that sort of thing. Even when I had a syndicated TV show, even when I was pulling in like four times what my dad ever made, she would leave newspapers on my bed with jobs circled. She believed in me, just...not *too* much.

We're at our lowest moment. Beth and I are sleeping in my childhood bedroom. The puppet money has run out. And my mom says [*mimes reading the newspaper*], "Oh, they're testing down at the plumber's union." And Beth says, "Ha ha, Frank would never...."

But she has this look in her eyes. I don't know how many more nights of mac and cheese at my mom's house she has in her. So, I go to the thing.

I wait in line for three hours. Most of the guys around me are, like, actual plumbers. Working stiffs. I take a written test, and then they sit me down in front of these big guys with round heads and thick necks and crewcuts. War vets, you know? And one goes, "So, why do you want to be a plumber?"

And... I don't. What am I going to say? My lifelong love of pipes brought me here? My mom made me come. But I start thinking... why do I do anything? What's with the puppets and the movies? I could tell myself something lofty about giving back to the art forms that mean so much to me or about having something important to say that can't be expressed in words. That sort of thing.

But here's the truth: I was a weird kid. I knew it at the time, I'm not stupid, but it's not something I could change. You can't really change who you are. But whenever I would channel all that into art, there was a reason for it. It's not sad anymore. It's an origin story. Everything about myself that I don't like is a necessary part of a narrative about the creation of this thing. This movie, or puppet show, or whatever, exists because I was me, warts and all. Only Frank Nano could do it. And if I don't make that art, I'm just Jakey Najmanovich, a weird plumber.

I can't be me for no reason. That's not how movies work.

Anyway, I didn't want to fix toilets all day, so I got up and left. Right in the middle of the interview. They yelled at me, "You still have to pay for parking!" *[laughs]*

Beth: He loves telling that story, but he leaves out the part where he bombed the written exam, anyway.

Frank: I dropped out of high school. I can't do math!

The Nanos settled into a routine in Chicago. Beth started teaching preschool, and Frank worked as a janitor at the same high school he had dropped out of years earlier. Despite or because of their newfound stability, their Hollywood dreams seemed to be at an end.

Beth: One night, I'm making dinner, and the phone rings. This man says his name is Kenneth Sakai. He's a Hollywood producer, and he wants to talk to Frank.

No, "Man" is wrong. Boy. He's a kid. He sounds like he's fourteen.

Kenneth Sakai (producer): I was a business major at USC. I had just graduated. This young Japanese-American kid, top of my class, but with no experience and no industry connections. I wanted to produce films, but it was all old white guys then. Still is! Nobody wanted to talk to me.

One day, I saw this old puppet show being syndicated at five o'clock in the morning. *Nano Tales.* It was pretty funny and surprisingly advanced for a kids' show. I watched the credits, found the name Frank Nano, and eventually I got his number.

Frank: He wanted to meet with me about developing some projects. He paid for my flight, so I went.

Gertie: I tried to talk him out of it. Beth did, too. We were worried. Frank was flying to LA alone to meet with some random person. But I was going through my first divorce, and Beth had to teach the kids in the morning. Neither of us had the time or the money to go with him, and when Frank wants to do something, there's no stopping him.

Ken: I'm waiting in this diner. I spent all my money on his plane ticket, so I'm just drinking coffee. I've got my notes in front of me, a pen for each of us on the table. I've got a fresh haircut and I'm wearing my only suit. Frank had a syndicated show in the mid-sixties, so I'm expecting a middle-aged man, and I want to impress him. Well, the bell above the door rings, and in lopes this seven-foot hippie. *[laughs]* Luckily, we hit it off.

Frank: Yeah, I liked him. We're about the same age, so we grew up with the same movies and stuff. I pitched him what I had, and he got it immediately. I mean, he's still a businessman. He had a briefcase and a tie, and he wanted to know about the ratings and demographics from *Nano Tales*, something I should have paid more attention to when I was there. But when I talked about movies, he knew what I was saying, and that's rare.

Ken: I was upfront about it. I needed a semi-established yet affordable white guy to shop around. Frank needed someone to speak business to the people in charge of greenlighting projects. We were a great match.

Frank: He made a convincing argument, but let's be honest, I was an assistant janitor at my old high school. My boss was my mom. I was lucky that he was on the level because I would have agreed to anything.

Ken: We shook hands, signed some papers, and started a company.

Frank: The Frank Nano Company.

Ken: Just like that.

Frank: So, day one, he sits me down and says, "Now that it's too late to back out, I can be honest with you. Your problem is that you think too big." He said I was being too creative, which had never been a problem before. I was actually under the impression that was my entire job.

Ken: The movies he wanted to make were unworkable at our current level, which was the bottom level. We had no money. I convinced him to try doing some advertising work.

Frank: Commercials! Jesus Christ.

Ken: Frankie Frog started selling car insurance.

Frank: Insurance, ice cream, pop, uh, dryer sheets. Beer. The beer ads were weird. It was a long time ago.

Ken: Frank stayed out in LA, and we focused on advertising for a couple of years. He grumbled through the whole thing, but we gained two essential things from the experience: One, we got the puppets in front of millions of people, including—and this is important—adults. And two, we made a shit ton of money doing it.

Frank: I flew Beth and Gertie back out. First Class seats. That felt good. I sent my mom a photocopy of my SAG card, so she knew I was in a union.

Gertie: We were so against Ken at first, back in Chicago. We didn't want Frank to be taken advantage of, and those first few commercials were tacky. There was integrity to Frankie Frog when he was reenacting fairy tales and teaching kids the ABCs. He was a mean little jerk when he was selling potato chips. But when Frank flew us out and showed us the house, it became clear that whatever they were doing was working.

Beth: It's hard to argue with success.

Ken: Soon, we had offices in Burbank and a team of fifteen people. Frank had Beth there to do the puppets with him, but they needed a third hand, someone who could bring in some new ideas and characters.

Hugh Hurtt (puppeteer)**:** I was working as a stand-up, going from club to club around LA and, well, bombing. Before that, I had been a *[whispers]* birthday clown, and some puppets were involved. No follow-up questions.

Frank: He brought Dingus Dog with him. He was the only person to audition who had a puppet rolling around in his trunk, ready to go.

Ken: Hugh was perfect. We hired him on the spot.

Beth: Hugh was funnier than Frank, and it drove Frank nuts.

Hugh: Frank's a tall guy, so his puppets are all up here. *[raises arm above head]* I'm a bit more, er, stout, so they got me a stool to stand on. And because of the seat's height, Dingus Dog was a few inches higher than the others. So, I always played him big, a little higher energy than Frankie Frog, and his presence sort of pushed Frankie into a straight-man role, which Frank was *really* well-suited for, cause he's a crab ass.

Frank: He annoyed the shit out of me, and it made the crew laugh, so we worked it into the act.

Ken: Giving Frank someone to bounce off of besides his adoring wife brought things to another level.

Frank: I could come up with a simple premise, like, "Frankie Frog wants to sip his coffee," and then Dingus comes in like a wrecking ball, and I can just react to whatever Hugh was doing. I barely had to act.

Hugh: We spent a lot of time trying to one-up each other, and it would build and build until the puppets were both shouting. Frank would have Frankie on the one hand and the Mad Mallard on the other, and I'm wobbling on my stool with Dingus above me, cracking up where the cameras can't see.

Frank: We'd keep going after the cameras stopped rolling and the puppets were off. Just head to a bar and keep trying to make each other laugh.

Hugh: Those were the days, man.

Beth: Once the commercials became the Frank and Hugh show, there wasn't much for Frannie Frog to do. I started talking to Ken about getting the Nano Princesses going on a national scale.

Ken: The success of the ad campaigns had led to a revival of *Nano Tales* in syndication. We started getting some offers.

Frank: It was fun doing commercials, but it was a lot of work, it took up all my time, and in the end, you're selling soap. I didn't want to do it forever. And so, we returned to the movie studios, this time with more credibility.

Beth: We started pitching a series of *Nano Tales* feature films, each based on a fairy tale princess. This time, I worked with Frank on the scripts, so it wasn't all jokes and monsters.

There was actually a bidding war.

Frank: We had a little heat this time around. We could negotiate. I thought this might be my only chance to direct an actual movie. I told Ken that whoever lets me make a sci-fi picture for five million dollars can distribute all the *Nano Tales* movies.

And he got it. He got the money.

Ken: I got him *Time Breakers*.

"Aw yeah," Ethan muttered, "Here we go."

He had his phone tucked under the brim of his baseball cap, two inches from his face, which was the only way to see the screen as he stood in direct sunlight, waiting with his family to board the Fantasy Carousel. Pegasuses and unicorns, along with non-horse fantasy creatures like jackalopes and three-tailed foxes, galloped and trotted next to him, legs moving several inches off the floor. Realistic as these creatures might seem, they were still attached to the merry-go-round via a large golden pipe speared through their midsections.

Ethan's dad tapped the boy's hat. The line shifted forward, and Ethan tucked his phone away. The O'Brien family walked together, in a clump, for a total of two feet before stopping. Hailey stared straight ahead, white as a ghost and panting like a pug.

Maddie tugged her dad's shirt. "Daddy, I don't wanna go on the merry-go-round. I wanna see Princess Winnifred!"

"I know, Mads." The dad wiped his brow. "Let's just do this first, ok? Your sister's not feeling great. She needs a pick-me-up. Right, Hailey?"

The middle child hunched forward and vomited on the pavement in front of her. The guests ahead of them in the line, and the ones on the other side of red velvet ropes, edged nervously away from the expanding puddle.

"Dad…" Hailey ducked under the divider and ran over to the nearest garbage can, hands covering her mouth. She threw up again into the trash.

"Ah, man." Kevin exhaled through his teeth. "Ok. I gotta take her back to the hotel."

Ethan stumbled back as a janitorial crew in green-and-gray jumpsuits swooped into line ahead of him, seemingly from nowhere. They had mops and buckets at the ready.

"No!" Maddie said. "We can't go back! I wanna see princesses!"

"It's ok!" Kevin knelt down in front of Maddie. "Your brother's going to take you."

Both Ethan and Maddie looked at him like he was crazy.

"But I want you there!" Maddie shouted.

"Dad, you can't leave Maddie with me! She's not tall enough for Time Breakers! If it's only the two of us, I can't—"

"*Ethan.*" His dad said his name sternly, in a conversation-ending sort of way. "Take your sister to the princesses. I'll bring Hailey back to the hotel and then meet you over in Battlezone so you can ride your ride. Ok?"

"But..." Ethan knew what he was about to say would seem whiny—that the wait for Time Breakers was already three hours, that if he didn't get in line soon, he may never.

His dad nodded, somehow sensing everything Ethan didn't say. "Sometimes you gotta do things for other people. I'll meet you in outer space."

He went to help Hailey, who had collapsed on the edge of a trash bin while the other three were talking. The custodial staff was already done cleaning and disinfecting the barf and had dispersed into the park, vanishing into the woodwork until they were needed once more.

Ethan and Maddie stared at each other. Dad had walked away for ten seconds, and this was already the most time they'd spent alone together since Maddie was a baby.

"Here." The girl handed Ethan her princess wand, which she insisted on bringing and never wanted to hold.

He held up the sparkly piece of pink plastic—topped with a rainbow star—and let the sun shine through it. Beyond it loomed Frog Tower, and to the right of that, the top edge of the Cosmic Coliseum.

Ethan's ride was right there. He was so close.

"Do you want to go to the princesses right now?" he said. The sooner they got there, the sooner they'd be done.

"Yeah!"

Maddie ran straight under the red velvet divider and out into the park. Ethan swore as he clambered over the rope, following her.

6

Alicia rushed into the dressing room. She had her Princess Dee dress on, which meant she'd stopped at the lockers and changed, but she didn't remember doing so. Her mind was elsewhere. She sniffed her shoulder, realized how sweaty she was, and grabbed a stick of deodorant from the vanity.

Savannah and Greg were scrolling through their phones. Babs was helping Pasha with her wig. The sensors in there hadn't deactivated when her shift had ended, and Babs was peeling them from Pasha's scalp one by one. That happened sometimes.

Alicia stared at herself in the mirror. What the hell had just happened up in Frog Tower? What was that siren? Why wasn't it going off anywhere else? Was Barclay Bloom about to send her to LA to audition? What was she supposed to do with any of that? She'd been planning that meeting for months, and the result had been such a disaster that she would almost have been better off if she hadn't bothered going.

Almost.

She saw crow's feet in the corners of her eyes that weren't there a year ago. She reached for the concealer and dabbed some on her face. Maybe she should talk to Gertie? Bloom wouldn't be here tomorrow, but Grandma Nano would. She checked the clock. Two minutes. She stood.

"Hold up," Savannah said. "You're putting on a show."

She clutched her vape pen between her teeth as she reached forward and zipped the back of Alicia's dress.

"Thanks," Alicia said, "Fifth shift in a row?"

"Whatever the Big Frog needs." Savannah took a quick puff before pocketing her rig. "I'm very tired."

Alicia nodded. "Yeah."

"I'm off," Pasha said, her wig finally removed. She handed it to Alicia. "Good luck with this thing. Are you girls meeting at the Cantina later? Most of the royals are going."

"Hell yeah." Savannah raised her arms. Her long blond wig pixelated as it swirled into the air and settled around her head. "I need a drink."

"Alicia?" Babs was reading something on her tablet. "I just got a message from corporate. Did you go to a level of backstage you're not approved for? Did you...assault Barclay Bloom?"

Savannah and Pasha backed away from Alicia, gritting their teeth and pretending not to listen.

"Assault? No, I wouldn't–" Alicia winced as the princess wig attached itself to her head more forcefully than usual. "Grandma Nano was there. She can vouch for–"

"We need to talk after your shift," Babs sighed.

"Am I in trouble?" Alicia didn't like the expression on Babs's face. There was something she wasn't saying. "How much trouble?"

Babs shook her head.

"Ladies." Greg stood near the invisible wall, tablet ready. "Showtime."

"Babs." Alicia felt the blood drain from her face. She heard ringing in her ears. "Am I fired?"

Babs smiled wearily. "Let's take some pictures, Princess Dee. We'll talk after."

Winnifred gave her nanotech wig one last primp before passing through the wall. Alicia stared at Babs for a moment, and then she bit her lip and followed Winnifred. Her natural stride transitioned to a properly elegant princess glide.

Sunlight hit her face as she emerged into the Photo Pavilion. Princess Dee took her position on stage left. Two white kids—a middle school boy in a baseball cap and a little girl in a bright pink Winnifred dress—were at the front of the line, ready and waiting. Babs waved them over. The boy scanned his band on Babs' scanner and held up his phone to take pictures. The girl headed straight for Princess

Winnifred.

"Oh, uh," Babs went to redirect the girl. "This way, dear."

"Maddie." Ethan guided his sister to Princess Dee. "You gotta talk to this one first, ok?"

Maddie pointed. "But I wanna meet Winnifred!"

"Hello, Princess," Dee said to the girl, kneeling to greet her on her level. "That's a beautiful dress you've got."

Maddie regarded her suspiciously. "Are you a princess too?"

"*Ah sure ayam*," Dee said. "Is there anything more wonderful than that?"

"I love princesses." Maddie held up her sparkly plastic wand. "Did you see my wand? Isn't it cool? Are you sad?"

Princess Dee didn't understand. "Hmm?"

"You're crying."

Dee touched her cheek and felt the tear. She hadn't even noticed. She held the little girl's hand in hers. "Say, have you ever kissed a frog? Boy, I sure–"

A loud, low rumble echoed through the park, followed by a metallic groan, like two cargo ships scraping against each other. The whole Photo Pavilion shook. Ethan looked up from his phone.

Babs fixed her glasses. "What in the world?"

•○•

Over in the Puppet Paddock, Dingus Dog pretended to steal a small boy's nose, sticking his gloved thumb up between his fingers. The boy then grabbed the man-sized golden retriever's nose and did the same. Dingus held his snout in surprise and flopped onto his butt as the crowd in the queue laughed. Dingus jumped up, pointing at the boy, then jumped again. As he landed, the ground quaked. Windows around him shattered. Guests dropped their phones. In the cafe next door, drinks slid from tables.

Dingus scratched his head and gazed quizzically at his feet.

•○•

Outside Mermaid's Cove, a little girl gaped up at the statue of Mermaid Monica, confused as the face began shifting and changing. Each feature morphed individually—a new nose, a different mouth, eyes blinking at asynchronously as they swapped between other models.

Several guests noticed the problem, and within moments a crowd had gathered to gawk at the glitching statue. The mermaid's clothes changed, flipping from her original seashell bikini to a shirt, to a jacket, and for a brief moment, full frontal nudity. A few people snickered.

The statue turned its head downward, glowering at the little girl with dead yet ever-changing eyes.

She screamed.

•○•

A teenage boy stepped up to the ice cream counter in Retro Refreshments. "Can I get a large double chocolate Klutzy sundae? Hold the sprinkles."

The cashier spoke, but the boy didn't hear what she said. The letters and numbers on the menu board behind her had changed around, becoming blurry and incoherent.

He squinted at the letters. "What?"

A cold, wet hand made of ice cream burst through the glass below the teen and began strangling him. Brown, pink, and yellow cream oozed up from all sides of the freezer, pouring out into the rest of the restaurant as the staff and patrons fled.

The hand grew, dripping as it enclosed the boy's entire head.

•○•

A middle-aged man wearing shorts, black socks, and flip-flops approached one of the map kiosks stationed throughout the park. He pulled out a map, and as he went to walk away, many more maps blasted from the slot, shooting out the man's legs and knocking him to the ground.

He tried to crawl to safety but kept slipping on laminated maps, which continued pouring from the kiosk. Dozens, hundreds, thousands of paper maps rushed from the dispenser, burying the man alive.

•○•

Down in the hallways below the park, Pasha was getting an apple from a vending machine, still in her Princess Dee dress. Her phone cut out.

"Mom? Hello?" She checked the screen. Call disconnected.

There were a lot of sounds coming from upstairs. She couldn't tell what; the hallways were fairly well insulated from the sounds of the park, for employee sanity reasons, but *something* was going on up there. The hallway was empty except for her, which was also strange. There were always people down here.

The apple clunked into the bottom of the machine, startling her. Pasha reached down to get it, and as she did, the light four fixtures down the hall went out with a quiet plunk. Pitch-black darkness loomed beyond.

The next light closest to Pasha, three away, also cut out. She gasped.

"What..." she took a step back toward the machine. She was at the end of a hall. The encroaching darkness was the only way out.

She went to use her phone as a flashlight, but her shaking hands dropped it. As she reached down to pick it up, water flowed from the dark, and Pasha yanked her hand away as her phone disappeared into a pool of black.

Another light went out. Two remained. She held her finger to her ear instinctively to call Ron from security. She put her hand down. Alicia had the wig.

Splashing sounds burbled up from the end of the hall.

Pasha yelled, "Is anyone there?"

One more light plinked away. Only the bulb directly above Pasha, buzzing fluorescently, remained bright.

The screams upstairs seemed louder as Pasha stared up. The light flickered.

"Oh, no..." she whispered as the hallway went dark.

•○•

An air siren sounded from hidden speakers throughout the park. The pixelated head of Frankie Frog emerged at the top of Frog Tower. The guests stopped and stared at the glowing head as it spoke.

"Hey-yah hey-yah, park guests!" he shouted, louder than usual, "We're experienckkzing some shhhzzlight technical difficultieszzurktz! Please prozzkktttzeed to the emergency exitszzzk located at at at *at at at–*"

Frankie yelled louder and louder, throwing his head back and tilting his face toward the sky. The cloud of pixels that formed him grew sharper and more rectangular. His mouth dropped out of sync with the sound.

"AT AT AT AT!" the frog bellowed.

Bright red spotlights lit up the sky at every dock on the island. The park had three larger ships with multiple levels and dozens of small vessels sailing from its shores to mainland Florida at all times during park hours. Flashing red lights blinked on each of them as their engines roared to life. Every employee in the park received a signal on their nanobands. A gift shop cashier in her early twenties spoke first.

"Everybody, listen up!" she shouted over the frog, "We're going to need you to head east to the loading dock where you see the red lights! This way! Have a nanomagical day!"

"Please remain calm!" said the other cashier, an older woman. "Help anyone who needs assistance!"

As more and more employees spoke up, the panicked guests moved in more specific directions, converging on the docks at the park entrance. They held hands with their families, dragging souvenirs, strollers, cameras, and kids along with them.

Frankie Frog's head glitched out, dissolving completely before recombining.

"...at the nearest docking station!" he said. "Follow the red lights! Hey-yah! Hey-yah!"

The frog vanished, as it usually would after a message, then reappeared almost immediately.

"Follow the red lights!" he repeated. "Hey-yah! Hey-yah!"

•○•

Over in the Prehistoric Forest, Churro Charlie finished organizing his churro cart and popped his head out. Chaos reigned all around him. Plants merged into one another. Animals split and combined at odd angles. A trail of red lights pulsed toward the entrance. Guests and staff alike hustled in that direction. A wooly mammoth with two bodies joined at the neck—no head—stomped past, four of its eight legs wobbling upside-down above it.

Big Sam, the massive extinct ground sloth, lumbered out of the forest and over to Charlie. He seemed to be the only nanomatronic creation unaffected by whatever was happening.

"Well, Sam," Charlie said. "It's here."

He reached into his cart and pulled out his favorite: a sausage-and-egg breakfast churro. He took a bite and offered one to the beast. A torrent of water rushed through the trees, flowing up to Charlie's ankles. His shins. His knees.

He and Sam chewed their churros solemnly as the water level rose.

•○•

The riders on Danger Dragon wailed in mock terror as the cars hit a particularly intense loop. The laughter faded, and the screams became more genuine as the people rolled faster and faster through an endless loop. Many of them had ridden this roller coaster before. It wasn't supposed to move like that.

The tracks rocked like they shouldn't, wobbled and tilted sideways, angling the riders toward the ground. The people ducked as their cars rushed forward at increasing speed. Guests still in line hustled away, further from the tracks, as each line of cars flew through the ride entrance every few seconds.

The concrete-embedded steel beams supporting the coaster burst from the ground.

In the front row, the horrified riders watched as the tracks broke away and bent apart, aiming the cart directly at the ground. The screams grew silent as the realization spread and the car careened head-on into the concrete below.

•○•

Dingus Dog stood at the edge of the docks, holding a sign reading "This way!" and waving people toward the boats. Several other park employees were doing the same. Already, all three of the bigger ships had filled to the brim with bobbing heads in Frankie hats and dog ears.

Another deep shudder rumbled throughout the park. Dingus watched as part of the Cosmic Coliseum broke away. He turned his gaze to the Fairy Tale Kingdom, where the spires of the castle-shaped Photo Pavilion began to fall.

The anthropomorphic dog dropped his sign and ran.

•○•

Adults and children scrambled to exit the Photo Pavilion, fleeing as the building shook and shuddered around them. Greg, Winnifred's host, dropped his tablet and scurried off with the guests. Bits of plaster and drywall dribbled down as cracks formed in the ceiling. There was another loud screech as the floor fractured into two distinct plates. The Dee half of the room sank a few inches.

"Maddie!" Ethan grabbed his sister by the arms. "We gotta go!"

"Wait!" The girl pulled away from him. "I dropped my wand! I can't find it!"

"Forget your wand!" Ethan shouted.

"No!"

"Don't worry, children," Princess Dee held her wig closer to her head, right above her ear, "we're still going to have a nanomagical day."

Silence on her wig headset. No answer from Ron. No static, even.

"Have a nanomagical day," she repeated. Nothing. "Have a nanomagical day."

Ethan stopped searching for Maddie's wand and stared at her. "Why do you keep saying that?!"

Dee turned to Babs. "Ron's not answering."

The host nodded. She scanned the room. She reached for Maddie's arm. "Kids, we're going to go for a walk. Do you have an adult with you?"

"Princess Winnifred!" Maddie yanked her arm away as she yelled to the other princess. "Use your hair!"

Winnifred had pressed herself against the back wall, under a thin arch, with her arms and legs spread to keep herself from moving. She glanced at Maddie without turning her head and flashed the girl a fake princess smile.

"Can't," she whispered. "Terrified."

The park shuddered, and a sizable chunk of the ceiling fell, crashing to the floor in front of Ethan and knocking him off his feet. Babs helped him up and pulled him away from the rubble. Dee held Maddie back as she reached for the other princess.

"Use your magic hair!" Maddie shouted. "You can hold everything together!"

Winnifred shook her head, her pixelated mane flowing majestically around it.

Ethan blinked. Something was blocking his vision. He pulled off his hat and saw that a piece of rebar from the ceiling had speared itself in the bill.

"Son! Boy!" Babs held the boy by his arms and shook him. He looked at her.

"Where are your adults?" she said.

"They're…" Ethan blinked. "They're back at the hotel."

"Ok. Princess Dee, can you help me?"

"Darlin' girl," Dee said to Maddie. "We're going for a little boat ride, ok? We'll find your parents."

"Winnifred!" Maddie said, tears in her eyes. "Hurry! You need to-"

Another shudder and the rest of the ceiling gave way, exposing black roofing and rotted wood. Debris crashed toward Maddie, Ethan, and the adults before a wave of sparkling yellow hair spread throughout the room and held the broken ceiling aloft.

The blond princess stood at the center of the Pavilion, immaculate under an awning of her own hair, resplendent in her sequined pink ball gown. Maddie shrieked with delight. Winnifred grinned at the girl, wincing a bit from the strain on her all too human body holding up all that ceiling.

"Well," she grunted. "That just happened."

Suddenly, her hair glitched, sections of it bending and twisting away from the mass at polygonal angles. A few strands of hair fell, then more. Some plaster and rebar of the ceiling clattered to the floor.

"I can't–" Winnifred trembled, eyes wide with fear. "It's not listening. I don't–"

A thick strand of her blond wig whipped out and wrapped around her neck. The princess choked. Dee covered Maddie's eyes.

More hair wriggled around Winnifred, crawling away from the ceiling and trickling down into her mouth and nose. She stumbled to her knees, clawing at her wig with her hands. More plaster fell.

Another digital spasm from the hair. Winnifred convulsed, gagging.

Dee and Babs dragged the kids to the back of the Pavilion as the entire ceiling caved in on top of Princess Winnifred. The room filled with plaster, dust, and rebar, plunging into darkness as the mass of debris blocked the only exit. The screams and alarms outside grew quiet. Ethan could hear his own breathing. Maddie sobbed.

Now that she was in the back of the Pavilion, Dee remembered the other exit: the pixelated wall that led to her dressing room. She held Maddie in her arms and stepped into it, passing unobstructed until Maddie touched the edge. The wall rippled as both princess and girl were spat back into the dark Pavilion. A low chime rang on Maddie's nanoband.

"This area is for cast members only." said a pleasant robotic voice.

"No! They're with me!" Dee slapped the pixelated wall. It was solid as stone.

"Ok." Babs turned on her tablet, the only light in the room. "It's ok. We'll find another way out. Is everyone alright?"

Ethan limped toward the debris blocking the exit. He could see a point of light coming from one corner of the door.

Dee held Maddie close. "Son, come away from there. It's dangerous."

"I see daylight," Ethan said.

"We need a plan." Babs tapped her tablet, which showed only a white screen. "Dee, you go through the dressing room and find help.

I'll stay here with the—"

The floor shifted, and the concrete beneath Babs' feet crumbled away. The woman plunged deep into the darkness below.

"Babs!" Dee shouted.

Ethan staggered back as the floor between him and the others broke away too. Water rushed up from the new hole in the ground.

"Ethan!" Maddie reached out.

Dee beckoned to him. "Jump!"

The boy leaped, catching Dee and Maddie's hands just as the floor beneath his feet sank into the water, before resurfacing all broken, jagged, and unpainted. The three of them huddled by the back wall as the dark room around them undulated and churned like a stomach digesting meat. Behind them, the wall cracked, and the pixelated section—the hidden door—glitched out before solidifying into a jagged, dangerous-looking shape.

"What is happening?!" Ethan said. "What do we do?!"

Maddie wailed, crying. Dee held the kids. For a brief moment, the debris cleared from the exit, revealing Frankie Frog's head glowering over what remained of the park. As the frog's semi-translucent eyes met Dee's, more rubble fell, and the princess and the kids were in darkness once more.

7

That one was new. Princess Dee laughed a little, her accent dropping away momentarily. "What?"

The little girl giggled as she spoke. "They don't have butts, so they can't make poops, and they fill up with poop!"

They sat on the floor of the Princess Photo Pavilion, huddled with each other and surrounded by debris, lit only by some stray shafts of morning light peeking in through unreachable cracks in the roof. They'd been trapped there overnight. The sounds of destruction, the screams, and the mechanical rumbling had died down hours ago. Now they crouched alone in eerie silence.

Across the room, Ethan leaned against the wall, lit by the glow of his phone, which he'd plugged into the only accessible outlet to keep it charged. There was no internet or data, no way to call for help, but his ebook app worked, so he'd been reading.

"She's going through a poop joke thing," Ethan said, eyes never leaving the screen. "We're supposed to ignore it."

Maddie laughed maniacally. "And the frogs explode, and their poops go everywhere and—"

"Frogs have butts, Maddie," Dee said, "Right above their legs. How's your book, Ethan?"

"Good. It's the Time Breakers chapter, so I already know most of it. Did you know John Candy was originally supposed to play Doc Rocket?"

"I did not."

"Princess Dee." Maddie tugged on the princess's arm. "Can we go back to the hotel now?"

"We talked about this, darlin'," Dee said. "The magic door in the back is stuck, and all that wood and plaster is blocking our way out the front. It's too heavy for your brother and me, so we need to sit tight and wait for the helpers."

"But when are the helpers gonna get here? I'm *bored*."

"Well, in all my born days." Dee stood and brushed the dust from her dress, "Being bored is no reason to be sad! Boredom is an opportunity to use our imaginations! I declare! Surely there's a game to be had in all this."

"You don't have to do that," Ethan said. "You can drop the princess voice."

A buzz tickled across Dee's scalp beneath her wig. She raised her eyebrows at the boy. "And what voice should a princess use?"

Ethan locked his phone. "I just mean, like, you can be yourself. We won't tell your boss or nothing."

"What?" Maddie said. "What's he saying?"

"Ethan." Dee walked over to him. "This world can be a dark and dangerous place, full of things no child should ever have to experience. And in those times, having a grown-up you trust can be helpful. Someone good, and pure, and clever, and kind, and maybe a little magical. Someone who will never lie to you and never leave you behind."

He stood as she approached. She held his hands.

"Sometimes, you need a princess."

Ethan peeked over her shoulder at his sister.

"Yeah," he said, embarrassed. "Ok. Sorry, Princess Dee."

She smiled sympathetically as the buzzing in her head faded. The silence inside the room, and the silence outside, seemed more omnipresent than before. She felt the weight of it. There was a tug on her dress.

Maddie stood behind her, legs crossed. "I need to go potty."

Dee brought Maddie to a small alcove behind Winnifred's station, where there was a large potted plant and a long-disconnected landline phone. The princess helped the girl with her dress and dangled her above the pot.

"Princess Dee," Maddie said. "Am I the first kid to pee on this plant?"

"You know," Dee laughed. "You just might be."

As Ethan settled back into reading his book, the rubble blocking the entryway into the pavilion shifted. Dust and drywall trickled down. A few more small thin beams of daylight broke into the darkness. The boy shielded his eyes.

"Uh, Dee?"

"What is it, Ethan?"

"Someone's coming."

"Oh, my stars." Dee's head popped around the side of the alcove wall. She was still holding Maddie. "Are you almost done, baby?"

"Almost!" Maddie said. "Is it the helpers?"

Ethan shuffled to the light as more debris rolled away. The pavilion grew even brighter.

"Ethan, stay back!" Dee shouted. "We don't know what that is."

"Yes, we do!" Maddie pulled up her pants. "It's the helpers!"

Ethan scanned around the now-visible room. He picked up a broken piece of rebar and clutched it in front of himself like a baseball bat.

More substantial chunks of rubble moved away. A tall figure shifted in the doorway, backlit by the morning sun. Having cleared a large enough hole, the person or thing crawled into the pavilion. Ethan squinted at it, unable to determine what he was seeing as the figure rose before him, wobbling upright atop the rocks and drywall before dusting itself off.

"Who is it?" Dee said, finally able to leave the alcove. She squinted too. They'd all been in the dark for a long time. "Park security?"

"No, it's, uh…" Ethan rubbed his eyes with the back of his arm. "It's Dingus Dog."

The golden retriever in dirty overalls struck a heroic pose before falling onto his butt.

Dee let go of Maddie's hand and stumbled across the rubble in a slight daze as she moved toward the dog. As she helped him up, she felt the ketchup stain on his fur. She ran her fingers over it.

The princess fell into the dog's furry arms. He hugged her back.

"Hooray!" Maddie cheered. "They're friends!"

Dee wiped away a tear before the kids could see. Maddie and Ethan shuffled past her to gaze out into the sunlight.

"Is Frannie Frog here too?" Maddie said. "And Frankie? And the duck?"

Dingus shrugged and shook his head. He pointed outside and made a walking motion with two fingers.

"Children, gather your things," Dee said. "Ethan, help your sister. We're leaving."

"But I still didn't find my wand," Maddie said.

"C'mon," Ethan led her back to his phone charger, "Maybe we can see it now."

Dee leaned in closer to Dingus as the kids went to collect their stuff. "Are you ok in there?"

The dog looked at her with his big googly eyes and nodded.

"What's out there?"

Dingus stared at her. He shook his head before pointing at his mouth.

"Listen." Dee reached up and felt around the sides of his head. "I'm staying in character for the kids, but you can take the head off. I'm sure you're hot in there."

She frowned. Something was off. She couldn't find the seam between the neck of the costume and the mask. The dog seemed to know what she was thinking. He leaned forward and pointed at the back of his neck. Dee gasped.

"There's no zipper," Dee whispered. "What does that mean?"

Dingus shrugged dramatically. Dee took a step away from him.

Maddie and Ethan came back over. The girl pointed out into the park. "I see my wand!"

Ethan looked. Sure enough, a pink plastic wand glinted in the sun, propped up against a broken fire hydrant several yards into the courtyard.

"Wait," the boy said. "That doesn't make any sense. What's it– Maddie!"

The girl was already halfway out, crawling through the hole Dingus had dug. Ethan followed her.

"Children!" Dee said. "Hold your horses!"

The dog put his gloved hands on the sides of his head and wobbled in shock as the princess crawled after the kids.

8

Dee shielded her eyes as she stepped out into the sunlight. Dingus emerged from the pavilion behind her, the dust and dirt wafting from his golden fur. The princess scanned the area. *Where are they?*

The park was still recognizable, if a little worse for wear. A spiderweb of cracks ran through the pavement, with some sections raised or lowered, making the terrain much more treacherous than it was before. The trees were still standing. Mermaid Cove was partially caved in, but the restaurant and the gift shops were mostly untouched. Dee was expecting more damage after the night she'd spent in the Photo Pavilion.

A chill ran through her, and it took her a moment to realize why. She felt unsettled by the quiet. Whenever she came early or stayed late, cast members were already milling about, cleaning, prepping, and repairing rides. The park never closed. The after-hours were for maintenance. Nanoland was *never* quiet.

"I got it!"

Maddie stood on a particularly damaged spot in the pavement, holding the pink plastic wand victoriously above her head. Ethan paced behind her, arms folded, whipping his head around at every noise.

Dee waved to them and was about to yell when a soft furry hand fell on her shoulder. Dingus put his finger to his doggy lips.

"Dee!" Maddie said. "I found my wand!"

Dee raised her hands to keep the children quiet and beckoned them over. Dingus led her to a small alcove at the base of a tree, hidden on two sides by a fallen popcorn cart and a brick planter with a painted metal gate on top. Dee peeked over the top of the cart and waved to the kids again.

"What are we hiding from?" she whispered.

The dog didn't answer.

Halfway to the hiding spot, the ground beneath Maddie's feet gave way, and she slid forward, falling on one knee. Ethan went to help her, but she yelped as he pulled her upright.

"Ah!" Maddie wailed. "I'm stuck!"

Dee climbed out from the hiding spot and tottered over to them in her clear plastic high heels, lifting the hem of her ball gown so it didn't snag on anything. She knelt by the girl.

"What's wrong, baby?"

"My foot!" Maddie pointed with her wand. Her right foot was wedged between two chunks of concrete. "I can't move it!"

"Ethan," Dee said. "Go by Dingus. We don't know what's out here."

The boy hesitated and then nodded, clearly feeling too lost and overwhelmed to fight her. He hustled over to Dingus's hiding place. Dee hunched down and reached between the concrete slabs to loosen Maddie's foot. It was a little too far down, wedged a little too tight. She could almost touch the laces.

"Can you wiggle your foot? I can almost reach it."

"Princess Dee," Maddie said. "Where did all the horsies go?"

Dee looked up. The merry-go-round was empty: no unicorns, no pegasuses, just two big metal disks with a single pole in the middle. Dee didn't have an answer.

"Try pulling your foot out again," she said.

Maddie grunted. "Still stuck."

"Ok. Let's take your shoe off."

Dee lay on her stomach and reached deeper, gritting her teeth as her arm scraped against the broken street. Her fingers brushed against the girl's laces. She could touch them, but she couldn't grip them in any useful–

"Dee! Maddie!"

Hushed voices called to them. Dingus and Ethan were frantically waving their arms. Dingus pointed over Dee's shoulder.

She turned her head.

A unicorn stood alone in the fantasy courtyard, twenty feet away from them. It was mainly a unicorn. The fiberglass beast was filthy, with bits of cotton candy, popcorn, twigs, and plaster sticking out of it. It seemed to have absorbed some of its surroundings into its skin.

The creature snorted mechanically and trotted toward them. The golden rod that had once connected the unicorn to the carousel dragged beneath it, scraping on the ground like a loose muffler.

Dee forced her arm deeper into the crack, reaching desperately for Maddie's shoelaces. The unicorn grew closer. Dee could see that the top half of the pole, the part that protruded from the beast's upper back, had flopped and curled across its torso, like the dorsal fin of an orca whale in captivity. Maddie inhaled to scream, but Dee covered the girl's mouth with her other hand. She didn't want to spook this thing. Maddie's muffled screech did little to change the unicorn's trajectory. It stared past them with empty black eyes as it approached.

Ethan stood to help his sister, but Dingus held him back. The boy struggled against his fuzzy arms, but the dog was surprisingly strong.

Dee got two fingers on the girl's shoelace and tugged at it. She freed her arm from the ground and hugged the girl, covering her eyes. She closed her own.

The unicorn stopped in front of them. It lowered its head by tilting its entire body, its snout inches from Maddie's face. It smelled like a fried battery or burnt plastic. Something hot and industrial. Dee leaned back and angled the girl away from it as best she could.

A cloud of gray pixels—nano dust—misted from the horse's face, which stretched along with the dust as it drifted tentatively toward Maddie. The end of the cloud brushed against her cheek like an insect's antennae. The girl whimpered.

Shlunk! A golden rod speared through the unicorn's abdomen straight to the other side. Three metal points drove themselves into the broken asphalt. The horse flailed silently, almost in slow motion, its sparkly pink horn bobbing on its head. The beast dropped onto its side and kicked, running in place momentarily before falling motionless.

"What is it?" Maddie said. "I can't see!"

The three golden points dislodged from the ground, loosening the rocks around Maddie's foot. The unicorn shifted, grinding against the asphalt as it slid away from them. It stopped after a few feet.

Dee recognized the trident impaling the unicorn. She glanced at where the mermaid statue should be, finding only an empty pedestal.

The creature slid again, faster this time, all the way across the courtyard, yanked by a chain on the end of the trident. Finally, it reached an open utility hole, which was in no way big enough for a unicorn. The beast slammed into the concrete surrounding the hole before bending and twisting apart as some unseen force hauled it downward. There were soft, wet sounds, like waves lapping on a shore, then silence.

"What happened?" Maddie said.

"Nothing much," Dee spoke in a harsh whisper. "We should go inside."

Ethan ducked away from Dingus and hustled over to the girls before the dog could grab him again. Dee pushed on one rock pinning Maddie's shoe down, and it shifted slightly. She turned to Ethan.

"I'm going to hold this, and you lift her up. Ready?"

The boy nodded and held his sister under her arms. Dee shoved the rock with both hands as Ethan hoisted the crying girl up, stopping after her foot wedged into the rocks again.

"Bless my biscuits!" Dee swore, keeping the rock pinned up with one hand and reaching into the gap with her other. She snagged Maddie's shoelace and tugged it free.

"Wiggle your foot, baby."

A herd of mutated merry-go-round horses—maybe a dozen—clopped out from behind Mermaid Cove, dropping leaves, trash, and silver dust behind them, their support rods dragging loudly along the concrete. The pegasuses flapped their wings but stayed grounded. The herd stomped right past Dee and the kids, heading south toward Nostalgia Bay.

"Something spooked them," Dee said.

Sounds of banging and scraping came from behind the mermaid ride.

"Ok," Ethan said, lifting his sister again. "Wiggle faster."

The girl shook her foot, desperately trying to free it from its shoe. Dee covered her mouth, stifling a scream, before putting her hand on Maddie's.

Ethan saw it too. "Holy shit."

The Danger Dragon roller coaster lumbered out from the shadows. It moved like an enormous centipede, with two dozen steel beam legs slamming into concrete in a rolling wave. Two coaster cars stuck out at the front, wheels in the center, poking curiously at the air like pincers. Other than those, it had no discernable face. The ride's fiberglass dragon head was somewhere in the back.

Ethan yanked his sister upward, and her foot popped out of her shoe.

"I'm free!" Maddie said.

The cars waved in the humans' general direction. It seemed to sense them somehow. Several of its legs stamped their way.

"Run!" Dee shouted.

A metallic clanging from the left. The creature shifted its eyeless gaze toward Dingus, who repeatedly banged on the downed popcorn machine with a stick. He pointed at the gift shops.

"Head for Treasures & Trinkets!" Dee said.

She grabbed both kids' arms and gunned it, dodging broken ground and fallen decorations. The coaster creature skittered after them faster than anything that big should have been able to move, its steel feet driving into the ground with each step. It dipped its pincers toward them, only to get caught in the branches of a tree.

Dingus caught up to them as they reached the shops. Dee threw herself at the door, which only opened an inch. It was unlocked, but something was blocking it.

"Ethan! Dingus! Help a princess out!"

The boy and the dog lined up next to her, shoulders out, and they all slammed their bodies into the door.

Ron, the security guard, went flying backward into a rack of light-up wands. Dee, the dog, and the kids spilled into the gift shop, one on top of the other.

Someone shouted, "Those kids are human!"

Another security guard stepped forward and dragged them all further into the room while a third guard slammed the door behind them, blocking it with a shelving unit once again.

Dee stood. She fixed her dress and tiara. Five or six people were hiding in the gift shop, surrounded by toys and clothes and other knick-knacks. One guard helped Ron up. Gertie Nano was sitting on a bench, seeming relatively untouched. Reggie, the man with the lab coat from Frog Tower, was eating an ice cream sandwich.

Barclay Bloom leaned against the checkout counter, swiping pointlessly at a blank cell phone. His white suit was still immaculate. He glowered at Dee from over his sunglasses.

"I can see why you're ready to leave this place," he said.

•○•

Pasha wandered alone in the hallways below Nanoland. The water level was up to her waist and seemed to still be rising—slower now, but consistently. The power was out, and she sloshed along in complete darkness, keeping her right hand on the wall at all times. It had been hours. Or it felt like hours. It was hard to tell in the dark. The only sounds were splashing water and her own breathing.

When she was little, back in Indiana, her parents would take her to these corn mazes at the county fair. If she ever got lost, they told her she should keep her hand on one wall and always turn in that direction, and eventually, she would find her way out. She didn't know if this was true, but it was all she had right now.

"Well, I declare," said a familiar voice.

Pasha stopped. That sounded like Princess Dee, which was, of course, insane. She peered into the dark. "Hello?"

"Aren't you a sight for sore eyes," said the voice.

"Alicia?" Pasha said, "Is that you?"

"I was hoping I might find you down here," said the voice. "How are you?"

"Oh, thank God," Pasha said. "Oh, God. You don't know how long I've been underground. The power's out, even the emergency lights. Do you know how to get out?"

"Just head toward my voice, darlin'. That's a lovely dress."

Pasha laughed nervously. "Yeah, I was at the vending machines. I didn't have time to change."

Pasha kept her hand on the wall as she waded forward. The surrounding water grew warmer. Obviously, Alicia was staying in character to keep her calm, which was a little strange but also precisely what Alicia would do. She was a Nano obsessive if ever there was one.

"A beautiful blue ball gown, bright as the sky, shining your way home. It really is a lovely dress."

An electronic buzz. A flash of light. A face glowed in the darkness directly in front of Pasha. Princess Dee's face. The nanomatronic Dee from the parade, a little bit larger than life, animatronic skeleton exposed at the joints where the pixel layer grew thin. The water around the robot princess boiled into steam.

"Unfortunately…" the princess smiled a sinister, pixelated grin. "It's *my* dress."

Pasha screamed.

9

The moment they shut the door to the gift shop, two security guards grabbed Dingus, pinned his arms back, and slammed him against the door. The dog struggled silently, his googly eyes wobbling to-and-fro. One guard drew a pistol from his belt and aimed it at Dingus's head.

"Goodness!" Dee shouted. "At ease, boys! The dog's with me!"

"Guys," Ron said, wiping his mouth. "I think I know him."

"Yeah!" Maddie said. "That's Dingus Dog!"

Gertie stepped forward and snatched the gun from the guard with shocking speed for an elderly woman. She popped out the clip.

"You will not be drawing this weapon with children present," Gertie said, returning his empty gun. "Do you understand me?"

The guards stared at her as she hunched down to speak to Maddie.

"Where's your other shoe, dear?"

The girl pointed outside. "It's stuck in the ground! No! A unicorn pooped on it!"

She giggled.

Gertie took the girl by the hand. "Well, that won't do, will it? Come on, we'll find you something."

She led Maddie toward a rack of child-size sneakers. As she did, she turned to Ethan and pointed to the freezer. "There's ice cream if you're hungry."

The boy was. "You got any Mallard bars in there?"

"Hell yeah, we do." Reggie tossed him one.

The guard closest to Dingus's face leaned in to speak to him.

67

"What's your name, dude?"

Dingus just stared.

"He can't talk," Dee said. "His gob's buttoned up tighter than my corset at the town hall ball."

The guard glared at her. "What?"

Ron seemed to consider this for a moment, before saying, "Hold her."

One guard moved away from Dingus and pinned Dee's arm back.

"Get your hands off of me!" she shouted.

"The thing is," Ron said, "Every other costumed character has attacked us on sight. What's your name?"

"You know my name," Dee said.

"I do. We've known each other for years, and you're talking like Colonel Sanders. I need you to say it."

Dee looked around the room. Reggie and Ethan huddled by the ice cream freezer, Barclay by the checkout counter. Shelves filled with toys, clothes, and other merch surrounded the big display—a green golf cart with Frankie's big googly eyes at the top. Maddie and Gertie were on the other side of the room, trying on shoes.

The princess spoke in a hushed whisper. "I've worked here for ten years. I sneak the wine in on Employee Nights and kick your ass in the Cosmic Coliseum. I was at your daughter's wedding. The fish was too salty, but the cake was excellent. Now take your goddamn hands off me."

Ron relaxed a little, but not entirely. "Why are you still in character?"

"That little girl saw Princess Winnifred get crushed to death under her own hair. I'm keeping her sane. What do you want from me?"

"Savannah's dead?" Ron gestured to the others, and they released their grips on Dee and Dingus. The dog rubbed his arm and made a *Naughty, Naughty* motion with his finger.

"Babs, too. Where were you? You were supposed to protect us."

"I got called in to escort Gertie and Bloom out," Ron said. "All available hands, five minutes before the whole park wigged out. Executive override. Nothing I could do."

Dee rolled her eyes.

"What about him?" Ron pointed at Dingus.

The dog noticed his own tail and spun in a circle, trying to get a closer look.

"He's in there somewhere," Dee said. She waved to Barclay, who watched with great interest as Ethan pulled out his phone to read his book as he ate ice cream. "Mr. Bloom! Always a pleasure."

The CEO snatched the phone out of the boy's hand.

"Hey!" Ethan reached helplessly for it as Barclay held it away.

"I need this," he said, swiping on the screen. "Why does your phone work?"

"It doesn't," Ethan said. "It's in airplane mode or something. There's no signal."

"Everyone else's bricked when the, uh, 'event' happened." Reggie pulled out his phone and showed it to Ethan. Black screen. "What do you have on there?"

"Games and stuff. I don't know." Ethan stole his phone back from Barclay, who let him take it. "What event? What's going on? Why are we hiding in the gift shop?"

"I also have those questions," Dee said.

Dingus nodded in agreement.

Reggie sighed. "We don't know much. The—"

"It's confidential," Barclay said firmly.

Reggie continued anyway. "The park is—"

Barclay stood. "That is confidential information, Dr. Cundey."

"So fire me! Sue me! Whatever! We got them into this. They have a right to know!"

Barclay slammed the counter with his fist, fuming. The engineer stood, too, holding his ground. The CEO snorted before turning away to stare at a rack full of keychains.

"Go on," Dee said.

"Nanoland has been running on the same software since 1989. It controls the pixels coating everything inside the park, from the rides to the landscaping to the neural interfacing in your costumes, all from one central hub at the top of Frog Tower. It's a hundred years ahead of its time. The pixels have advanced, but we've never had a reason to update the software."

He paused, pulling another ice cream sandwich from the freezer. He offered it to Ethan, who declined. Reggie unwrapped it and took a bite, continuing with his mouth full.

"Except, we've been getting glitches for the last few months. Pixels where they shouldn't be. Things moving around. We don't know how to fix them. There are no errors in the code. There's no reason this should be happening. And yet...."

Murmurs behind Dee. The three security guards huddled together by a framed park map, working something out. Dingus had wandered to another part of the store.

"Last night, we had a major event." Reggie tossed the empty wrapper over his shoulder. "Cascading software failure. Every pixel in the park glitched out at once. And since then...."

He paused. Dee and Ethan glanced at each other.

"Since then, it's like the pixels are operating on instinct. Absorbing information from whatever's around them. Overlapping with each other. I'm sure you saw the Danger Dragon."

"We've been holed up in here," Ron said, standing with his arms crossed next to Dee. "Every couple of hours, we get another wave of costumed crazies trying to break in. But, like, weird ones. Extra arms, missing eyes. Ice cream and french fries oozing out of the seams."

Dee frowned.

"We incapacitate them, and the living rides clean up the mess. You can see why we were a little edgy around you."

Dee ignored him as she turned to the man in the lab coat. "Reggie, right?"

He nodded.

"How do we fix this?"

"I wish I knew. You have to understand, the park mostly runs itself. My team and I, we're like white blood cells. We just run around scooping up problems and throwing them away. This is completely unprecedented." Reggie sighed. "If I can get to the top floor of Frog Tower, I might be able to shut down the server. Knock out all the pixels at once."

"That's out of the question." Barclay turned to face the group. "You told me—"

"Sir," Reggie said, "With all due respect—"

"*You* told me," Barclay said, "that same software also controls the streaming service, it runs the merchandizing, it green-lights which films get made, it navigates the goddamn cruise lines. The accounting team told me we'll lose 2.07 million dollars a minute while it's down. How long does it take to reboot?"

Reggie bit his lip. "Nobody knows. It's never been turned off. It may not turn back on."

"We've got investors, man," Barclay said. "If we shut that off—"

"If we don't shut it off, we'll be eaten by a roller coaster!"

"Check out my shoes!" Maddie strutted up, showing off her brand new Princess Winnifred-themed sneakers. She hopped up and down to make the pink lights in the heels flash. "They light up!"

All the adults oohed and ahhed, pointing, clapping, and complimenting the little girl on her fashion choices. Gertie stopped by Reggie.

"Don't turn it off," she said. "Please. Frank wouldn't want you to."

Ethan finally realized who she was. He sat on his hands and fought the urge to ask her a series of detailed questions about her brother.

"He told me before he died that he wanted this place open every single day, with no exceptions. This is his legacy. This is his gift to the world."

"Ok, great," Reggie said. "So what do we do? Stay here in the gift shop and watch the place slowly get worse? Wait for the glitching pixels to reach the mainland? We don't know what'll happen if…"

Barclay removed his sunglasses and wiped them with a handkerchief. "You know as well as I do those things konk out the moment they leave company property."

"Look out there!" Reggie said. "I don't know anything!"

As they continued to argue, a furry three-fingered hand tapped Dee's shoulder. Dingus handed her a pullover hooded sweatshirt and a pair of sneakers in her size. The shirt had a big picture of Princess Dee's face, the words "Hop into your Heart" surrounding her in curvy green letters. The dog bowed dramatically before backing away.

Dee smiled and pulled the sweatshirt over her head. The Princess Dee dress was designed to look great for fifteen minutes at a time. It was not intended for long-term active use. There was tape involved. She reached down and pulled the clear plastic shoes off her aching feet.

Maddie climbed onto Ethan's lap, surprising him. He was unsure whether to hold her, so his hands hovered at her sides. She spun her princess wand in her hands.

"You boys have kept this place running for forty years," Gertie said. "I don't understand how this happened, I'm mortified that it happened, but there has to be another way."

"Ma'am," Reggie said. "You of all people must understand–"

"We're not shutting the park down." Barclay shook his head. "Stop talking about it. Stop thinking about it. It's not happening!"

"Alright, everyone, listen up." Ron turned to face the others with his arms behind his back. The other two security guards lined up on either side of him.

"Regardless of what's causing this and how it should be dealt with, our priority is to get the remaining civilians and staff safely to the mainland. Do you all agree?"

Murmurs and nods of reluctant approval.

"Luis, you worked the emergency unit." He addressed the man to his left. "What's the protocol?"

"Well," Luis removed his black baseball cap and rubbed his bald head. "In the event of a terrorist attack, natural disaster, or, uh, this, guests and staff are immediately sent to the boats. Once the initial wave is off the island, all alternative emergency ports are sealed."

"Why?" Ethan said.

Reggie fixed his glasses. "The Frank Nano Company's got a lot of proprietary technology in this park that we don't want leaving the island. On its own, or otherwise."

Ron nodded. "The point is, the only way on or off park property is through the main gate in Nostalgia Bay. There's an emergency exit and a storage closet with a few escape rafts in the main entrance area. They're supposed to leave some rafts, no matter what, for any stragglers who get left behind. They're on autopilot. They'll take us straight to the mainland."

"Nuh-uh." Maddie waved her wand at them. "We're supposed to wait where the helpers can find us."

Dee shushed her.

Ron smiled. "We are the helpers, kid. But we can't defend this location forever, so let's head to the exit. We'll all be safer when we're off this island."

"Don't forget," Barclay said. "I also have a fueled-and-ready helicopter sitting on the pad over there."

Ron said. "How many people fit in that thing?"

Barclay bobbed his head. "There's a passenger seat."

"Are you all waiting for an invitation?" Dee said. "Let's get to gettin'."

"Well, here's the problem. The arch between Fairy Tale Kingdom and Nostalgia Bay is blocked," Ron said. "We checked earlier."

"Two people didn't make it back," said the third security guard quietly.

"The roller coaster built some kind of nest in the arch. So, either we go the other way and circle around the entire park, fighting through God knows what, or we head down to the first floor."

Dee shuddered. "I do not want to know what the Prehistoric Forest is like right now. Are we sure it's safe in the tunnels?"

"We're not," Ron said. "We also don't know how to get down there. The entrances keep moving."

"What do you mean?"

The third security guard gestured to the back wall. "There used to be one in here. The door's just not there anymore."

Dee thought of the hidden door in the Princess Pavilion going solid the moment the crisis occurred.

"There's an entrance behind Mermaid Cove," Ethan said. "We could try that one."

Everyone looked at him.

Ron laughed. "No, there's not."

Ethan held up his phone. "It's in the map in my book."

Ron took it and pinch-zoomed on the image before holding it away from his face so he could squint at it.

"This map has backstage entrances throughout the park. We don't release that information to the public." He gave the phone back. "None of these are accurate. Which book is this?"

"*Nanolandia*. Gertie Nano's in it."

Gertie laughed. "Am I?"

"Hey," Ethan said, "Is it true that—"

"If it's about my brother," Gertie raised her hand, stopping him. "It's all true. All of it."

She winked. Ethan grinned.

"Ok," Ron coughed. "We've all been through a lot. Everyone's seen some strange things out there, but I want you all to know there's nothing to worry about."

"There is a tremendous amount to be worried about," Reggie said.

"I've been with the company for fourteen years. My associates and I have been working security for a collective forty-five. We've been through hours of extensive crisis training. You're in good hands. No matter what we encounter out there, don't be afraid. This is all under control. We're going to get you all home."

As Ron spoke, a shadow loomed from outside the window behind him.

"No one, I repeat, *no one* else is going to get hurt."

The head of the steel centipede smashed in through the glass doors and snatched up all three security guards in its roller coaster car pincers. The entrance to the store collapsed around it, sparks flying as the creature guided the men further into its mouth.

Dingus shoved Dee toward the counter where Barclay and Reggie stood with the kids. The interior of the steel beast, visible between the pincers, was a cacophony of girders, sliding and grinding against each other. Dee watched in horror as Ron and the others were torn apart, screaming, by the guts of a living theme park ride.

The pincers scraped against the floor and snapped at the princess but stopped before they could reach her. The creature was caught in the doorway. Dee kicked the mangled roller coaster car in front of her, which let out a hollow *bong!*

The insectoid beast, frustrated, jerked itself free and stomped off after a few scattered merry-go-round horses. Fresh air wafted in from the new hole in the wall.

Dingus crawled from the rubble, shaking like a real dog to shed himself of dust and dirt. Dee checked the kids and Gertie for injuries. Reggie peeked out from where he was cowering behind the ice cream freezer.

Barclay Bloom, still sitting on the counter, was the first to speak.

"So," he said. "Do we have a plan that doesn't involve them?"

10

Hours passed in silence as the survivors waited for either a sign of
rescue or evidence that the Danger Dragon roller coaster had moved
on. Neither happened. They all watched through the big hole in the
wall as the park's new pixelated ecosystem flourished in man's absence.
The steel beast was out there now, doing its horrendous skitter-stomp
toward an oblivious unicorn, which had been grazing on a small patch
of cotton candy grass. The roller coaster pounced, pincers slamming
into concrete moments too late as the horse galloped off, dragging its
golden rod on the ground beneath it.

Barclay reached into the freezer, rooting past several empty
wrappers until he found one of the last ice cream sandwiches. He
looked at it, frowned, and dropped it back in.

"I can't do it," he said. "I can't sit here staring at that thing and
eating ice cream. We gotta get out of here. Tell me how we kill it."

"It's not alive." Reggie was lying across the checkout counter, his
head propped on a Frankie Frog backpack. "It's roller coaster parts
dipped in a thin nanite shell."

"How long until it runs out of power?"

"The pixels are solar." Reggie ran the numbers in his head. "If
nothing changes, that big bug will be out there eating horses long after
we're dead."

"Shame on you." Gertie slapped his forehead as she paced past. She
pointed at Maddie, who was curled up in a pile of stuffed animals.
"Keep it positive in front of the kids."

Reggie sat up, rubbing his temple. "She's asleep!"

A few notes of music echoed in the wind outside, followed by a metallic screech.

Dee looked up from the princess-themed board game she was playing with Dingus. She'd been trying to suss out how much of her boyfriend was in there. The results, so far, were inconclusive. The dog rolled the dice and moved Winnifred two spaces before gaping at Dee expectantly.

She patted his head and stood, stretching before heading over to the battered entrance. She crouched next to Ethan, who'd been sitting there watching the coaster for some time. What was once the Danger Dragon loomed over the merry-go-round, poking at it with its steel pincers. The empty carousel spun a bit. Deep, out-of-tune music dribbled out of it. The centipede shuddered, backed away, then skittered close again, poking at the flamboyantly colored discs more gently.

"It likes the music," Ethan said.

"Or hates it." Dee smiled. "Makes sense. That roller coaster has been listening to the same three songs on a loop for its entire life. There's days *I* wanna rip that merry-go-round apart with my big metal pincers."

Ethan nodded, rubbing his chin. Dingus sat next to him, nodding and rubbing his chin in the same way. Ethan glared, leaning away from him.

"Does your map still show the backstage door behind Mermaid Cove?"

"Yeah, I think so." Ethan checked his phone. The door was still there on the map.

"If we can draw that thing south toward Nostalgia," Dee said, "we might get everyone across the courtyard and into that door without being eaten. You got any princess music downloaded on there?"

"No." Ethan shook his head. "I'm, uh, I'm twelve and a boy."

Dee thought it over. She did a quick head count of the people in the room and did an inventory of what resources they had at their disposal. Endless piles of shirts, toys, and hats, a handful of housewares, a shelf full of shoes, and one novelty golf cart shaped like Frankie Frog's head. She glanced at Dingus, whose tail wagged slightly. She frowned. That tail wasn't supposed to wag.

"Treasured guests and cast." She addressed the room. "I'm a day and a half late for my magical tea time. Gather your belongings. It's about time we move on."

•○•

The roller coaster centipede lowered its mandibles around the top of a tree and munched on the branches as it fed the entire plant into its grinding mouth. A small engine revved, and the creature paused. A branch fell. Unicorns scattered.

The golf cart burst from the gift shop, tires squealing on the asphalt as it whipped around a toppled balloon cart that had partially fused into the ground.

Dingus swung the steering wheel, which was a bit lower than his knees. He honked the horn.

Hey-yah, Hey-yah!

Dingus looked down at the horn, surprised by the sound.

The steel beast shifted its eyeless gaze to the speeding cart, its pylon legs aligning in a wave. It wrenched the rest of the tree from the earth, and its pincers twitched as the roots disappeared into its body.

Princess Dee stood upright on the back of the cart as it whirred along. She cleared her throat and took a deep breath. Then, she began humming a tune.

Dee hadn't sung it professionally in a few years, but she'd done it hundreds of times in the Nano Princess stage show before they replaced it with an expanded queue for Mermaid Cove. She sang a song she had been listening to, alternating with two other princess songs, every single day inside the Photo Pavilion for ten years.

She sang "Hop into your Heart."

"I've been dreaming all my life
Of a world beyond the swamp.
Where the skies are bright and clear
And the little bunnies romp."

The centipede shuddered with recognition, and it roared. Bits of wood and fiberglass flecked from its gaping maw. The air reeked of metal and oil.

Dee hit the refrain.
"Hop into your heart, and you will see

All the magic and wonder you can be!
Close your eyes, and you will find
All the dreams you left behind!"

The steel beast charged.

•○•

Down in the tunnels, the nanomatronic princess zipped up her long blue dress, sequins sparkling in the light of her glowing face. A muffled voice reverberated down the hall.

She froze.

Someone was singing her song.

•○•

Princess Dee hit a high note as the golf cart swerved around a drinking fountain, which had grown tall and gnarled like an old tree. Dingus honked the horn at a herd of grazing unicorns, zigzagging around them as they scattered.

The roller coaster centipede trampled toward them, destroying everything in its path. It lunged and snapped its pincers, narrowly missing Dee. The princess squeaked in surprise.

She saw, beyond the coaster, the other people from the gift shop hoofing it across the courtyard. Barclay was out in front, alone, running full speed. Reggie helped Gertie, who shuffled along with her cane as quickly as her elderly legs could carry her. Ethan ran behind with Maddie on his back, her arms clenched tight around his neck.

Newly motivated, Princess Dee kept singing, heading into the bridge of her song:

"I'll hop over mountains and cross the sea,
'Cause my frog-loving heart is always free!
And though my path may twist and turn,
My heart will always burn!"

The roller coaster roared, metal turbines grinding inside its open gullet. The force of its roar hurled the golf cart forward. Dingus stuck his legs out to the sides to stabilize them and held Dee's waistband with one hand.

The dog turned a corner, around the empty merry-go-round and back toward the gift shop. The centipede chomped again, catching the hem of Dee's dress. She stopped singing and grabbed the sides of the golf cart, wrapping her arms around the poles holding up the frog-themed awning. The cart stopped as Dee was hoisted into the air. Dingus kept the pedal to the metal. The front tires squealed as the back of the cart lifted off the ground.

The princess screamed.

She slammed her foot onto the pincer and pushed. Her dress tore! The golf cart crunched onto the ground and immediately peeled across the pavement.

Barclay slowed as he approached the hidden door—or at least, the spot where Ethan's map said a secret door would be. Gertie, Reggie, and the two kids were right behind him.

The CEO brushed the dust off his white suit. He pushed up his sleeves and nervously pressed his hands to the wall. They passed into the bricks like a spoon in Jello. Barclay winced, closing his eyes as he forced himself the rest of the way in. Ethan and Maddie waved at Dee and beckoned to her. All clear.

Dee slapped the side of the golf cart. "Move along, little doggie!"

Dingus gave her a big thumbs up and spun the wheel. The golf cart swerved on two tires and would've toppled completely if Dee hadn't reached out and pushed off a wall. Dingus hit the gas, and they zoomed straight beneath the roller coaster's legs.

Dee looked up. The steel beams had arranged themselves like a rib cage, with legs extending from the sides. Metal churned inside the centipede's torso beams, swirling around and tearing apart concrete, wood, and fiberglass in an endless mechanical tornado. This thing was horrible, but it was also, in its own way, beautiful.

Gertie was next through the door, guided by Reggie, who followed her in. Ethan stopped, hesitating. His sister squeezed his neck.

"We have to wait for Dee!" she said.

The boy turned back.

Dee and Dingus passed under the back of the roller coaster, where the dragon heads were. They were almost to the door. Ethan and Maddie waved.

The steel beast stomped around to face them, then stopped. It roared, its interior pylons screeching against each other.

The bushes across the courtyard, over by the Photo Pavilion, rustled. Leaves and sticks fluttered to the ground. The centipede noticed.

A man sat up in the bushes. He wore a Hawaiian shirt and had a Mad Mallard puppet on his hand.

Dee groaned. It was that weird guy from earlier, Trent. The one Roy had escorted out of the pavilion for being a creep. Was he drunk? How long was he in those bushes?

The man searched around, bleary-eyed, and sniffed before his gaze settled on the three-story insect made of roller coaster parts staring at him from across the courtyard.

He screamed as the creature barreled in his direction.

Dingus pointed at the man.

Dee said. "Do we have to?"

The dog gave her a stern googly-eyed look.

Dee sighed. "Yeah, I know."

Dingus spun the cart around again, sending them back toward the centipede. Maddie climbed down from Ethan's shoulders to watch.

"What are they doing?" she said.

The cart weaved around the creature's steel legs and rushed like a rocket toward Trent as the roller coaster lowered its pincers at him. They weren't going to make it. Dee stood and sang:

"Hop into your heart, and don't you fret!
Your heart's melody is the best duet!
Give it all you got and then one day,
You'll hop right on your way!"

The creature paused, listening. Dingus dove from the golf cart. Dee did the same. Both rolled out onto the asphalt, and just as the centipede was about to gobble the man up…

Wham! The cart crashed into the roller coaster's pincers. The beast stumbled to the side and caught itself with several steel legs. It shook its head, snapped its mandibles together to adjust them back into place, and turned back to Trent.

He was gone. The beast roared.

Dee and Dingus raced across the courtyard, each holding one of Trent's arms. The man ran like someone who'd been unconscious in a bush for hours.

"W-what's happening?!" he blubbered, "What the hell is that?!"

"Don't ask!" Dee shouted.

The centipede lumbered toward them, smashing through trees and carts and what remained of the gift shop as it turned its enormous body around.

Dee huffed as she ran. She was glad she'd changed her shoes. They were still yards from the hidden door. The kids were shouting at them, telling them to hurry.

The centipede was coming faster than they were going. She was out of breath. She couldn't sing again. She didn't have another song in her.

The princess closed her eyes.

Music—trumpets and snare drums—blasted from the speakers throughout the Fairy Tale Kingdom. Trent tripped, falling on his face and pulling Dee and Dingus down with him.

The roller coaster centipede shrieked, then scurried away, squeezing itself between the outer wall and the back of the Photo Pavilion in a space that it should, by all rights, not have fit. Dee could still see the tops of some of its legs poking out from behind the castle.

"Wait," Ethan said. "I know that music."

Maddie smiled big. "It's the parade!"

Dee turned. The path to Nostalgia Bay was blocked by the centipede's nest, a two-story mass of twisted steel and debris harvested from surrounding buildings and wreckage from the initial event. That was the route the parade usually took.

The rubble shifted. A flower, a daisy, popped up from behind a wooden beam and lifted itself over with its little leaf arms. It marched down the path to the beat of the song. A chipmunk followed, squirming from the shadows, then a robotic dancer made up to look like a human in a fish costume, then bagpipes, walking along on pipe legs, the bag dragging behind them. Princess Winnifred crawled out, robotics exposed on her arm, her dress torn. Her holographic face glowed serenely as she began to dance.

Dozens of characters were crawling from every shadow, every crevice, all dancing along with Winnifred to the song on the speakers. Frannie Frog used four arms to wriggle her way out of an upstairs window. A headless prince walked on his hands, his feet bouncing above him to the beat. A swarm of lumpy, misshapen fairies twirled in all directions, flashing like lightning bugs. The centipede's nest bulged as a flower-covered princess float burst through.

"Get up!" Dee shouted. "Run! Go!"

She and Dingus pulled Trent upright just as the pressure of the parade burst through the nest, flooding the courtyard with characters.

Frogs, birds, and woodland creatures, their features mangled and twisted, marched alongside pixies and fairies and mirrors and teapots, all singing, all marching, all blending together, swirling around the flower-covered float and flowing as one mass toward the last humans on the island.

Maddie leaped into Dee's arms as she approached. She pointed at Trent's left hand. "Is that a real puppet?"

"Huh? Oh, uh," Trent held up Mad Mallard. The puppet brushed itself off. *"Cracked Crackers!"*

The girl laughed. "Yay!"

"Can we do this later?" Dee guided everyone toward the hidden door. "We'll have plenty of time for that when we're—"

The moment Maddie and Ethan entered the wall, their nanobands buzzed. Then, a force pushed the five of them back out into the courtyard.

A woman's voice came from the bands, warm yet artificial. "This area is for cast members only. We apologize for the inconvenience."

Dee rolled her eyes. "Oh, for the love of—"

"I do declare!" said a familiar voice. "Can no one rid me of these meddlesome doppelgängers?"

The nanomatronic Princess Dee pirouetted above the crowd of the manic parade, dancing atop a quivering float made of roses and octopus tentacles. Her eyes locked onto Dee's, never drifting from her gaze even as she spun. The human princess's heart pounded in her chest. A cold, clammy sensation spread across her skin. She'd always hated that robot.

"You stole my face, darlin'!" shouted the artificial Dee. "False one! Usurper! You'll never be a—"

"Princess!" Ethan shouted.

Dee looked at him.

"What do we do?"

She was at a loss. "I...I don't—"

Barclay Bloom's head emerged from the wall. "What's the holdup out here? Who's the dude with the puppet?"

The wave of parade characters caught up to where the humans were standing. Frannie Frog reached for Dingus with two of her four arms, and he kicked her away with his oversized paws. A cluster of fairies swarmed on Trent, and he batted away at them with his puppeted hand. Ethan grabbed his sister and backed away as a mass of woodland creatures—chipmunks, robins, bunnies, a single deer—writhed as one in their direction.

"Bloom!" Dee said, "Hire them!"

Barclay seemed put off. People rarely yelled at him. "What?"

"They can't go backstage! Hire them!"

"For what?"

"Anything!" A three-winged fairy buzzed in Dee's face. She punched it. "Make it sound official!"

"You're just like that frog!" shouted the robotic Dee.

She raised her arms, and a flock of mutant birdies gathered around her, lifting her gracefully off the platform she stood on. The princess with the glowing face floated toward the human Dee, eye contact never breaking.

"You think you can take whatever you want," said the robot. "But there can be only one Princess Dee!"

"Bloom!" Dee shouted.

Barclay stammered. "By the, uh, the power invested in me as Chief Executive Officer of the Frank Nano Company, I solemnly swear that uh, that young boy is my new personal assistant. Officially."

Ethan kicked a bunny away and stuck his hand inside the wall, where it passed through unimpeded.

"And the toddler is his assistant!" Barclay said. "The little girl!"

"I'm a big girl!" Maddie said, right before Ethan dove the rest of the way into the wall, taking the big girl with him. Dingus grabbed the back of Trent's shirt as the man flailed helplessly at the fairies swatting at his face.

"Right," Barclay said. "And that guy is, uh–"

"Puppeteer in the Puppet Paddock," Trent said, slapping a fairy with the back of his duck. "Head Puppeteer!"

"Custodial staff," Bloom said. "Part-time. Get in the damn wall!"

Dingus shoved the man, and he stumbled forward through the wall. Dingus followed him, and Dee followed the dog.

"Fool!" shouted the robot. "I'll tear that stolen face from your–"

The music, the creatures, the whole parade fell silent the moment Dee was through the wall. She was in a cool, dark space, surrounded on all sides by people. She felt Maddie's hair brush against her hand. A dot of white light hit her eyes as they were adjusting.

Ethan had turned on his phone flashlight. Bloom, Gertie, Reggie, Trent, both kids and Dingus were all standing within reach.

Dee felt the wall behind her. Solid once more. She leaned against it. "Why're y'all standing so close?"

Something cold touched her foot. They were all on a small metal grate five steps above the hallway. Water was seeping up through the grate and sloshing against their feet. The whole hallway was dark and flooded with pitch-black water.

"It's underwater," Reggie said, "The whole lower level."

"I see," Dee said, "Well, don't that put a fly in our puddin'."

11

Time Breakers opened in the summer of 1977 to moderately positive reviews and mediocre box office. Critics hailed the groundbreaking special effects but were mainly confused by what one critic from the *Chicago Tribune* called an "overindulgence of narrative."

Frank: I did my passion project. Nobody cared. *[shrugs]* Ok. What's next?

Ken: The deal had been worked out prior to *Time Breakers* for a series of *Nano Tales* features. As long as we brought them in on time and under budget, the studio was committed to releasing three films whether they liked them or not. This was good because the studio and Frank were experiencing a certain amount of, uh, creative differences.

Frank: People ask me why there's no *Time Breakers Part 2.* I had a script. 120 pages. The studio people came back with 128 single-spaced pages of notes. Eight pages longer than the script itself. So, you know. Forget it.

Beth: After that movie underperformed, and Frank found out he couldn't continue the series without getting studio approval, he got a lot more protective of the puppets. He'd always been careful not to sell away the rights to anything—Ken was very good about that—but after *Time Breakers*, Frank was almost evangelical. He wouldn't do orange juice commercials starring Frankie Frog without final cut and full ownership in perpetuity of any characters created for the spot.

We had the rights to a lot of talking oranges.

Frank: We owned the puppets outright. That's kind of *all* we owned, so I wanted to make sure we had creative control. It's my hand inside the frog, right? It's my voice coming out of his mouth. I won't make Frankie do disco just because disco is popular that summer. I'm only adding celebrities to the cast if they fit the part. I'm trying to make art here.

Hugh: *[Frank impression]* "I'm already holding a puppet; I don't need a hand up my ass, too."

Gertie: Frank's not someone who can turn it on and off. Frank, is Frank, is Frank.

Winnifred's Magic was released the next summer, followed by Mermaid's Tale less than a year later. Both films were modestly successful, buoyed significantly by merchandise sales and, in the mermaid's case, a hit single version of "Aquatic Love". Then, as the eighties dawned, production began on The Little Princess.

Ken: Those first couple of princess films were all old-fashioned puppeteering—hand puppets and marionettes mixed with some early animatronics. Remote control robots. For the late seventies, they were pretty cool.

Beth: It was a lot like when we did daytime TV, except now we had an actual crew made up of professionals, most of whom had stuck around after *Time Breakers*, Lord knows why. Having a real team means you can do a lot more, but it also means someone has to explain to a large group of people what we'll be filming today. It took Frank weeks to come out from behind the monitors on that shoot.

Hugh: He was like, "Can you go tell that guy to move those lights?" and I look where he's pointing, and it's Gregor Alonso, the Oscar-winning, legendary director of photography, who had taken a pay cut to work with Frank on his first feature film. I'm like the third-billed puppet man, and he's using me as his go-between. I'm like, "Frank…you *have* to talk to people."

Gertie: He understood that he needed to step outside his comfort zone if we were to keep working in this business.

Frank: Beth made me talk to them. It sucked.

Beth: Frank always drew storyboards for every project. He was a great artist. But starting with the princess features, every morning, he would bring all the camera people, the sound crew, and everybody up to the conference room and act out the entire scene we were shooting that day. Playing all the parts, doing all the voices, and crawling around on the floor when he's an animal.

Hugh: Then we would start shooting, and Beth would ignore every single thing Frank had done.

Beth: He gave all the jokes to whatever male characters were standing near the princess. The women just go *[squeaky voice]* "Oh, wow, Frankie!" No, no. We're not doing that.

Hugh: We only had three or four puppeteers on those early features, so I played twenty characters per movie. All the background goofballs. It was fun.

Beth: Frank was the main creative engine. But let's not downplay Gertie's role.

Gertie: Ken spent most of his time dealing with outside interests, so I became the de facto production manager around the office. Making sure everything was on the calendar and every department knew what needed to be done. Get the shot list to the crew in the morning, take notes on the dailies at night, cut them out and paste them into this little binder so Frank had a record of everything. Someone had to keep things on track and moving along. If it was up to my brother, he'd fiddle with one project for fifty years.

Frank: "Art is never finished, only abandoned."

Gertie: When we started *Little Princess*, we had 114 employees, and Frank and I were racing around between two buildings all day. Frank was so busy managing everything at the creative level that he finally came out of his shell.

Hugh: I made him my Best Man, which I expected to be ceremonial. I had a brother who could step in if necessary. But on the day of the wedding, he's out front laughing with people, shaking hands. He hugged my mom! The man never touched another person willingly in his life.

Beth: That Frank was always there inside him. He just had to relax.

Hugh: To become a real human being, some people need over a hundred employees who are financially obligated to only talk to them about movies.

Frank: So, *Mermaid Tale* was a solid hit, in exactly the way the money people wanted. I thought we could get creative and push the boundaries a little in *Little Princess*, special effects-wise. We could go bigger on the third one. Develop some things we could use in later pictures.

Phil Tobin (*head of effects*)**:** Frank comes into the shop one morning and says, "I need you to build a dragon." I say, "Sounds good, Frank. How big?" and he says, "Dragon-sized. No sticks, no wires." I'm like, Jesus, how are we going to do that with puppets?

Back then it was all analog. We had puppets, paintings, models, and makeup. We had some rudimentary animatronics. Jittery things. Didn't look too great up close, you know? I told him as much.

Frank: I told Ken, "Somewhere in the world, there's a weird guy nobody's heard of, and because of whatever extremely specific thing he's obsessed with, he can make us a photorealistic dragon. I need you to find him and bring him here."

He said, "You're dreaming."

And I said, "Dream big."

Ken: I wrote that down. *Dream big.* Eventually, we had it trademarked. It became our tagline. We used that in commercials, on billboards, and on t-shirts. It's going to be on Frank's tombstone one day.

Frank: If I had known how often I'd be saying it afterward, I never would've said it.

Beth: Everyone in Frank's life teases him about it. I like to say it when he goes to bed. "Dream big, darling."

Hugh: Whenever I sip a drink near Frank, I cheers him and say, *[winks]* "Dream big." It's a hilarious joke that only gets funnier every time, and Frank absolutely loves it.

Ken: I put some feelers out that we were looking for people in engineering and technology. Actual tech people, not movie people. Movie people were going to give us movie solutions. It doesn't go anywhere for weeks, but then I read an article about these advanced robots being developed in Italy: tiny little robots that can take any shape. Two days later, I'm in Europe, in a factory outside Milan, meeting with Sal Destro.

Silvio "Sal" Destro (*inventor of Nanotech*)**:** I work at a, eh, unnamed water treatment plant in Lombardy. They asked me for a solution to the pipes breaking down too quickly, inside and out. I think the pipes, they are bones, but they have no skin! The cells of the body, they heal their wounds. If we teach these pipes to repair themselves, this will never be a problem again.

Ken: A crazy person. He takes me to his little lab, down this dark, forgotten hall in the factory. He's got these pipes slathered up with this shiny metallic glaze and there's a bunch of wires running to a wall of computer terminals.

So, he pulls out an ax.

Sal: The plant doesn't want my robots; they say it is too expensive to use for every pipe. I think, Ah! American movies! Hollywood! They have money.

Ken: He swings this ax over his head and hacks a pipe in half. But then...the glaze ripples like water and each end of the broken pipe reaches out for the other. In seconds, the pipe is good as new.

I was particularly taken with the way it moved. It was like magic.

Sal: I tell him any color he wants. Any shape he wants.

Ken: This man created artificial life.

Phil: Ken brought Sal to LA, straight to our shop from the airport. This hairy little guy walks in. He still has his luggage with him. He'd never been more than a few miles from whatever village in Italy he was from.

And he's got a jar full of this stuff. It's like liquid aluminum foil, and he's got it in a mason jar you'd keep jelly in.

Ken: I gave the two of them a week to make a dragon together, a little one, a model to show Frank. Sal had the technology, and Phil was a gifted designer. Phil would make the traditional animatronic structure for the inside, and Sal would coat it in his tiny robots to give it life. Within four days, they had a blocky little sky-blue dragon that could walk, blink, and flap its wings.

You wouldn't know it looking at him, but behind all that beard, Sal was like twenty-four years old. Phil was twenty-six. I was twenty-nine. We were all too young to know we were doing the impossible.

Frank: They brought it to my office, and the damn thing stood up on my desk, flapped its wings, and hovered in front of me. Flew around in a little circle. No sticks. No wires.

So, months later, they built the full-size dragon. The actual animatronic is two stories tall, and it's already the most advanced creature, the most advanced *anything* we've ever developed. Again, Phil did a fantastic job.

Phil: I worked out a control system where Frank could puppeteer it himself like he insisted. So he's standing in a little booth two rooms away, wearing the control rig and watching on a little monitor. We, the crew, are behind two feet of glass, watching next to the camera.

We had to take a lot of precautions because we didn't know what was going to happen. I built this thing to withstand the robots, but, like, it *might* explode. The entire set might go up in flames, or this goop might melt through the floor and clog up the sewer system. Brand new tech, who the hell knows?

Sal: I open the ceiling, turn on the hose and apply the Destrotech. When I come to America, I bring 0.8 kilos. Now, it's 42 kilos. Big difference.

Phil: Sal's at the computers, yelling at his assistants in Italian, even though they absolutely do not speak Italian. They cover the whole animatronic in the glaze. And for a minute, nothing happens, and I think I'm screwed. I'm flying back to San Jose to work at my dad's stationery store.

But then, slowly but surely, just like we planned it, the liquid metal ripples and changes color. The blue dragon forms. Scales, teeth, semi-translucent wings. It breathes. It blinks. Its nostrils flare.

The damn thing bends down and turns its head toward the camera, toward me. It looks me dead in the eyes. And this dragon says, in Frank Nano's voice, "We're putting this shit on everything."

Beth: There's nothing done in post. There are no tricks. If you were on the set, a live dragon stood there, stomping its feet and flapping its wings. I found it utterly terrifying.

Sal: After that film, they give me an office and a team, and we get to work. We add Destro bots to the sets, to the puppets, to the camera equipment. For each microscopic machine, I get paid. It's good money!

Frank: You paint that stuff on a prop, and it can move and change colors. You can add little movements to the puppets and add extra life to their faces. You can build extremely simple backgrounds and change them on the fly. Incredible, impossible locations in days. We could film anything!

Ken: That one jar of bots cost twenty-two thousand dollars. That's in 1980 dollars. The dragon alone cost over a million. We had to use it judiciously. At first, anyway.

Sal: I wanted to call them Destrotech. I am Destro. They are Destrotech. But Frank Nano says that it sounds like a bomb.

Frank: We're making kids' movies here. The demo piece is a talking dragon. We can't call something Destrotech. Explodotech. Stabbotech. The man's out of his mind.

Sal: Frank decided my robots should be called Nanotech because he thinks he is God. Everything in the world should be named after him.

Frank: I want people to know what they're getting. Nano also means "small." It's a good name. What should they be called?

Hugh: Everyone called them "pixels," anyway. Like the little dots on a TV.

Ken: Sal Destro invented a programmable swarm of miniaturized robotics. The Frank Nano Company developed the combination of those machines with existing film production technology to create the illusion of life on film. If Sal disagrees with that, he certainly didn't when he signed the contracts and worked with us for eight more years.

Sal: He named the fucking frog "Frankie."

The Little Princess was· a blockbuster hit, earning four times its budget opening weekend, opening at #1 and keeping that spot for an unprecedented sixteen weeks throughout the summer of 1982.

Phil: They invited me to the premiere, but not the rest of the effects crew, so I skipped it out of solidarity, and we all went out drinking instead. We liked this bar about a mile from the Chinese Theater, so we went there, and we couldn't get in because the line to see *The Little Princess* passed right in front of it. Streets were closed. Thousands of people were standing around waiting to see our show.

I should've gone to that premiere.

Beth: We tried to see it at a mall when it went wide a month later to see how it played with ordinary people, but it was sold out everywhere, even in the suburbs. Frank's the director, I'm the Little Princess, and we couldn't even get in.

Ken: *[grins]* That was a good weekend.

Frank: By then, we were already working on *Froggy Princess*, which would bring together the Nano Princesses and Frankie Frog. I wanted it to be the first film set in a fully nanotech world.

Ken: We had established the princesses on film, so with this picture, we could sort of backdoor pilot Frankie and Frannie Frog into their own feature. Usually, Frank resented that sort of thing, but he was primarily interested in the tech at that moment.

Frank: With nanotech filling the stage, we could set a picture anywhere and film them all in the same studio. We could film whatever we wanted and do it unbelievably quickly.

Phil: We had to expand upon what we'd done with *Little Princess* while also working around the main characters, which were regular-ass felt puppets.

Frank: I wanted the vibes to clash. Putting felt puppets in a fully nanotech world would draw attention to how photorealistic the nanotech looked. The puppets grounded the whole thing.

It was a little unpleasant to shoot, but I thought it would all be worth it to show audiences something brand new. Beth and Hugh disagreed.

Beth: I hated the pixels. I was used to fabric, doll eyes, tiny clothes, and maybe a little wood. Homemade. Handmade. This was different.

Phil: Early nanotech was a lot more dangerous than it is now. There was a layer of super-heated bromine on the surface of each little robot. It would burn right through your skin if you touched it with your bare hand. So for a long, long time, we couldn't combine it with live actors. Even with the puppets, we had to coat the felt in a protective solution.

Beth: It smelled like battery acid, and I could still feel the little creeps crawling on my skin through the felt. It was like sticking my hand up into a bucket of spiders.

Phil: From the wrists down, they wore full radiation suits.

Beth: And then, just to be sure it's safe, we had to stand in these giant plastic tubs with our hands sticking out of two little holes on the top.

There were still accidents.

Sal: No one has ever been killed from my Destrotech. This, I am very proud of.

Hugh: Dingus Dog's tall, so I had to stand on a stool and really stretch my arms out there. Every day, I'm rubbing the suit on the edge of the hole in the tub. I tore a seam right at the shoulder, didn't know about it, and a trace amount of the bromine got in. I had a rash from neck to elbow that peeled off and became a scar. I still have it. *[pulls up his sleeve]* See?

Our only consolation was that Frank was in the tub, too, wearing the radiation suit and doing it with us.

Frank: Yeah, that happened to me too. I've got a scar on the back of my neck. We created a universe that audiences had never seen before. A photorealistic wonderland. What's a few rashes?

Beth: We were making fairy tales! Kids don't care about how realistic it is. If you put a pair of wings on a puppet and call it a dragon, and invest it with as much personality and craft as possible, they'll believe it. They just want good stories.

I told Frank I wanted out. No more pixels. I didn't enjoy working with them and was uncomfortable with the risks. It was probably our first real fight.

Frank: I didn't want to do all this without her. I'd never done anything without her, but she didn't get it.

Ken: We'd been talking to some networks about getting *Nano Tales* back on TV in some capacity in the wake of Little Princess. So we set Beth up with her own show, *The Nano Princess Hour*, sans Frank.

Beth: Little, human stories for children and families. No pixels, just puppets. Back where we started.

Ken: Beth was a perfect fit for that.

Hugh: You know, this all got exaggerated after the fact. It was unpleasant filming with the pixels, but I kept doing it. Frank kept doing it. We brought in new people, and they climbed into the tub and did it. It wasn't about that. I think Beth wanted to scale her life back a bit.

I kind of assumed she was pregnant. She talked about kids a lot.

Beth: We filmed *Princess Hour* down in Irvine, which was a two-hour drive from Burbank on a good day. Hugh would drive back and forth twice weekly to puppeteer for both of us. Gertie went back and forth. Frank never did. Frank was hardly involved in the show.

We barely saw each other, to be honest. And this was after spending all day together, every day since we were teenagers.

Hugh: How did Frank feel about all this? Who the hell knows, man. I was his closest friend, but we didn't get beers after work anymore. Once he had the pixels, there was no more "after work."

Ken: *Froggy Princess* came out, and it did well, but less well than *Little Princess*. We had the princesses on television now. It was time to do something else in theaters.

Frank: Beth was busy with her show, and I wouldn't make princess pictures without her. That was her thing.

Beth: "Her thing." I was turning thirty, I hated the direction the movies were going, and I wanted to scale work back so we could start a family. *That* was my thing. It just wasn't Frank's. And I thought maybe if I kept hinting at it, kept pushing him on it, eventually...

Frank: Of course, right when we're granted this magic substance, this goddamn genie that can create special effects from nothing, she decides she wants to slow down. I couldn't slow down. I had art to make! The art was what it was for. That's what *I* was for. That's what I was here to do.

I couldn't be a father. The only thing fathers do is die.

Ken: We shifted the company's primary focus away from princesses and frogs, away from puppets and more onto Frank himself and the nanotechnology. So, first up was *Jungle Jack.*

Frank: I wanted to do an old-fashioned adventure serial like I used to watch on TV, and I thought nanotech would be great for making realistic prehistoric animals and exotic scenery. We did a lot of research. Other books have been written about that picture.

Phil: Once we had a certain amount of nanotech always at the ready, we could reuse it for different purposes. Settings, props, creatures. The remaining crew could work fast with the time and money we saved on locations and labor.

Ken: We started producing four or five films per year.

Frank: No sequels. I was adamant about that. They had burned me with *Time Breakers.* When something works, all the money people will come in and ask you to do it again. Resist them.

We were in a privileged spot at the Frank Nano Company. Audiences were responding to what we were making. We had an obligation to keep moving the medium forward and giving them new things to watch. I didn't want to do the same thing over and over. If you do that, you might as well be a plumber.

Ken: After *Jungle Jack,* we did *Mystery of the Moon, Gnormus Rises, Odd Odyssey, Adventures of Zog...*

Hugh: Frank Nano, unmoored by Beth and costs, is a firehose of things that little boys like.

Ken: *Train Boy, The Legend of Bandito, Sam Fights the Mole Men...*

Frank: I was in a position, with the money and the technology, to write and direct every idea for a movie I'd ever had since childhood. Did I go overboard on a few pictures? *[shrugs]* Maybe.

Ken: The first draft of *Space Squad,* Frank's original version that he dropped on my desk, was 375 pages long. Most scripts are about a page per minute, so 120 pages tops. We turned that into three different films. That's how you get Frank to do sequels; it was all one thing.

I told him I wanted him to do a Frankie Frog movie; we needed to revitalize the brand since it had been a number of years. So, he comes back with a script. 512 pages.

For the first time since I'd known him, I wondered if he was on drugs.

Frank: Movies is my drug.

Gertie: Frank was so focused on work I don't think he even noticed how restless he was. He was always working, all the time.

Mom died around then. I took a month off to fly home and make all the arrangements. Frank flew in on the day of the funeral. He came to church, went to the cemetery, and flew back. Didn't talk to anyone. He was in Chicago for about two hours.

Frank: Right around when my mom died, I started getting these chest pains, right here, under the breastbone. *[taps his chest]* This was when I was regularly working eighteen, nineteen-hour days. I saw a bunch of doctors. No evidence of anything.

Beth: For someone so worried about having a heart attack, he certainly wasn't trying to keep his heart rate down.

Ken: Beth asked me to talk to Frank. I asked him to take a week off. He took one day and went to a carnival like a weirdo.

Frank: There was a summer festival that popped up once a year a few blocks from my house, so I went there on my day off. I always liked that kind of thing, even when it was terrible. And they were usually terrible.

So I'm walking around alone, eating a churro. The rides roaring past, the games, the food. Kids and families running around and having a good time. They had film scores playing on the speakers outside the haunted house. One of those Halloween tapes. You didn't hear movie music in the wild back then. I don't know. It was nice.

Here's the thing: I was in my mid-30s. I had spent my entire life trying to break into Hollywood. And I did, but they weren't really my kind of movies after the first one. So, I worked and worked until, eventually, they *were* my kind of movies. All my dreams came true. You'd think I'd be happy, but...

Even with our tech, you spend months making one picture. Even if you write and direct and puppeteer and edit the thing yourself, hundreds of other people are involved. It's a massive operation. Actors, cameras, sound, and gaffers all work together to help make this thing in your head *real*. And when it's done, you have this series of images flickering on a screen twenty-four times a second. It's as corporeal as a fantasy can get, but it's in a box. You can't touch it.

Sam the Sloth, from *Jungle Jack*, was four times as complex mechanically as the dragon in *Little Princess*. It took three people to operate the animatronics and another four to program the pixels, and only the front half of him exists. We never showed his back legs. It was real, but it *wasn't*.

And I thought, if I only have a certain amount of time left, I want to make something real.

Ethan looked up from his phone. His eyes slowly adjusted to the darkness as he tried to gauge the reality of the world around him. Princess Dee stood with her back to him, staring into the water. Barclay Bloom was lounging against the wall that had briefly been a door. Maddie was playing patty cake with Dingus Dog. They were all still on that metal grate an inch above the water.

Gertie sat across from Ethan. She smiled at him in the way old people sometimes did when they wanted kids to talk to them.

"Uh, Ms. Nano?" he said.

"Yes, dear?"

"How come you never made another *Time Breakers*? My book says there's a script."

The old woman leaned in and beckoned him closer. "Can you keep a secret?"

Ethan nodded.

"There's no script."

"Really?"

"He lied. Frank hated sequels. Are you a Time Breaker? Are you here for the last day?"

"Yeah. It's my favorite," Ethan said. He wondered if the ride was even still there.

"That was his favorite, too. Every morning, before the park opened, he would stop over there and ride it a few times. He said it helped get his head on straight, to remind him of where he started, but I think he just liked it."

"Do you miss him?"

Gertie nodded. "He was only forty when he died. I'm sure that sounds old to you, but…we were all young then. Now he's been gone almost as long as he was alive, but he's still here. In this place. I see him everywhere."

Maddie slapped Dingus's hand, and the dog held it, feigning pain. The little girl laughed.

"Everything my brother loved is here on this island," Gertie said. "This park was his whole life. He'd be horrified if he knew what was happening now."

Dee stared at her reflection in the water, barely visible in the red emergency lights. She tried to ignore the muffled sounds of the parade vibrating through the wall. Every other costumed character had attacked the survivors. She'd seen a few of them. Frannie Frog. Prince Teacup. There were people in those costumes, actual living human beings. She probably knew them. But she was still herself.

Wasn't she?

She reached up and lifted her wig before glancing back at Maddie to see if the girl noticed, but Maddie was caught up in her game with Dingus. The dark ketchup stain was still barely identifiable on his furry chest.

"Hey." Barclay pushed himself off the wall and stepped toward her. He had his sunglasses hanging on the collar of his shirt now that they were underground. "You were pretty good out there. Singing under pressure."

Dee smiled. "We always sing under pressure. One wrong note, and there's someone else in the dress tomorrow. Did you tell them to fire me?"

"Who? No. Why? Did you get fired?"

"I don't know." Dee scraped a chip of paint off the railing and flicked it into the dark waves. "Maybe."

"I mean, it was probably someone below me. I don't make those decisions." He paused. "You *did* sneak into a restricted area and yell at me. You're not supposed to do that."

Dee nodded and said, "Am I still up for that audition?"

Barclay raised his eyebrows. "You still want to be a princess? After all this?"

"I've been here since I was a teenager," Dee said. "It's all I know how to do. Can I ask you something? Did you know this was going to happen?"

Barclay sighed. "If I knew, I wouldn't be here. I thought this would be a fun trip. I tried to bring my daughter. Can you imagine?"

"Why didn't you?"

"My ex won't let her ride in the helicopter." He shrugged. "Too dangerous."

Someone made a triumphant trumpet sound with their mouth. Everyone turned and looked. Reggie sat cross-legged atop a floating upside-down hollow plastic card table. Trent Santiago was on another table behind him. Both were using the walls to push themselves forward. They were sopping wet from the waist down. Trent had the Mad Mallard puppet raised in front of him.

"Cracked crackers!" said the duck, "I know I'm a waterfowl, but this is ridiculous!"

"There's a storage closet a few yards down," Reggie said. "There's a bunch of these tables. They're hollow. They float. We can use these to get through the tunnels."

"Can they carry all of us?" Barclay said.

"I think so. What am I, a table expert? This one carries me."

"Well," Dee said, trying not to glare at Trent. "The door's closed, so we can't go back outside. Do you need help?"

"We could use some people to help us gather the rest," Reggie said. "We could have brought more if someone would take off his stupid duck puppet."

Trent coughed, laughing nervously, before making the duck also cough.

"He can't get me wet!" said the duck, "I'm a collector's item!"

Dee nodded dismissively. "Ethan, you and Barclay go with him."

Ethan stood, his legs stiff after sitting for so long. He took a careful step into the dark waves.

"Wait!" Maddie said. "I wanna go too!"

"That water will be over your head, darlin'," Dee said. "We have to take care of Gertie."

Barclay frowned. "Why should I go? This is a four thousand dollar suit."

"I don't know what you think this dress is gonna do in water, but it won't be pretty. And Dingus's costume weighs forty-seven pounds dry."

Dingus gestured to himself.

"Gertie's in her eighties and Maddie's five."

"Five-and-a-half," Maddie said.

"C'mon, Mr. Bloom," Ethan said. "It's not that cold."

"That's not…" Barclay held the bridge of his nose, sighing. "Fine."

He removed his leather loafers, set them near the wall, and sloshed grumpily into the water. The four men waded down the tunnel, vanishing into the dark.

"Watch out for poops!" Maddie shouted.

"I don't like him," Gertie said. "You can always tell with these business people which ones truly love movies and which ones might as well be selling washing machines. Barclay Bloom's a salesman down to his bones."

"Grandma," Dee said. "What is this? What is happening here?"

Gertie looked at her. Her glasses glinted in the red lights. She was always old, as long as Dee had known her, but now she seemed worn out, tired in a way she'd never been.

"My brother had a dream," Gertie said, "but I think that dream is over."

12

A line of four tables floated along the flooded hallway, legs pointed to the ceiling, linked only by the hands of the people riding them. The hall was still dark, illuminated only by the red emergency lighting, which led to exits that, thus far, no longer existed. Reggie and Ethan were up at the front, navigating. Ethan consulted his phone regularly to check the maps in his ebook, which only showed the surface and the hidden entrances that, thus far, also no longer existed. Dingus was pushing debris out of their way with a broom he'd found floating in the black waves.

Gertie and Barclay shared the second table, followed by Dee and Maddie, with Trent Santiago bringing up the rear. The man with the duck puppet on his hand was the only one with no connection to any of the others, and he seemed distracted by something. He kept to himself, silently pushing against the walls with his foot to keep their rafts moving.

The halls were all at the same level, but the depth of the water kept changing. The table legs would scrape against the ceiling, and everyone would duck. Occasionally, they would pass a loose glove, a chunk of circuitry, a prop from one of the rides, but the hallways were strangely empty considering the chaos above.

As they drifted on, there were some odder sights. Fiber optic cables drooping like vines. Stuffed animal fur growing on the walls like moss. A soft pretzel shaped like Frankie Frog's head being picked apart by spiders made from nanobands.

"Princess Dee?" Maddie absent-mindedly dangled her wand in the water. "Are we almost there?"

"Oh, I'm sorry, darlin'. Not yet." Dee held the girl in her arms. "Your big brother is finding us the most perfect spot to go back upstairs."

"He's really not," Ethan muttered, flipping his phone around.

A low, mechanical hum rumbled ever louder as they approached their first open door of the adventure. Inside, pipes and wires crisscrossed around massive industrial washers, which grew from the floor and walls in clusters like mushrooms. Some were sucking in water, and others were barfing it out. Mascot heads and costume pieces floated among uniforms and linens.

"Laundry room?" Reggie said. "That's still under Fairy Tale. We should be way past that."

Ethan flipped his phone around to read the map from a different angle.

The sounds of the machines faded into music, punctuated by laughter and the sounds of squealing tires. To the right, partially obscured through a hole in the wall, was a flickering projection of Frankie Frog and his friends, each in their own go-cart, racing down a rural track. The screen was at an odd angle after having collapsed through the floor. Frankie's cart bumped against the camera, and the hall shook, water sloshing onto the table boats. The mismatch of the motion on the screen and his own movement made Ethan feel ill.

"That's Dingus's Doofy Drivers, right?" the boy said, closing his eyes and swallowing, "That's in the Puppet Paddock."

"It's usually a little higher," Dee said.

"This makes no sense." Reggie consulted Ethan's phone. "Are you sure we're going east?"

"Christ," Barclay sighed. "Are we floating in circles?"

"Have we turned at all?" Dee said.

"No. Yeah," Ethan said. "Dee's right. It's more like we're going in a straight line, and the island is moving around us."

Water sloshed behind them. Dingus's ears went up. Dee heard it, too. She turned and caught a dark shape right as it sank back below the waves.

"Something is back there," she said.

Trent spoke without looking up from his lap. "It's been following us for a while."

She glared at him. "What is it?"

"I don't know," he said. "But it's getting closer."

They all coasted along silently, listening for more signs of their mysterious follower.

"Dee." Maddie wiggled in the princess's lap. "I need to go potty."

"Again?" Dee managed, barely, to appear cheerful and not frustrated. "Now?"

"Surprised she made it that long," Ethan said. "She has to go like twice every time we go to Target."

"Ok." Dee lifted the girl up. "Uh…Alright. Mr. Santiago, avert your gaze."

The puppeteer nodded and turned away. Dee moved into a position where she hid Maddie from the others so the girl could pee off the side of the table. The princess was, unfortunately, facing Trent Santiago, and the situation was awkward enough that it seemed to require conversation.

"So, what'd you do?" she said, "Take a picture of me and search online?"

Trent frowned. "No, I, uh, there's a Nanoland fan forum where they list cast members' real names. I picked you cause you seemed nice. I know that's kind of creepy."

"You stalked me, asshole." Dee glanced at Maddie. "*Sugah. Darlin'. I do declare.*" She continued in more hushed tones. "You invaded my privacy. It's very creepy!"

"I'm sorry! I've been trying to get a gig at this place for over twenty years. But, you know, the puppeteers in the paddock never leave until they retire. Most of them were hired by Frank. And there's certainly no work for a puppeteer outside of Nanoland. Kids don't want the Mad Mallard at their birthday parties anymore."

He lifted his puppet hand and said, in the duck's voice, "I haven't been in a movie in twelve years!"

"I don't like Mad Mallard," Maddie said, adjusting her pants. "He's too shouty."

"I got a little desperate. I thought maybe if I had a personal connection to someone on the inside, I could get somewhere. You know, ninety-nine percent of show business is networking."

Dee turned away. She made eye contact with Dingus.

"That's what they say," she said.

"Mr. Bloom, is that job offer real?" Trent sat up, peeking over Dee's shoulder at Barclay. "I'm backstage, so I'm an actual cast member, right?"

Barclay was leaning against a table leg, sunglasses back on, relaxing. "If you help get me off this island, you can have whatever part-time minimum wage job you want."

"It's always the money with you guys," Gertie said, "This man is an artist. He doesn't care how much it pays."

"That's great," Barclay said. "We can both agree that that's good for us."

The water level rose, and Barclay hit the back of his head on the ceiling, knocking his sunglasses off.

"Hey, boss!" the Mad Mallard shouted. "Don't forget to *duck*!"

Trent did a double-take at the puppet. He put his hand down. Dee squinted at him. Had his mouth moved when the mallard spoke?

"I'm just saying," Gertie said. "If you're going to run this company, you can't think in terms of paychecks and earnings and financial statements. Frank knew there was more to Nanoland than money."

"Ms. Nano," Barclay rubbed his head. "With all due respect, your brother died when I was in third grade."

Gertie sneered at Barclay with the practiced gaze of someone who'd been dealing with bureaucrats for decades. "Did he."

"We can go on about magic and dreams and the innocent smile of a child hugging a man in a frog suit, but at the end of the day, the Frank Nano Company is a multinational corporation that exists to create value for shareholders. Ken Sakai understood that."

Trent pinned the puppet beneath his leg and tried to remove his hand. He saw Dee watching him struggle and turned away to face the darkness behind them.

"Somebody has to make sure all these dreams are funded," Barclay said. "Ken kept the company going for thirty years without Frank. Do you think Frank could've done that without Ken?"

Gertie shook her head. "You never even met Ken."

"I read his book," Barclay said, pausing before adding, "Most of it."

"Oh, well, in that case—"

A small object landed with a wet flop on the table in front of the old woman. She let out a soft "Ooh!"

Maddie pointed. "A froggy!"

A tiny lifelike frog croaked up at Gertie. Its skin and eyes shined in the red emergency lights.

"Red-eyed tree frog," she said. "We must be under the forest."

Vines and roots were growing in and out of the walls, crawling with insects and wildlife. Kelp grew up in bunches in the water. A green baboon crouched in the vines, eating a yellow flower bulb and glaring at Maddie as she floated past. A dragonfly buzzed across Dee's view, then another. The princess raised her hand, and a colorful butterfly landed on her finger.

"It is getting a little biological down here," Dee said.

The butterfly bit her with sharp little teeth. She flicked it away and sucked on her wound.

As the frog stared at the old woman with its round eyes, a third eye sprouted between the normal two. It opened its mouth.

"Grandma!" Dee said. "Watch—"

A barbed tongue shot toward Grandma Nano. Dee caught it as it was about to slash the old woman across the face. Asymmetrical bat wings curled up from the creature's back, and it fluttered into the air, its hiss of fury drowned out by Maddie's scream. It flicked its tongue backward and caught Dee's arm, and the princess released her grip. Just as the bat-frog swooped at her, the end of a broom slammed down on top of it, and the amphibious chimera splashed into the water.

Dee rubbed her arm. Gertie handed her a tissue to wipe the blood. Dingus held his broom like a bat, ready to strike any other weird animals that attacked his friends.

"The creatures are blending together," Reggie said from his spot up front, "I think I get it."

Ethan looked at him. "I don't."

Reggie turned to Ethan. "Their programming is out of alignment, so they're picking up each other's signals. The nanotech, the pixels, they're like stem cells. If you put them into a lung, they become lung cells. If you put them in a kidney, you grow more kidney…meat. I'm not that kind of doctor. They can be anything, right? But now they're behaving as though they're everything."

Barclay perked up. "So what? Can you fix them?"

"Yeah, I can fix them. It's easy. I can't believe I didn't think of it before." Reggie peered into the dark, trying to see the end of the tunnel. "We need to go back to the surface."

"I'm trying," Ethan said. "But this place keeps—"

Reggie stopped him. "Do you hear that?"

Dingus turned toward the front. His ears went up.

The sound of rushing water grew louder and louder as the waterfall emerged from the darkness. They'd reached their first intersection underground, and a torrent of waves gushed down from above it. Yet the pool surrounding the waterfall was strangely unaffected by the flood. As they approached, Dingus, Barclay, and Dee reached out and grabbed onto vines, stopping their table boat caravan before they could float under the falls.

"That explains all the water!" Barclay shouted over the roar.

"Why isn't it pushing us?!" Ethan dipped his fingers into the stagnant pool. "It's weird!"

"That's not water!" yelled a voice from above.

Dingus clutched his head in surprise. He pointed up and waved excitedly.

"Churro Charlie!" Dee said, "As I live and breathe!"

Charlie was shirtless, half visible through a jagged hole beside the top of the waterfall. He was in a better mood than he had been in all the time Dee had known him. He was practically giggling.

"Don't drink that shit!" he said. "It's all pixels! Pixels that think they're water! You're under Plummet Falls! You're floating in a simulation!"

Dee put her hands on her hips. "How you holdin' up, you old frog dog?"

"Ah, I always knew it'd be something like this!" he said. "Hang on, I'll throw down a vine!"

"What did he say about the water?" Trent said.

"Don't drink it!" Dee said. "Did you drink it?"

Trent stared at her with a worried look on his face.

"Trent!" she said. "Good gravy! Did you drink it?!"

"Heads up!"

A vine dropped down behind Dee's head, almost clocking her. She grabbed it and was about to climb up when she remembered she was wearing a ball gown.

"Dingus!" she said, "You head up first to help the rest. Anybody else good at climbing a rope?"

"I'm actually great at it," Ethan said, pocketing his phone. "I don't know why. I'm usually bad at gym."

Dingus hoisted himself up the vine with ease, which was a little surprising since he'd been wearing a wet mascot costume for a couple of days. Ethan held the end, and seeing Dingus reach the top, climbed up after him.

"Plummet Falls." Reggie held the bottom of the vine for Ethan as he ascended. "Ok. We're close to the end, Mr. Bloom. I've got it all worked out! All we need to do is—"

Thunk! A copper trident speared through the engineer's chest, and the heavy chain connected to it clanked onto the table boats. Barclay fell backward, using the wall to stabilize himself. Maddie screamed.

Dee stared at Reggie in shock.

The man trembled. His eyes drifted down to the trident in his chest. He coughed, and a trail of blood dribbled down his chin. He let go of the vine, and the tables drifted in the water.

The chain went taught, and Reggie was yanked face-down onto the tables, which wobbled furiously as the man in the lab coat slid past Barclay and the women. He smashed into a surprised Trent as he hit the end of the tables, and both went splashing into the dark water.

The tables floated away from the spot where he'd vanished. Ethan lost his footing and hung loose on the now-swaying vine.

"Ethan!" Maddie shouted.

"What's happening?!" he said.

Trent surfaced, flailing. Gertie and Maddie scrambled across the tables to the last one and reached out for him. He caught Gertie's hand, and the old woman was almost pulled into the water with him. Barclay crawled across the boats to help.

A dark shape rose from the waves behind Trent.

The metallic statue of Mermaid Monica glared at them with eyes that constantly shifted, each a unique shape and size and never matching the one next to it. All of her facial features were in constant motion, blurring together, blinking between noses and mouths and eyebrows belonging to actors who had played the mermaid in the past... or perhaps would someday. Her body spasmed, expanded, and contracted, morphing into marginally different physical shapes and never keeping one for long. The design of her clothes also shifted unpredictably, transforming into different styles from different eras with each passing moment.

As the surviving humans watched, the mermaid's face twisted in fury. Her mouth opened to reveal a host of razor-sharp teeth, each one glinting in the red light.

Monica shrieked in a hundred voices. She slashed at Trent with the terrible claws on the end of her human hand. Barclay kicked her in the stomach, and the surprised mermaid redirected her attention to him.

Reggie bobbed up from the water, eyes wide open, gurgling and moaning with what life he had left in him. The mermaid snarled, snatching him up in her hands and diving back into the black.

Dee shook her head, having been briefly entranced by the mermaid's grotesque beauty. The boats were moving quicker now that they were past the waterfall. Ethan dangled alone, halfway up the vine and out of the others' reach.

"Guys?!" he said.

"Go up!" Dee shouted. "Meet us in Nostalgia Bay!"

"Ethan! No!" Maddie wailed. "We can't leave him!"

The boy felt himself rising through no effort of his own. He looked up. Dingus and Churro Charlie were hauling up the vine. He wrapped his legs around it and held on tight.

Working together, Gertie and Barclay dragged Trent back onto the rear table. He coughed, sputtering. As he did, the Mad Mallard puppet on his hand pushed itself upright with its tiny hand-like wings and shook off some of the water.

The duck turned to Barclay and said, "Is this a good time to ask for a raise?"

Barclay lowered his sunglasses and peered at Trent, who was still coughing.

"Neat trick," he muttered.

Dee caught the leg of the rear table, watching as the frontmost one, now empty, drifted further and further away from the group. The water—pixels, whatever it was—seemed to pick up a lot of speed. Dee felt her stomach drop in fear. The surrounding air was getting colder. They were moving away from the waterfall, but the roar hadn't stopped. It had gotten louder.

Water sloshed up onto the rear table. There were too many people on that one, weighing it down. Gertie and Barclay clambered over to the middle. Trent remained alone in the back. Maddie started to cry.

"It's alright, darlin'." Dee sat and patted in front of her. The girl climbed into the princess's lap. "We'll find your brother. This place isn't as big as it looks."

The empty table in front of them dropped out of view. As they approached, they saw it careen down the rest of the hall at a steep angle, banging off the walls as it fell. One of its legs snapped off, and the whole thing cracked in half before sinking into the rough waters.

"That's impossible," Dee said. The lower level of Nanoland was one floor. It was a series of hallways. There were no steep drops. She held Maddie close and grabbed the table leg next to her. Barclay and Gertie did the same. The water around them became increasingly erratic, rushing at an obscenely high speed.

Dee's table dipped downward.

13

Ethan emerged from the cave, blinded by the light of the afternoon sun. As his eyes adjusted, he peered down at what had once been the Prehistoric Forest. Trees, in all directions, grew not only from the earth but also from each other, their branches knitted together in a tangled green web. Their misshapen trunks twisted at odd angles, some inverted as if growing upside-down, their roots groping toward the cloudless sky. Strange creatures roamed unseen through the twisted forest in the shadows of the leaves.

Something drifted into Ethan's field of vision. A hot dog with butterfly wings fluttered along, pausing to regard the boy with its shriveled sausage face before bending its pure beef body downward and disappearing into the woods.

Dingus stumbled out of the dark behind Ethan, rubbing his eyes dramatically. He pointed over Ethan's shoulder and held his mouth in a silent gasp.

The boy staggered back as a gargantuan prehistoric sloth, a Megatherium, strode into view. It towered above the forest, which crumbled under each step of the slothian leviathan.

The creature seemed to be absorbing the surrounding greenery. Its back was a living landscape. Trees and bushes clung to its fur like barnacles, their roots embedded deep into its gray hide. Birds and miniature pterodactyls flitted among the foliage. Weeds and vines draped over the sloth's sides, creating a green gradient that ran down its arms and legs.

Ethan's gaze drifted to its head and he locked eyes with the beast. The sloth regarded him, and for a moment, the boy sensed a flicker of understanding pass between them. But just as the connection seemed to solidify, a hand clamped onto his shoulder.

"You remember Big Sam," Churro Charlie said, stretching his back. "Gives piggyback rides to all the little kiddos."

"He got bigger," Ethan said.

"Every time I look at him." Charlie held out his hand. "Charlie." Ethan shook it. "Ethan."

"Don't worry about Sam. He won't hurt you. We go way back."

The boy nodded. "We need to get to Nostalgia Bay. Meet up with the others. My little sister's with them."

It dawned on Ethan what he'd done. He left his five-year-old sister in a murderous theme park with complete strangers. He felt the guilt settle into a pit in his stomach. "Jesus, I left her down there."

Charlie was busy rummaging in the child-size backpack he had slung over his shoulder. "We can cut backstage next to Frog Tower. Nostalgia Bay's right on the other side. It's gonna be a long trek through the jungle. We might have to take shelter halfway. It'll be night soon."

"What happens at night?"

"It gets dark." Charlie handed Ethan something, a tube in a crinkly wax paper wrapper. It was a churro.

The man held one out for Dingus, too. He looked the dog over and measured his height, holding his hand above Dingus's head then his own. He stared into the dog's googly eyes.

"Jimmy?"

Dingus cocked his head in confusion.

"He doesn't talk," Ethan said.

"No..." Charlie considered this. "No, I suppose he wouldn't. Are you sure there's a person in there?"

Ethan wasn't, but he didn't want to say that in front of the dog. "Princess Dee trusts him."

"Yes…" Charlie considered this, too. "Yes, I suppose she would. Alright. We've got a long walk through dangerous territory."

He pulled out a churro for himself and clinked it against Ethan's like he was cheersing a beer.

"Gotta keep your energy up. Nanoland runs on dreams, but you don't. So…"

He paused as if waiting for something. Ethan didn't know what the man wanted, so he took a bite of his churro. All he'd eaten in the last 24 hours was four ice cream sandwiches, so it tasted pretty good.

"...'So grab a Fun Sun Orange.' Damn it, you kids never know commercials anymore. Frankie was in those! Are you a nanofan or what?"

"Uh…" Ethan was distracted by Dingus repeatedly trying to stuff a churro into his fake mouth. "Kind of. Mostly just *Time Breakers.*"

"*Time Breakers*! Old school!" Charlie started to descend the mountain, gripping splinters of wood and metal as he moved. "Are you here for the last day?"

Ethan and Dingus followed directly behind Charlie, mimicking his movements.

"I was yesterday. Too late, huh?"

"Ah, you never know. Battlezone X has been dark ever since things went cuckoo."

He stopped climbing and pointed. Ethan looked. Darkness loomed beyond the trees to the East.

"But there's one light in the back, right where your ride should be."

Ethan peered into the distance. "You think it's still running?"

"Could be. The whole thing's analog. Even the park benches here have pixels, but Time Breakers: The Ride is completely nanobot-free. It always has been. It's what Uncle Frank wanted."

Ethan saw it now. A small oasis of light amid the black.

"Maybe you can stop on your way out," Charlie laughed as he continued on.

Ethan kept glancing at the light as he climbed after Charlie. Nanoland was broken. Nothing was working. People were getting killed. He himself had almost been eaten by a roller coaster. He wasn't going to go on a ride right now. That would be crazy.

"Wouldn't it?" he muttered.

He turned to Dingus, but the dog just shook his head.

•○•

The three-table caravan hurtled down the steep corridor, repeatedly slamming into the walls as the rapids raged around them. With Maddie secure in her lap, Dee gripped the two table legs in front and attempted to steer them clear from the encroaching walls. It wasn't working. Gertie and Barclay were on the middle table, clinging to the sides for dear life.

"Keep us together!" Dee shouted over the rush of water. "We don't want to get separated!"

"We gotta go back for Ethan!" Maddie said. "He's my brother!"

"Sure thing, kid!" Barclay shouted. "Let's turn these tables around!"

Gertie elbowed him. "That's not helpful!"

Behind them, Trent's table thrashed violently, caught in the wake of the others, but also because he was only holding on with one hand. He raised the Mad Mallard puppet on his free appendage.

"Cracked crack—"

A golden trident erupted through the center of Trent's table. The puppeteer gave a startled yelp and lost his hold, lunging forward onto Barclay and Gertie's table as his own was dragged downward, swallowed in an instant by the churning waters. The remaining table sank slightly under the added weight, struggling to stay buoyant.

Mermaid Monica emerged from the depths, her eyes ablaze with fury, her shape-shifting torso heaving with wrath. She brandished her trident, with Trent's table still impaled on it, and smashed it against the wall, filling the air with plastic shards.

Dee cast a quick glance over her shoulder. They couldn't outrun that thing. She gingerly wobbled the table she sat on, bouncing to test its sturdiness.

"Maddie!" she said. "Go back by Gertie!"

The girl released her grip on Dee's dress and crawled precariously across the front table, her tiny fingers clutching the grooves in the hollow plastic. But just as she reached for the second table, they collided with a wall, and she went rolling sideways.

Barclay reacted quickly, snatching her hand and hauling the girl onto the rear table. Maddie scuttled over to Gertie and nestled against the older woman.

The mermaid dragged her monstrous claws along the wall, igniting a shower of sparks that illuminated the endless corridor. She submerged, and her shape drifted closer before surfacing again, now alarmingly near the huddled humans.

Dee finished folding down the legs of the front table and joined the others on the remaining one, which sank even further under the water. Only their momentum kept them afloat.

With a piercing shriek, the mermaid aimed her trident directly at Trent's heart. The puppeteer recoiled in horror, seeking refuge among his companions.

Dee heaved up the empty front table and held it with two hands. She tilted it forward until she thought she had the right angle. She took a breath, watching the mermaid's looming form.

As the enormous aquatic statue reared back to strike, Dee plunged the table into the water with all her might.

Wham! The table burst from the waves behind the group, colliding squarely with the mermaid's jaw. The sentient statue toppled tail-over-head back into the water, her screech dwindling into a gurgling whimper as she went under.

"Good aim!" Barclay said.

"She was gonna kill me!" Trent stuttered, pale with shock.

His Mad Mallard puppet wiped its tiny brow. "I oughta smooch you, Princess!"

Dee shook her head, her attention snapping back to what lay ahead. The last table had sunk a bit, but strangely, it seemed to have settled on something solid. It didn't make sense. They were still careening down the corridor, so how could they be touching the floor? The park only had two levels. It was on a small island. They should be in the middle of the ocean by now.

As she studied the wall beside her, her eyes narrowed. They rushed past a doorway, then another, and another. Was that the same door? She noticed a small piece of plastic rattling against the wall but moving at the same speed as Dee. No, that wasn't right. It was rattling, but it wasn't moving.

"It's fake!" Dee turned to address the group. "It's Nano magic! We're on a ride!"

Barclay didn't get it. "What?"

"We're not moving! It's a simulator!" She grasped one of the table legs and bent it forward. "We're shaking side to side while angled down. The water's sloshing around, and the walls are sliding past, but it's a digital projection! Something's propping us up and keeping us in one spot. Help me with this leg!"

Barclay rose and lent his weight to the table leg, forcing it further off the table's edge.

"A brand new ride..." Gertie considered what Dee had said. "The first original attraction since–"

"Wait!" Trent seemed worried. "If we're not moving, then–"

The metallic mermaid surfaced once more, slowly this time, with a more sinister purpose. She slashed at the wall, shattering an electronic display panel. The pixels around the damage flickered and adjusted, repairing the illusion.

As she raised her clawed hand again, a glittery pink princess wand rose at the center of the table. The mermaid faltered, her ever-shifting eyes fixed on the sparkling rod.

Little Maddie stood, her wand held high above her head.

"Monica just wants shiny things!" she said. "It's in her movie!"

And with that, the girl sang:

"I want to walk,
On the sandy shore.
Where seagulls take flight
And my spirit can soar."

Dee and Barclay counted to three and, with a single bold effort, wrenched the leg free from the table with a jarring snap. Dee dropped to her knees and plunged the metal bar deep into the water, poking around blindly for something solid.

Maddie's song continued, and slowly, the shifting statue of Mermaid Monica began to sing along, her many voices blending with the girl's in a strange, harmonious duet. Together, they reached the chorus:

"Shine like the sun, with treasures I've won.
Glisten like diamonds, a new life begun.
The light that I crave, beyond the waves,
Signaling brighter days."

As she sang the last few words, Maddie stepped forward, offering the wand to the mermaid as a sign of peace. The mermaid hesitated briefly before snatching it from the little girl's hands. The creature sniffed the sparkly plastic.

Then she took a bite.

"No!" Maddie shouted. "Don't eat it!"

The mermaid, startled, let out a jarring howl that echoed in a dozen different voices. Beneath their makeshift raft, Dee's table leg clanked against something firm. She leaned in, applying pressure, and felt the table glide off the concealed platform—or whatever it was—and back onto unfettered water. They were swept along in the surging waves, accelerating as the illusion became reality.

The mermaid pounced, only to be ensnared in the intricate tangle of gears and pulleys composing the simulator ride's inner workings. The sentient statue thrashed against the confining mechanisms, her fury reverberating through the corridor.

The sensation of floating down a steep tunnel for real was a stark contrast to the simulated experience. Dee scooped Maddie into her arms, holding her close. Each of them secured their grip on the table or a leg, bracing for what lay ahead. The walls zipped by with increasing urgency. Their raft dipped and bobbed, occasionally disappearing beneath the water before resurfacing as it rocketed down the passageway.

Gertie was the first to notice the impending danger, her voice barely a whisper. "Oh, Lord."

Barclay caught sight of it next. He removed his sunglasses and tucked them into his jacket pocket before clutching onto a table leg with both hands.

Dee looked ahead, and her heart fell. They were barreling toward a wall, a dead end, at an alarming speed. She shielded Maddie's head and threw her own body onto the rear of the table, praying that it would bear the brunt of the impact.

Crack!

The world spun into a disorienting blackness as Dee was catapulted into the water. Her stomach churned with panic. Maddie was no longer in her arms. She was alone. Shards of shattered plastic swirled around her in the murk. She flailed, disoriented until a faint red glow flickered at the edge of her vision. She propelled herself toward it, her heart pounding in her chest.

The princess burst from the churning water, gasping for breath as the current slammed her back against the wall they'd collided with. Her feet found the bottom, and she hauled herself upright. The water barely reached past her waist. In the gloomy red emergency light, she frantically scanned her surroundings for the others.

"Maddie!" Her voice bounced off the damp walls.

"Dee!" The muffled reply came from a few yards away, where Maddie was battling against the water, her small frame barely staying afloat. "Help!"

Dee pushed off the wall and plunged into the water, powering through the waves toward Maddie. She emerged moments later with the little girl clutched tightly in her arms.

"Oh, darlin'!" Dee said, cradling her. "Are you ok? Are you hurt?"

Maddie coughed, sputtering between tears, "She ate my wand!"

Barclay emerged from the shadows, a stark gash on his forehead bleeding down onto his collar, staining his white sport coat pink. Trent trailed behind him, looking like a drowned cat. His puppeteer arm hung limply by his side, and he cradled it with his free hand. The Mad Mallard puppet bobbed upside-down in the water. Someone was missing.

"Where's Grandma?" Dee demanded.

Barclay seemed confused. "Who?"

"Gertie Nano! Who else would I—Grandma!" Her voice reverberated through the cavernous tunnel.

They searched the dark corridor for signs of another person, but the elderly woman was nowhere to be found. The Mad Mallard's high-pitched, nasal voice cut through the roar of water.

"I spy a ladder!" the puppet squawked. "Our ticket outta here!"

Trent stood at the foot of a ladder leading out of the flooded corridor. He didn't wait for a response before starting to clamber up.

Dee hesitated. She couldn't just abandon Gertie.

"Dee." Barclay already had one foot on the ladder. "Let's go."

"She can't have gone far." Dee searched the dark. Nothing but walls and red waves. "She was right next to us."

Before Barclay could protest, a dreadful shriek reverberated down the hallway, freezing them in their tracks. It was the mermaid, and she was getting closer.

"Alicia," Barclay said sternly.

The princess looked at him. Maddie looked at her.

"We have to keep moving." Barclay turned away and climbed up after Trent.

The shriek pierced the darkness again, louder this time. Maddie whimpered in Dee's arms. The princess cast one last desperate glance at the churning water and then reached for the ladder.

14

Gertie: Every great man eventually builds his pyramids.

Frank: We had this technology that could create anything we wanted. I'd been using it for special effects, for movies, but it looked photorealistic on the set. I'd been kind of wasting it, you know? I could make an entire fantasy world, but a camera can only point in one direction.

So, I bought an island.

Ken: He didn't tell me until after he bought the damn island. We were setting up pre-production for *Legend of Bandito*, and he was like, "Oh, by the way, we own some land."

Frank: It's a small island. 500 acres, a little less than a mile across in any direction. Forty minutes west of Naples by boat. I got it for cheap. There had been an unpublicized oil spill by a company that I signed a big stack of documents agreeing not to name.

Ken: We spent half the initial budget scrubbing rocks and burying dead manatees. Terrible location. He should've asked me.

Frank: I told Ken before anybody else because I knew it would be expensive. I wanted there to be a, uh, a place where people could go and walk around inside our movies. Something like a carnival, a year-round fair with rides and restaurants and shows, but Sam the Sloth is there, Frankie Frog is there, everyone's there, and it's all real. We had gotten the nanotechnology to the point where it was safe enough. You couldn't touch it directly yet, but you could stand in the room with it and your skin wouldn't melt off.

This was the future. Not just film and TV. We didn't have to be confined to the glowing rectangle. It could all be real.

Gertie: It's very Frank that his idea of the most incredible and wondrous thing he could do with a technology that can create any object imaginable would be to go inside his own movies.

Hugh: I thought he was losing his mind. His wife did, too. Gertie was on board one hundred percent from the word go.

Gertie: I loved it. We used to go to the St. Roch's carnival every summer in our old neighborhood. I would take him on Saturday, and Mom would take the day off—the *only* time she took a day off—to come with us on Sunday, so we could do it as a family. We'd load up on funnel cake and then ride the Tilt-a-Whirl. Frank would drag Mom around to show her all the new rides. We didn't spend much time together as a family, but we did that.

I think he built Nanoland for Mom. He would never admit it. He probably doesn't even know it. But that's what I choose to believe.

Frank: It would have to have a traditional theme park base, regular old buildings, and roller coasters and what not, but then we could use pixels to, you know, zhuzh it up.

So, at first, we went outside to architects and engineers.

Ken: Frank doesn't speak architect. The designs they presented were too practical. It was not a practical project.

Frank: When that didn't work out, I thought, we're the biggest special effects studio in the world. Let's use our guys.

Sal: He is given the gift of my Destrotech, and he uses it for what? A circus! Frankie Frog Island!

Phil: How did I react when Frank asked me to build a theme park? How did I respond to anything Frank said? First shock, then resignation, then I got to work. Until then, we'd only ever had the pixels in one big room. We'd never used them outdoors. Now he wants to cover a mile of rock in the middle of the ocean and have kids run around on them.

It wasn't just the nanotech, that was my responsibility, but you gotta deal with electricity, plumbing, and transportation. Just getting people there would be a nightmare.

Frank: I sat down with Phil and drew up a map. There would be a differently-themed area for each sort of movie. We made a puppet zone for the little guys to meet the characters and see Frankie Frog in real life. There was a prehistoric jungle full of extinct animals: Big Sam, wooly mammoths, dinosaurs. Fairy Tale Kingdom for all of Beth's princess stuff. I'd directed a picture called *Space Squad*, and there was a lot of hype around it, so I put the Cosmic Coliseum in its own area. I figured we could tie in the park's opening with the film's release, which was a spectacularly bad idea. We had to delay the film by over a year.

Phil: My contribution was to arrange it in radials that all led to a central hub: a big tower with Frankie Frog's head at the top. No matter where you are in the park or whatever magical world you're in, you see Frankie and know how to get home.

I'd been to Paris as a kid, it's arranged like that. All the roads lead to the Arc de Triomphe.

Frank: I wanted to tell the company's story in theme park form. You enter through Nostalgia Bay, a portal back into childhood for all the parents. We gotta get them in the right mindset to spend a day doing all this kids' stuff. So, it's the fifties again. There's a soda shop, and there are classic cars. A record store. A sock hop. A theater. Then you go from puppets to princesses, *Jungle Jack, Space Squad*. The future of movies, the beginning of theme parks. That was the plan. Everything got rearranged for structural reasons, but walk around a little, and you get it.

Phil: Frank goes straight for the details. The color of the dragon as the sun glints off of it. The feel of the fur on the sloth. The smell of popcorn in the air. A lot of fragrances.

Frank: There are no smells in film. I'd been saving up smell ideas.

Phil: I can't draw smells on a map, but eventually, against all odds, we had something to show people.

Ken: Frank calls me to his house. Not his office, not one of our world-class sets and sound stages, but his home. He's got this moving model in his basement that he and Phil Tobin rigged up with nanotech.

Frank: I wanted to work on it at 3AM. People judge you if you sleep at work too much.

Ken: You can walk through it. All the rides are moving. There are ocean waves projected on the walls. He didn't need to win me over. It's his company. He did all that for himself.

Frank: Then we sat down with Ken and worked out the math. It was going to cost a, uh, ludicrous amount of money.

Ken: What Frank wanted was, essentially, his own island nation. A Frank-themed Vatican City in the middle of the ocean. That's expensive.

Frank: Ken had been trying for years to get me to sign off on using our nanotechnology outside of the entertainment industry.

Ken: We had an army of microscopic robots that could be molded into any shape, size, or color and programmed to move in any way. That's an excellent product to own the patent on. There are industrial uses. Medicinal uses. Construction. Food production. Biotechnology. I told Frank if he wanted to fund Nanoland, we needed to diversify our investments. We could be a trillion-dollar company.

Frank's an artist. He doesn't care about that.

But *I* do.

Frank: I said, no military, no guns. Nothing bad for the environment. I don't want to hurt anybody. Other than that, I gave him free rein.

Ken: We were off to the races.

With the funds being raised through various new non-media divisions of the Frank Nano Company, construction on the park began in early 1984. By the end of that year, the company had already spent three times the initial budget with no end in sight.

Ken: It would've taken longer and cost more if we hadn't been developing nanotech construction equipment simultaneously. The new divisions fed into each other. New inventions were passed back and forth. It was an exciting time in the company.

Frank: I designed a *Time Breakers* ride. Well, that's not true. We had the ride people create the ride part of the ride, but I wrote the story for it. I wanted that one to be a little more old-fashioned. No pixels, just old special effects. Nobody was clamoring for a *Time Breakers* ride in 1984, but hey. That one was for me. I was going to put it up front in Nostalgia Bay, but that got moved, too.

Ken: We licensed out the rights to our film library for television broadcasts, and in the process, I managed to get Frank a primetime spot introducing the movies and hyping up the park.

Frank: *The Grand Land of Nano.* Sundays at 8 / 7 Central. It was weird being on TV without a puppet to hide behind, but all I had to do was go on a set and talk about Nanoland, talk over some B-roll, and show off our little moving models. I spent most of my time doing that anyway, so I could do it in front of a camera.

Ken: He was famous before that, but that show was when America really fell in love with "Uncle Frank".

Gertie: He was good on TV. He could always talk to kids. He got kids in a way most adults don't. He spoke their language.

Frank: "Dream big, 'cause the morning's almost here." Then, one day, it was.

Nanoland opened its gates for the first time on July 3, 1985. By this point, crowds had been gathering around the docks in mainland Florida for days, camping out on the beach and the surrounding streets to be among the first to buy a ticket.

Ken: When we opened, we couldn't physically get them all on the boats, so people were sailing out on their own, in sailboats, pontoon boats, a canoe. I saw a canoe. That's a long way to paddle.

We eventually figured out ways to, uh, redirect unauthorized seafarers away from our island, but that first day had a lot of gatecrashers.

Patty Vaughn-Busiek (*first guest*)**:** I was the first person to ever enter Nanoland as a guest. My mother was a huge nanofan going back to the puppet shows in the 1960s, so she'd worked hard to score tickets for herself, my brother, and me. The three of us waited in line for days. We were all fairly ripe by the time they let us in. *[laughs]*

I remember standing behind this big turnstile. It's right at eye level, so I can't see inside. The lady standing there takes my ticket, and they lead me into this magical world. Everyone's clapping, and there's Frank Nano, in the flesh, with Frankie Frog in his hand, waiting to take a picture.

Frank: She wouldn't go anywhere near the puppet. Some kids are like that.

After the photo-op, we filmed a live special with me and Hugh running around as Frankie and Dingus, going on all the rides, trying the food, and interviewing people. That sort of stuff. The problem was, by then I had made myself too famous, and nobody would look at the frog anymore. They all looked at me.

Hugh: I had nothing to do with Nanoland. I was primarily working on Beth's show, so hanging out with Frank that day was fun. But I don't think I had quite grasped the scale of this thing before then. You can see it in my performance. Dingus Dog was gobsmacked.

Frank: It was a challenging shoot because it was live, and we were trying to make the place seem like the ultimate vacation destination while literally everything kept breaking down.

Patty: I had never seen so many people in one place in my life. It was *very* crowded. We didn't make it past Nostalgia Bay that first day.

Frank: Danger Dragon broke down four times. Mermaid Cove got stuck for over an hour. Sensors were off a little in Battlezone X. The top score in laser tag that day was, like, three. Part of Plummet Falls collapsed, away from the guests, thank God.

There were too many people. We weren't ready.

Ken: If we let any more people onto that island, it would've sunk.

Frank: The nanomatronics were getting all warped from the weight of the guests. Too many kids climbed onto Sam the Sloth's back at once, and they pulled his face down low enough that some kid touched it. Burns all over his palm.

Ken: We had complex and costly software we'd developed in-house, operating the whole park from a series of servers hidden from the guests in Frog Tower. One central data hub. Because everything went wrong, we had at least three people up there fixing bugs twenty-four hours a day, seven days a week, for the first month.

Frank: That kid with the burns was our first injury, and hopefully *[knocks on wooden arm of chair]* he'll be our last.

Sal: They are having trouble with the Destrotech, so they have me—Sal Destro—and my whole team come to Florida. Brilliant engineers from all fields of science flocking to this ridiculous place! Still, everything is broken. It's too much. Too much broken.

Ken: I'd worked with computers in college before I got into business, and soon, I was up there too. I've got a whole company to run, all these new divisions, and I'm in Frog Tower calibrating leaf levels in an imaginary jungle.

Thankfully, Gertie's staff was down at the primary level keeping the guest experience running smoothly.

Gertie: All the guests loved it. I loved it, too. Everywhere I looked people were smiling, laughing, and gasping in awe.

Patty: It was a truly magical experience. We'd never seen anything like it.

Hugh: This was the eighties. We didn't have words for this sort of thing. I'd been in the bucket with my hand stuck up into the pixels, but most people had never seen it up close. When it got written up in newspapers the next day, the reaction was almost biblical.

"Frank Nano has created life."

Frank: I wanted Nanoland to be a living thing, constantly changing, always new.

Ken: Attendance was booked solid for the first eighteen months. Every day, full capacity. The place was a hit. The one criticism we got over and over those first few months was how the park had an unfinished quality to it. We still had blank spots on the map where new rides could be built. Frank released a statement that said, "As long as I'm around, the park will always be unfinished."

Frank: Right now, Nostalgia Bay is meant to evoke the fifties, but we can update it to the sixties in ten years. Bring in some peace signs and bell bottoms, whatever that generation of parents was into as kids. That's the real advantage of using nanotech. We could rearrange the same materials into different attractions. We were still making new pictures. There's always new material. Once we got going, we could have tie-in rides out the same week as the movie.

Nanoland should keep changing. The moment this place gets locked in stone, it's not an amusement park. It's a mausoleum.

Less than a week after the opening of Nanoland, **The Nano Princess Hour** *won its 4th consecutive Emmy Award for Outstanding Individual Achievement in Children's Programming. As Bethany Nano stood to accept the award, audiences noticed a conspicuous absence at the ceremony. Beth had come alone.*

Beth: I had no involvement whatsoever with Nanoland. The year—a year and a half?—where they were building the park, Frank was going back and forth from film sets and Florida, and I was shooting my show. We weren't living together.

A marriage isn't a done deal after the wedding. It is an ongoing conversation, and you need to keep having that conversation. We weren't. We weren't speaking.

Frank: I was afraid of her. It's not like I wasn't thinking about her. It's not like I didn't realize what I was doing. I knew. Beth always told me when my big ideas were dumb, and Nanoland was a very big and especially dumb idea, but I needed to see it through anyway.

Beth: I had talked to a lawyer. I had divorce papers ready. I don't know if I ever intended to use them, but... it seemed prudent. I didn't realize how sick he was at the time.

Frank: I was still having chest pains: this like, squeezing, stabbing thing, right in the middle of my chest. Years earlier, the doctor said it could be stress, and I was opening a theme park with my name on it, so I sort of let it go.

Gertie: A month after the park opened, I came to collect Frank at his apartment in Florida, we were going to some meeting somewhere, and I found him curled up on the floor, clutching his chest. Frank was two years old when our dad died, he doesn't remember it, but I do. I know what a heart attack looks like.

I wasn't going to let him do this to me. Mom had just died. I wasn't losing anyone else.

Frank: The doctors at the emergency room run a bunch of tests: EKG, stress test, all the usual stuff. Nothing. My heart's fine. But then, like, on a whim, probably because I'm rich, they scan my head with this big round machine. This brand new cutting-edge thing. They print out this picture of my skull and show it to me, and there's the black lump...

I had a brain tumor pressing on my spinal column. That's what was causing the chest pain. It's rare, but it's a thing that can happen. The tumor is still growing, and it's completely inoperable.

The doctor said I had six months. Probably less.

A fly made of straw wrappers and confetti buzzed near his head, and Ethan swatted it away without looking up from his phone.

He trudged along, ignoring the surreal environment surrounding him. The once well-trodden footpaths had been subsumed by towering ferns and dense shrubbery, with bits of food and electronics mixed in. Trees bore fruits that resembled stuffed animals. Branches sprouted fiber optic cables from their leaves. Glowing cheeseburgers dappled the undergrowth like luminescent mushrooms. Twice, they passed a nanomatronic creature—first an allosaurus, then a saber-toothed tiger—which had fused with the trees, their pixel-coated forms frozen in time and interwoven with ivy and moss. There were bugs, so many bugs, flitting and buzzing around, their bodies a mix of any available small debris.

Up ahead, Churro Charlie forged a path through the vines, slicing through the biomechanical vegetation with a sharpened pair of churro tongs. Dingus Dog stalked behind him, hacking ineffectively at the same vines with a stick he'd found.

Ethan, trailing at the back, was so engrossed in his book that he walked right into Dingus when the dog came to a sudden stop. Ethan dropped his phone into the technicolor underbrush and stumbled to the side, gasping as he saw the deep, cavernous gorge he was about to fall into.

Dingus caught him by the shirt and pulled him back to safety.

"T-Thanks," Ethan stammered.

The dog tilted his head, sending his googly eyes wobbling.

Charlie picked up Ethan's phone. He saw the screen. "Are you reading a book?"

"Yeah, sorry." Ethan snatched the device back.

Charlie grinned with disbelief. "Are you bored?"

"No, it's, uh, it's about Frank Nano,'" Ethan pocketed his phone. He needed to hold onto that thing. "It could be useful, right? Did you know he had a brain tumor?"

"Kid," Charlie said, "If you want to learn about Frank Nano's brain, you're standing in it."

Ethan looked back to the gorge, his eyes tracing the seemingly impassable chasm. The top of Frog Tower poked above the trees beyond. "How are we going to cross this?"

Charlie responded, "Oh, that's easy." and before Ethan could process the words, the man gave him a light push into the gorge.

Ethan screamed in horror as he tumbled into the abyss, but his fall was brief, his body meeting solid ground sooner than seemed possible. Peering upward, he found Charlie and Dingus perched at the edge of the gorge, only a few feet above him, laughing.

Ethan stood, confused. The canyon was a shallow trough, painted to seem deep from above.

"Forced perspective." Charlie explained. "It's an optical illusion. Paint it right, and you can make a bunny hill look like Mount Everest.

Give an old man a hand down, eh?"

Charlie extended a hand toward Ethan, bending to climb into the fake gorge after him. Ethan reached up, and just as their fingers brushed, a sudden rumbling sound reverberated through the air, the distinct vibration of heavy footfalls making the earth beneath them quiver.

Charlie opened his mouth to swear, but a wooly mammoth crashed out from the trees before the sound left his lips. All of its fur had been replaced with popcorn, and the lumpy beige elephant leaving a trail of popped and unpopped kernels in its wake. It trumpeted through its snack-encrusted trunk, and Charlie stumbled into the pit, landing with a thud beside Ethan. Dingus, with a silent, ungainly flail, managed to leap out of the creature's path.

A full-size triceratops composed entirely of smaller toy dinosaurs erupted from the forest, hot on the mammoth's heels. The tiny, multicolored figures that made up its body clinked and rattled as it moved.

With a sudden, swift motion, the triceratops' horn gored into Dingus, lifting the stunned dog off his feet and carrying him away into the dense undergrowth.

"Dingus!" Ethan shouted.

Charlie scrambled upright, concern etched across his face. He raised a finger to his lips, signaling Ethan to be silent. The boy followed Charlie's gaze to the trees on the other side of the gorge. He could see silhouettes beginning to emerge in front of the setting sun. Heads, hands, and the distinct shape of spears bobbed above the bushes.

Ethan froze. "Who are they?"

"Cannibals. Natives," Charlie answered in a hushed tone. "They're from the *Jungle Jack* stunt show."

Ethan shook his head. "They closed that last year for racism reasons."

Charlie nodded briefly, his eyes still fixed on the figures looming above them. "Looks like it reopened. When I say go, you need to run."

"What?" Ethan said. "Wait–"

"Run!" Charlie yelled. "Now!"

Ethan ran.

15

In a quiet enclosed corner of the park, a manhole cover popped up and slid to the side. The Mad Mallard peaked out of the hole, rubbing his little plastic duck eyes at the sight of the sun.

"All clear, featherless fools!" quacked the puppet, signaling below. Trent coughed as he followed his own hand out onto the surface, stumbling a bit as he stood. He wandered unsteadily over to a blank wall next to a gift shop and leaned against it.

Barclay was the next one out. He scanned around as he stepped out onto the concrete. The walls around him were painted bright, friendly colors. He saw an empty window with a blank black void inside. "I think we're in the puppet place."

He turned and reached down to help the others. First, a tight bun rose from the depths, and then a tiara, glinting in the golden sunlight as Princess Dee emerged with Maddie on her back.

"Perfect," Dee said, setting the girl on the ground. "Just a short walk to the docks from here. Right past the sword in the stone."

The little girl stood for only a moment before crumpling like a ragdoll onto her butt. "I'm *tired*. I don't *want* to walk anymore!"

"I know, darlin'." Dee rubbed her bare shoulder. She'd ditched her wet sweatshirt underground and was back in full princess mode. "I'm more tired than a grizzly bear in November. Could you use your own feet for a bit?"

Barclay brushed off his white pants and knelt down.

He patted his back. "Hop on."

Maddie glanced at the princess for confirmation, and when Dee nodded, she put her arms around the man's neck.

"I used to carry my daughter around like this when she was little," he said as he lifted the girl. "Let's see if I've still got the muscles."

"Is she here?" Maddie asked.

"No, she's fine." Barclay smiled. "I'm here for work."

"Do you think she's worried about you?"

Barclay seemed taken aback by this. He pondered the question. "I hope so."

"You said it wrong." Trent was still leaning against a wall, facing it, several meters from the others. A puddle slowly expanded beneath his dripping clothes.

"How you doin' there, bud?" Barclay said.

"It's the 'Puppet Paddock,'" Trent spoke without turning to face the others, "Not 'puppet place.' This park has a history. It means so much to so many people, and you–"

He broke into a coughing fit, bracing himself against the wall for support. The Mad Mallard coughed, too, slightly out of sync with Trent.

Dee leaned over to Barclay and whispered, "He drank the water."

"The pixelated sewer water? Why would he…" Barclay sighed before yelling to Trent, "You take a breather, ok? We're gonna look around."

Trent gave Barclay a *go-away* wave with his non-puppet hand as he continued to cough.

Dee and Barclay ventured further into the heart of the Puppet Paddock. The usually bustling central courtyard met them with an unnerving stillness. They were encircled by a ghost town of pint-sized facades - storefronts and quaint little houses punctuated by one to three hollow, black windows. On a normal day, these windows teemed with life as Frankie Frog, Dingus Dog, and all their friends performed shows, replayed beloved routines, and walked the grounds greeting guests in the form of costumed characters. Now, the windows sat vacant.

The paddock was empty.

The Froggie Flyers rotated in silence, the empty miniature planes bobbing in an endless, pointless ballet. Dingus's Doofy Drivers was eerily absent, a flat slab of concrete in its place. Apparently, that ride was still underground.

Dee thought of her own Dingus, who had escaped up that vine with Ethan and Churro Charlie. She hoped he was safe, wherever he was, and she realized, at that moment, that she'd referred to him as "Dingus" in her mind and not his actual name, which was...

Was...

Maddie broke the silence. "Frannie Frog has a letter."

She pointed over Barclay's shoulder. A round fountain stood in the heart of the courtyard, once filled with water and coins, now reduced to a barren basin of arid stone. Frankie and Frannie Frog were suspended in an eternal pirouette at its center.

A piece of looseleaf paper was bound to Frannie's hand with a weathered rubber band. Dee shared a look with Barclay before she clambered onto the fountain's rim. She carefully reached up and, before the statue could come to life and eat her, plucked the paper from the female frog's stone grip.

Carefully, she unfolded the paper and held it so they could all read it together.

It said: *Gone Paradin'*

"Alright, I'm done here." Barclay craned his neck. "Which way's the entrance?"

As they turned to exit, they were met by the soggy, grim figure of Trent Santiago, blocking their path. His clothes clung to him, sodden and dripping, his face smeared with grime, his eyes bulging with a desperate intensity.

"Cracked crackers!" said the duck on his hand, "Leaving so soon?!"

"Trent." Dee addressed him, her tone steady. She saw King Arthur's sword over his shoulder and, beyond that, the gateway to Nostalgia Bay. "It's time to go."

"We're not going anywhere," Trent growled. "I've been dreaming of performing here since I was a kid, watching *Nano Tales* reruns on TV, making my own puppets out of scraps and socks. I've worked so hard for this. This is my destiny, and I've been denied long enough."

"Look, uh, Trent," Barclay started. "We can talk about this when we're–"

"Shut up, Bloom!" shrieked the Mad Mallard, cutting him off mid-sentence. "Shut the hell up and let him finish!"

"I have a gift," Trent said, "And I'm going to share my gift with you..."

At that moment, the black windows of the courtyard filled with the small felt figures of the *Nano Tales* characters, each emerging from the obsidian darkness behind the tiny storefronts and houses. They murmured amongst themselves.

"...even if it kills you."

The puppets began to crawl out of the windows, falling limply into lifeless felt heaps on the barren ground. Then, slowly, the piles spread as the puppets dragged their flat, legless torsos away from their stages and across the courtyard, slouching relentlessly toward the terrified trio of humans. Maddie screamed, burying her face in Barclay's shoulder.

"You know," Barclay said. "I've never liked puppets."

•○•

Ethan and Charlie hustled down the length of the fake gorge, tripping and stumbling as they went. The canyon was designed to be seen from above, not run through, and the various boulders and outcroppings were very much in the way. Tribal yells followed them as the native cannibals gave chase, throwing spears and blowing darts that whistled past their heads and lodged into the canyon walls with frightening force.

Ethan stole a look back. The figures chasing him were all men, their cultural origins intentionally obscured by the park designers. Clad in minimalistic loincloths, their bodies were a disturbing medley of organic and artificial elements. Beneath patches of pixelated skin peeling away like decaying fruit, the harsh angles of animatronic parts were exposed, glinting under the setting sunlight. Bits of refuse—twigs, wrappers, remnants of food—were enmeshed in their surface. Their movements were strangely mechanical, their legs stiff and unbending, giving them an awkward, limping gait.

"At least they're slow," Ethan said.

"No knees!" Charlie replied between breaths as he huffed along. "They never had to walk in the stunt show."

Two natives sprang into the gorge astride what appeared to be mutated sabretooth tigers, each sporting an insectile set of six legs. Their grotesque mounts bore them swiftly forward, fast encroaching on the fleeing humans.

Ethan reached the end of the gorge, followed shortly by Charlie, and they scrambled out onto an overgrown patio. They stood in a dining area adjacent to Big Sam's Burger Slam. The tables and chairs were strewn about. Some were toppled on their sides, others buried under encroaching vegetation. Traces of abandoned meals littered the area, uneaten.

A six-limbed tiger pounced at Ethan, who barely had time to react. The boy dove across one of the tables, and the momentum tipped it forward just as the tiger crashed into it. The tiger scrabbled at the obstruction, its paw smashing through the wood.

Regaining his footing, Ethan snatched up a chair, brandishing it in a pitiful attempt to fend off the monstrous creature. As it staggered over the remains of the table, Ethan realized with a jolt that the native rider seemed to be a part of the tiger itself. No legs distinguished the man from the beast; they were fused together into a single entity at the waist.

Swinging the chair with all his might, Ethan connected with the tiger's side, but the beast merely swatted the makeshift weapon away and let out an irritated growl. The native grinned maliciously, revealing a mouthful of rotted teeth.

Ethan turned and darted into the restaurant, knocking over chairs and tables to slow the predator. The creature gave chase, slipping and skidding over the scattered furniture, only to crash against the counter as Ethan vaulted over it.

The native pushed his tiger half upright with his human arms. Peeking over the counter, the native gasped as a frying pan swung into view, striking him square in the face. Ethan struck again, and again. A screeching, electronic howl filled the air as the native clutched at his glitching face. Ethan shoved the native back and bolted out of the restaurant and back into the jungle.

Outside, he found Churro Charlie embroiled in a standoff with the second tiger-man, wielding his tongs as a sword and a lunch tray as a shield. Ethan brandished his pan as he approached.

The wounded tiger emerged from the restaurant, its pixelated fur bristling as it closed in on Ethan and Charlie. As the two humans braced themselves for the imminent attack, a creature of terrifying biomechanical beauty—a pterosaur—plunged from the sky.

Its wings stretched to an intimidating fifteen feet, water droplets shimmering on its semi-metallic skin. In an instant, it clamped its jaws around one of the natives, jerking its head back to swallow the human half of the tiger-human hybrid in a single gulp. The tiger half collapsed lifelessly onto the overgrown patio.

The remaining tiger-human recoiled, horror on both faces, before turning tail and fleeing into the undergrowth. But the pterosaur had already fixed its hungry gaze on Ethan and Charlie. A sense of defeat washed over Ethan, and his grip on the frying pan slackened.

As the pterosaur was about to strike, the triceratops made of toys burst from the foliage. It charged the pterosaur, skewering it with its three plastic horns. The flying reptile squawked, beating its wings as it took off, fleeing to the safety of the orange sky.

Mounted on the triceratops's back was Dingus, who seemed to have tamed the makeshift creature. The dog man waved happily.

"Dingus!" Ethan shouted. "You're ok!"

More cannibal natives, the ones lacking tiger parts, closed in. A sharp *foonk* pierced the air as a stale churro sailed past, embedding itself into a tree next to Charlie's head. He gazed at it in disbelief.

"Churro darts? Is that cinnamon sugar?" Shaking his head, he muttered, "What a waste."

He ducked as a barrage of darts followed. Dingus motioned for Ethan and Charlie to join him, and they clung to the sides of the triceratops as it charged forward into the forest.

The conglomerate dinosaur barreled through the trees, reaching the edge of the Plummet Falls River. It turned and continued running, its plastic feet splattering wet mud into the air. Ethan could see Frog Tower above the trees on the other side of the water.

"We need to get across the river!"

Charlie shook his head, his expression grave. "Can't go near the water, kid. The Ice Cream Man will get you."

Ethan looked at him, "Ice Cream Man?"

A sentient blob of ice cream, its many colors and flavors swirling together in a rough approximation of arms and a head, burst from the water. Ethan, Dingus, and Charlie leaped to safety as the all-dairy nightmare seized the triceratops in its frozen arms, dragging the squirming dinosaur into its creamy depths beneath the waves.

A churro dart thudded into the earth near Ethan. The cannibal natives had caught up to them. The trio found themselves trapped between the natives and the river.

The Ice Cream Man resurfaced with a menagerie of toy dinosaurs poking out of its cold, gooey body.

A shadow spread from overhead. A green, fur-covered paw, as large as a four-door sedan, descended onto the cannibals, crushing them under its weight. The Ice Cream Man, intimidated, retreated to the safety of the rapids.

Ethan, Dingus, and Charlie gazed upward to see their savior—it was Big Sam, the towering megatherium. He had grown even more massive since Ethan last saw him.

"Sammy!" Charlie shouted.

The enormous prehistoric sloth gestured with his eyes toward his three-toed paw. The three of them climbed into his moss-riddled fur, clinging on as the gigantic sloth slowly raised them off the ground. He brought them to his face, fixing them with his big, blank eye.

"What took you so long?" Charlie asked, his tone filled with relief. Big Sam's gaze didn't waver. "Yeah, I know. You're a sloth. Nostalgia Bay, Sam. Step on it!"

The leviathan turned toward the entrance of the park as the last bit of sun dipped below the horizon.

16

Maddie let out a terrified squeak as the sentient puppet horde swarmed around her. She scrambled higher onto Barclay's shoulders to escape the encroaching wave of felt. Dee moved closer to the others, keeping her eyes locked on Trent as the puppets blanketed the ground around her, crawling and writhing like earthworms drowning in the rain. Two larger figures stood out from the crowd—empty costumes of Frannie Frog and Klutzy Kow, each missing a few body parts. Like the puppets, they were flattened and lifeless, yet they slithered onward regardless.

Gradually, the puppets came to a halt, aligning themselves in neat rows surrounding the humans. Their hollow eyes stared unblinking at Trent, and the courtyard fell silent.

Trent coughed. He straightened his posture, grinned out at the captive audience before him, and began his show.

The Mad Mallard cocked his head to the right. "Cracked crackers, Frankie! A dragon? Are you sure?"

He fell silent, nodding along as though Frankie were responding.

"Strategy, shmrategy! We just need some dragon-flavored bird feed!"

The surrounding puppets trembled with silent laughter. Trent joined in, but he seemed uncertain as his eyes flashed across the humans, gauging their reactions.

"No way!" said the Mallard. "That's never gonna work!"

He paused, nodding again.

"Yup! It'll be the biggest 'quack-up' in history!"

Barclay leaned over to Dee and whispered, "Is he just doing the duck half of a skit?"

Dee shook her head. "The Mad Mallard's never been a one-man show."

The Mad Mallard laughed, a bitter squawk, before adding, "When that dragon chases its own tail, we'll–"

"Hey, wait," Trent interrupted nervously, "This... this isn't what I had in mind."

The puppet on his arm swiveled its head toward him. "Cram it, blood sack! I'm in charge now!"

"N-No," Trent whimpered, shrinking away from his own arm, "You're just... There's no Frankie here. This doesn't make sense."

"You don't make sense!" the mallard shot back. "You've got the Chairman and CEO of the Frank Nano Company here, and you want an hourly job at the theme park?! You should be the real deal!"

"The real deal...." At this, Trent seemed to regain some of his composure, a smile creeping onto his face as he nodded to the puppet's words. He liked the sound of that.

Maddie screamed as she noticed a small monkey puppet that had perched itself on her shoulder. She dropped from Barclay's back and darted into the maze of miniature puppet theater buildings.

As Dee and Barclay instinctively moved to chase after Maddie, the Mad Mallard bellowed at them, "Hey!"

All of the puppets simultaneously turned to face them. The two humans halted in their tracks.

Trent's puppet continued. "Who's the joker who's been playing Mad Mallard on TV shows and movies these days?"

"I..." Barclay inched away from the puppets nearest to him. "I don't know that offhand."

"Cal Loduca," Dee called out, losing sight of Maddie among the buildings. She hoped Trent hadn't noticed the girl's absence. "He's been doing it since the late nineties."

Trent grinned. "Right! Duh! Cal Loduca," he said, chastising himself. "See, I was–"

His puppet cut him off mid-sentence. "Fire him! That's Trent now! He's your Mallard!"

Trent's nod of agreement was almost violent. "The real deal!"

Barclay rolled his eyes. "Listen, I don't know what you people think a CEO does, but I can't hand down an order to cast you as the Mad Mallard! That's not my job!"

"Barclay," Dee whispered through gritted teeth, "Lie to the puppet man."

"Hey, but I'll tell you what…" Barclay started to take a step forward, then stopped. Too many puppets. "I shouldn't tell you about this, but there's a secret audition in LA."

Dee turned and glared at Barclay.

"An… audition?" Trent said.

"A secret one. We don't want people just showing up. It's a short list. First Tuesday of next month. I'm sure once they see this… thing you do, they'll–"

"Liar!" the Mallard wailed, "Stop lying to him! Do you think he's an idiot?! Do you think he's never been to a fake audition?!"

The puppets surrounding the humans began to convulse, their felt bodies trembling and thrashing violently.

"Wait!" Trent seemed to rally, grabbing his wrist and attempting to wrest control back from the puppet. "I want to go–"

"He's lying to you!" The Mad Mallard's torso clenched around Trent's hand. The puppeteer fell to his knees, screaming and clutching his wrist. "Cracked crackers! Show some backbone, Santiago!"

Trent's resistance faded. His body went limp. The puppets on the ground started to lift, floating as if caught in a whirlwind, drifting and twirling toward the Mad Mallard on Trent's hand and adhering to it as if magnetized. The oversized costumes, Frannie Frog and Klutzy Kow, rolled and tumbled into the air before colliding with the other puppets.

The felt animals crawled around each other, disappearing into the grotesque assemblage as it throbbed and expanded, slowly molding into a familiar shape. The mass grew arms, two little wobbly ones on either side, as it flopped against the ground like a fish on land. The end of the puppet pile molded itself into a round blob, which sprouted a curved protuberance that coalesced into a beak. What was once a featureless bundle of felt was now a twelve-foot-tall multicolor Mad Mallard puppet with an oversized head, gaping voids for eyes, and dinky little wings.

Before it had fully formed, the puppet monster let out an unnatural quack-roar and dragged itself toward the two humans, with Trent's limp body towed along behind like a rag doll.

Dee and Barclay both turned tail and ran. Dee went right. Barclay went left. Just as the prodigious puppet's mouth was about to close around the CEO's midsection, he dove into a nearby puppet house, crashing into the black cloth and collapsing into a heap in the small wooden box.

The swarm of puppets surged forward. A semi-solid mass of felt and fabric flowed into the puppet house, and within seconds, Barclay was pulled out, his body suspended upside-down, held aloft by a single leg. He yelled and flailed, his hands swatting helplessly at the air.

"Hey!" Barclay shouted. "Take it easy! This is a four thousand dollar suit!"

Amid the chaos, Trent's eyes fluttered open. He seemed confused. Dee, having sought refuge in the fountain behind the stone statues of Frankie and Frannie Frog, shouted to him.

"Trent, you have to fight this thing!" she said.

Trent's eyes found Dee's. He seemed surprised by the monster tethered to his wrist.

Dee pleaded. "This isn't you!"

Trent's face hardened.

"You don't know anything about me," he responded, his voice low. "But I know all about you."

Without warning, the mass of puppets discarded Barclay, tossing him sideways into a puppet post office, which collapsed under his weight. The wave of animated fabric rushed across the courtyard and crashed into Dee, shattering the fountain she hid behind and sending the princess sprawling to the ground, pinned beneath rolling waves of felt.

"Cast straight out of high school." Trent continued as his puppet swarm carried him to his prey, "Two years in the *Frogged Up* stage show. Three years in the parade. Cast Member of the Month twice. Always quick with the Nano trivia, always, *always* in character. Do you know what they call you online? 'The Real Dee.'"

As he spoke, the Mad Mallard's oversized tongue lashed out, the felt appendage whipping inches from Dee's face as she held the loosely assembled beast back.

"But I know the truth," Trent spat. "You're like Barclay Bloom. A fake!"

"FAKE!" the amalgamation of puppets screamed in unison.

"A phony!" Trent said.

"PHONY!" the puppets reiterated.

"I've been coming here regularly for years," Trent said. "Did you ever notice me before yesterday? Have you ever remembered me?"

The puppets pressing down on Dee seemed to tighten their hold, their combined weight forcing the air out of her lungs. Gasping for breath, Dee could do nothing but stare up at Trent.

His grin was wide and unsettling. "You'll remember this."

"Behold! An heir has been found!" The voice of the Mad Mallard, not Trent's version but Cal Loduca, the actual Mad Mallard, sounded across the courtyard. "All hail Princess Madeleine of Madison, Wisconsin!"

Five-year-old Maddie O'Brien came charging through the Puppet Paddock, a gleaming replica of Excalibur from *Nano King Arthur* held high above her head.

With a battle cry of "Bad duck!" the girl thrust the sword into the side of the enormous fowl. Wet puppets spilled out of the wound like blood as Trent and the monster screamed in unison.

"Bad duck!" Maddie repeated. "Poop duck! Bad duck!"

The colossal mallard swung at Maddie, and its gaping beak snapped inches from her face just as Barclay swept her off the ground and bolted back toward the village. Maddie's grip on Excalibur loosened as Barclay carried her away, and the sword clattered to the pavement. The girl stuck out her tongue at the puppet creature, which roared in response.

Freed from the oppressive weight of the monster, Dee sucked in a ragged breath of air as the beast lurched after Barclay and Maddie. Her gaze fell upon Excalibur. Rage flared within her as she picked up the fallen weapon. A pack of stray blood puppets came slithering toward her, and she swung the sword with deadly precision, cutting them down with a few swift strokes.

She smiled.

Barclay darted in and out of the miniature buildings of the puppet village, carrying Maddie securely in his arms. The monstrous Mad Mallard puppet crashed through the structures, obliterating them in its wake, with Trent limping awkwardly behind it.

Barclay turned a corner and found himself at a dead end, sandwiched between two unyielding walls in the corner of the Paddock. There was no escape. A shadow fell upon them as the puppet monstrosity approached.

With a swift, brutal arc of Excalibur, Dee severed Trent's hand at the wrist. The puppeteer let out an ear-splitting shriek, echoed by a shrill wail from the puppets.

"Thanks for stopping in," Dee said, "Have a nanomagical day."

The Mad Mallard's pained cries slowly morphed into a low, sinister chuckle. Puppets flowed like a torrent from the rear of the Mad Mallard, rushing to Trent's bloody wrist before reconnecting with it.

A vicious wind whipped through the courtyard. The metal structure of the abandoned train ride tore free from its moorings and hurtled toward the Mad Mallard, the tracks twisting around the monster's felt body to form a skeletal framework. Dee ducked as the stone statues of Frankie and Frannie Frog were yanked from their pedestal and vacuumed up into the mix. Debris from the destroyed puppet stages also tumbled and blended into the enlarging beast.

The transformed Mad Mallard slammed its enlarged fist onto the ground, shaking the earth beneath it. The puppet monstrosity had grown twice its previous size, and its anger had doubled with it.

"CRAAAA...CKERRRRS," it rumbled in a deep, otherworldly voice.

Barclay lowered Maddie to the ground. He lost his footing and stumbled backward. To his surprise, his back met not a solid wall but air, and he fell through the false facade and into a dimly lit hallway.

His head popped back out of the fake wall. "Princess! Backstage door!"

His hands emerged, snatching Maddie from her frozen state and dragging her safely into the hidden corridor.

The enraged Mallard took a mighty swing at Dee, its massive fist colliding with the asphalt as she dodged to the side. Dee retaliated with a slash of the sword, slicing away several puppets but causing no real damage. She barely evaded the mallard's next blow and burst across the courtyard. With a leap, she dove headfirst through the pixelated wall.

The Mad Mallard roared.

Barclay and Maddie helped Dee to her feet. It was dark and quiet. For a fleeting moment, they had found a brief respite in the dim backstage hallway.

Dee smiled, and the trio shared an uneasy laugh.

The grotesque wing and head of the Mad Mallard surged through the concealed door, crushing the group against the cold wall.

Maddie's scream was abruptly muffled as the little girl vanished within the mass of puppets. Dee was equally consumed as a wave of wet felt creatures enveloped her entirely. Barclay managed to spit out three words before being fully engulfed by the puppet horde.

"Trent!" he said as his mouth faded from view. "You're fired!"

A calm robotic voice drifted through the corridor. "Unauthorized guest detected."

The hidden door solidified in an instant, severing the sentient flood from Trent's arm, and the Mad Mallard went limp, collapsing into a sprawling pile of moist puppets and fragments of the destroyed park. Dee, Barclay, and Maddie slowly clambered out from the mound of felt and debris, gasping for breath.

Barclay picked a puppet off his shoulder and shook a few out of the sleeves of his jacket. "Which way's the exit?"

Dee pointed without looking.

"Good." Barclay replied, walking in that direction. "I'm getting the hell off this island."

Maddie stood frozen in her Princess Winnifred dress among the wet, lifeless puppets, her young eyes wide with shock. She seemed younger than she had a moment ago. Too young. The trauma was getting to her. Dee moved toward her, sinking to her knees to meet the girl at her level. She held out the sword, the gleaming replica of Excalibur.

"I saved your royal blade, your majesty. You know, the Princess of Nanoland gets to have a tea party with all her favorite characters. Free ice cream at every shop for you and your whole family."

"Princess Dee?" the girl said, ignoring the sword, her voice barely a whisper. "This isn't all pretend, is it?"

•○•

Dee, Barclay, and Maddie stepped out from a hidden door behind an old stand-up video game cabinet in an arcade. The games were still running a day after the event. The room was bathed with neon light and filled with the beeps and boops of video games popular thirty to forty years earlier. The trio weaved through the old consoles warily before finding themselves outside, standing on the main strip of Nostalgia Bay.

The lights were still on, but there were no characters, no cast members, no guests. Cracks ran across the paved streets, and half the windows in the Gift Emporium had shattered, but otherwise, the Bay seemed to have escaped the worst of it.

"Where's Ethan?" Maddie said. "Ethan!"

"We're up here!" Ethan shouted.

The three of them looked up. Across the street, a dozen feet from the ground, an impossibly large green sloth paw was drifting ever so slowly downward. Ethan, Dingus, and Churro Charlie sat in its palm. The claw was attached to a gargantuan, semi-botanical version of Big Sam, the Ice Age sloth from the Prehistoric Forest, who had grown so huge that he stood across two sections of the park: his front in Nostalgia Bay and his rear in the Fairy Tale Kingdom.

"He's been lowering us down for like ten minutes," Ethan said. "Hang on. Help me out, Dingus." He grabbed the dog's arm and began climbing down the claws to speed the process along.

"Oh, thank God," Barclay said. "Chopper's still there."

His white helicopter was resting untouched on the pad. Maddie slipped from Barclay's back and ran to her brother, who was dangling from Dingus's arm ten feet above the ground.

"You can't fit everyone in that thing," Dee said. "Let's go out the front and take the escape rafts like security said."

"I think we should chance it," Barclay said. "Cram you and the kids into the passenger seat."

"What about Charlie?" Dee said. "What about Dingus?"

"What *about* Dingus?"

The dog in overalls let go of Ethan's arm, and the boy dropped to the ground beside his sister. She pounced into his chest, hugging him.

"Don't leave me again!" Maddie said. "I mean it!"

"Yeah." Ethan hugged her back. "It's ok. I'm here."

Dingus pretended to fall, waving his arms wildly before climbing down after the boy.

Dee glared at Barclay. "My friend is in that costume."

"Are you sure?" Barclay said. "Why don't we ask him?"

Dee scoffed. "That's not fair."

Dingus jumped, and the moment his large, furry feet touched the sidewalk, all the lights in Nostalgia Bay cut out, leaving only a soft green glow. Maddie whimpered. Ethan held her closer.

Dee felt a tingle on the back of her head, not from the wig, just that feeling she got when someone stared at her. She turned.

Frankie Frog's giant head was back, perched above Frog Tower. The semi-transparent glowing puppet watched Dee through the branches of the tree above her.

"That seems bad," Dee said. "Charlie! Your turn!"

"Don't–" Churro Charlie coughed. "Don't you worry about me."

He sat upright so Dee could see the wound in his stomach. A dried churro protruded from his bloody abdomen.

"Oh," Dee said. "Charlie…"

Dingus Dog put his arm around her, holding her.

"These things were always going to kill me," he said. "It's alright. There are worse places to die than Nanoland. You kids take care of each other. C'mon, Sam…"

The paw raised up as the gargantuan sloth swooped its head back toward the Prehistoric Forest. As they watched it lumber off into the night, the hidden speakers throughout Nostalgia Bay clicked on.

A music cue, a synthetic disco beat, building from silence, as if approaching from a distance. A woman's voice, autotuned to oblivion, cooed into the night.

All the color drained from Dee's face. "Everyone off the road."

Barclay peered toward the helipad. There were colors at the end of the road, beyond the helicopter, at the bottom of Frog Tower. A kaleidoscope of colors, ever-changing, with shadows dancing in front of it.

"What is that?" he said.

The music continued to build. Dingus grabbed both kids by the arms and hustled them to the empty storefronts. Dee took Barclay's hand and tried to lead him off the street.

"Forget the helicopter, Mr. Bloom," she said. "We can't go that way."

"Why? God damn it! What is it?" Barclay said, holding his ground. "What's over there?"

The music hit the climax of its build and fell silent. The colors at the end of the road went dark.

Dee sighed.

"It's the Night Parade."

17

Pixelated constellations darted and swarmed across the night sky like fireflies before congealing into spotlights, which pointed their spectral fingers toward the impending procession. Colors and textures flashed under beams of light. The dark mass beneath Frog Tower moved as one single, amorphous blob. Only as the Night Parade began to draw near did details emerge: Frannie Frog's arm sprouting from the Mad Mallard's hip, Klutzy Cow's hooves growing from the side of a Space Squad trooper. Robotic warriors twirled with Princess Winnifred's magic hair sprouting from their chassis. The costumes, the puppets, and the nanomatronic characters had merged and blended, and they marched as one, throbbing to the rhythm that bled from the park's speakers.

The surviving humans watched in horror as the horde strutted toward them. Sequins and glitter flashed under the spotlights. Neon colors—screens, LED strips, and glowsticks—smoldered in the dark. These creatures had gotten dressed up for the event.

Dingus tapped his foot and swayed his hips to the rhythm. Dee put her hand on his shoulder, stopping him.

In the heart of the parade, structures heaved and swayed like ships caught in a storm. These floats moved of their own accord. Their elaborately decorated exteriors contracted with each lunge forward as though muscles flexed beneath their fiberglass surface. Characters and scenes sprouted from the floats' bodies at odd angles, all dancing to the same beat.

Grinning snowmen jostled for space with humanoid pineapples and waving skeletons. Seasonal items. It was as if every parade in the park, half a dozen different ones throughout the year, had erupted from the tower at once. They intermingled and overlapped, swirling like paint rinsed from used brushes.

Frankie Frog's big glowing head vanished without sound or warning from the top of Frog Tower.

"Where did Frankie go?" Maddie hugged her brother around the waist. Ethan just shook his head.

One entity rose high above the flurry of floats and characters. A monstrous octopus ascended. It spun in a languid, nightmarish ballet, its tentacles—speckled with merch and debris—thrashed and writhed as it went.

The floating spotlights converged upon the octopus. Stone terraces and towering pillars jutted from its grotesque form as if the immense cephalopod was growing a medieval castle from its chromatic skin.

A female figure emerged atop its pulsating cranium. She wore a ball gown shrouded in LED sequins that pulsed and changed in time with the music. The dress cascaded down twenty feet, enveloping itself around the octopus castle's head.

A gasp rippled through the survivors as the figure turned to face them. All but one. Dee knew who it would be the moment the parade had started.

The twisted, pixelated version of Princess Dee, the same doppelgänger who'd attacked them earlier, raised a microphone to her artificial lips, and with a voice that sailed across Nostalgia Bay shouted, "Are you ready, party people?!"

The blare of synthesized vuvuzelas punctuated her words. A swarm of birds and butterflies buzzed around her like gnats as she vamped, singing a series of wordless notes of excitement.

"Ok, the show's over!" The human Dee jabbed Excalibur in the direction of the park's exit, a rigid retro metallic structure lined with turnstiles standing stoically opposite the oncoming parade. "Head for the gates!"

Ethan nodded, turning his sister away from the madness but unable to look away himself.

"Wait!" Barclay protested. "We have to take the chopper!"

"You want to fight your way through that?!" Dee gestured at the tableau advancing on them. "Be my guest!"

Barclay frowned. "You don't understand."

"What don't I understand?"

Barclay turned away, saying nothing.

As the parade grew near, the distorted faces of the dancers came into eerie focus. Dee could hear them shuffling along, their legs and claws slapping the ground in unison. She could feel the heat of the pixels lining their mangled bodies.

"Right," the princess said. "Good luck with that helicopter, Mr. Bloom."

She gathered Ethan, Maddie, and Dingus and guided them toward the gates, casually at first, to not upset the nanomatronic dancers, but picking up speed as she went. Maddie couldn't keep up, so Ethan hoisted her onto his back.

Barclay was left standing in their wake. The pulsating technicolor parade reflected in his sunglasses. His gaze lingered on the distant silhouette of the chopper as he fastened his white sport coat, yanking the collar high around his neck. Hands shoved deep into his pockets, he took a breath and plunged into the crowd.

The mass of dancing robots and costumed characters converged around him, gyrating and lurching in synchronized fury. Their bodies twisted and warped, limbs stretching in abnormal angles and lengths. As Barclay pushed against the tide, a dragon in a top hat, Frannie Frog's high-heeled feet for hands, slammed into his side, nearly taking him off balance. A Halloween skeleton, its gaping mouth riddled with glowing LED panels, thrust into his path. Barclay dodged and weaved, but the creatures were closing in. He peered over the crowd. That helicopter wasn't getting much closer.

A troupe of dancers had begun to close in on the others, their bodies undulating to the beat. Bombadape—the Cosmic Ape—extended a gnarled, half-formed hand toward Ethan. Dingus swatted at the grotesque appendage with a swift jerk. More characters lunged for the kids, and Dingus fought them all away, but he couldn't do this for long.

Back at the frontlines, the relentless onslaught continued to batter Barclay. He ducked under one of the octopus float's tentacles, but the trunk of a wooly mammoth—attached to the belly of a snowman—knocked him off his feet and sent him sprawling onto the cold, wet asphalt. He attempted to crawl through the tempest, but the dancers kept coming, blotting out his view of his helicopter, then Frog Tower, then the sky. His scream of terror was drowned out by the synthetic orchestra.

Dee's feet hammered against the pavement. Ethan struggled to keep pace with her as the full force of the parade surrounded them. He heard a high-pitched screech as the weight of his sister lifted from his back.

A grotesque version of the prince from *Princess Bop* had Maddie in his arms, cackling as he twirled the girl into a hellish waltz.

"My princess!" he said, his voice deep and garbled, "I've rescued you!"

Ethan made a desperate lunge toward his sister, but the other dancers were there, their mismatched limbs striking him down with brutal efficiency. The prince laughed maniacally, his face burning with inhuman fervor as he spun Maddie around. The heat radiated off him, scorching the air around them and prickling uncomfortably against Maddie's skin.

A sword cleaved through the noise in a blaze of light and steel. The prince's head tumbled from his warped body in a shower of sparks and pixels, revealing Princess Dee's grim face.

As the headless royal crumpled, Ethan dove forward once more, catching his sister before she hit the ground. Dee brandished her gleaming weapon at the other dancers, pulsating neon reflecting off the blade. The closest characters slowed and backed away.

A sing-song voice rose above the beat. "Oh, my! Did you take that from the stone?"

A titanic tentacle effortlessly plucked the sword from Dee's hands, hurling it through the night air with a dismissive flick. The sword impaled itself in a 'Thanks for Visiting!' sign with a clang. The pointed tip pierced through a caricature of Dingus Dog right between his googly eyes.

The real Dingus clapped his hands over his mouth in shock.

"That sword is for the children!" From atop her luminescent perch, the nanomatronic doppelgänger of Dee cast her gaze down onto her human counterpart. "Did you think I forgot about you, darlin'? You've been wearing my face for quite long enough."

Dee searched the crowd. She didn't see the kids. The dancers were a whirlwind of chaos and colors, pressing in from all sides. She spied the exit sign and her embedded sword. She took a sharp breath and forced her way into the crowd just as the octopus tentacle slammed into the ground where she'd been standing.

"There's only room for one Princess Dee in this park," the false Dee shouted. "This is my kingdom!"

Meanwhile, Ethan and Maddie had become lost in the throng, all sense of direction erased by the dancers and lights. Dingus materialized out of the chaos and, with surprising strength, gathered both children into his arms and pumped his furry legs toward the exit.

Dee's progress was abruptly halted as a tentacle coiled around her, lifting her off the ground. But before she could scream, Barclay Bloom appeared, wielding a severed wooly mammoth trunk. He speared the trunk into the exposed inner workings of the tentacle, causing it to uncoil and drop Dee.

"Thanks," the princess managed.

Barclay offered a grim smile." Thank me in Florida."

They plunged back into the melee with the electronic scream of the fake Dee fading behind them. The music seemed to grow louder as they dodged flailing limbs and twinkling costumes. The colors and movement were disorienting, and each step was a battle, but their focus on the exit was singular. They pushed on until they caught a glimpse of Dingus and the others. The kids seemed relieved when they saw the adults. Maddie ran directly to Dee.

An immense art deco structure—the exit gates—stretched across the southern end of Nostalgia Bay. The turnstiles were each ten feet tall and all locked. Ocean waves loomed beyond, the smells and sounds of salt and sea wafting through the open air. They were almost free.

Dingus threw himself at the turnstiles, to no effect.

"He keeps doing that," Ethan said.

"This way!" Dee pointed. As the parade encroached, they veered toward a small door adjacent to the entrance—a tiny office room, seemingly untouched by the mayhem around it.

The five of them hustled to the—somewhat surprisingly—unlocked office and ducked inside, slamming the door shut behind them. The muffled din of the Night Parade rumbled outside.

With their safe haven momentarily secured, Dee and Dingus wasted no time fortifying the exit, barricading themselves in with any solid objects they could lay their hands on. Chairs, a small table, a potted plant.

Ethan, meanwhile, searched the room. Compared to the rest of Nanoland, this backstage office was unsettlingly ordinary. There were monitors displaying text documents, scattered papers, a coffee machine, and a printer. Normal, boring office stuff.

Maddie tapped a keyboard curiously. Barclay pulled her hand away. "Don't touch that," he said.

"Where's the emergency exit?" Ethan asked. "The one we're looking for."

Dee set one last chair on top of the pile of furniture in front of the door and gestured to the back of the room, where a big metal door stood surrounded by cabinets. It had the words' Emergency Exit' emblazoned in bright red letters.

"Right." Ethan started for the door, and Dee followed.

From behind them, Barclay said, "Alicia, wait."

Dee winced as a sharp buzz rippled across her scalp.

"Stop calling her that!" Maddie frowned, crossing her arms with a huff. "She's Princess Dee!"

Dee shook off the pain. She tried the door handle. It didn't budge. She leaned on the door, and Ethan did too, but the emergency exit remained stubbornly closed.

A crash shuddered through the room. Something had slammed against the entrance, causing a few objects to tumble from the pile. Dee noticed the frame around the emergency exit wobble slightly.

Dingus leaned against the barricade, holding up the pile of furniture with both arms.

Dee considered what she'd seen. She nudged Ethan's shoulder so he'd stop pushing. She grabbed the door frame with both hands and pulled. It came away from the wall with a surprising lack of resistance, revealing nothing but bare concrete behind it.

"There's no emergency exit." Barclay's voice came from behind her, confirming her fears. "This whole island locks down completely in the event of a crisis."

"You knew," Dee said, her voice low.

"Nanoland is filled to the brim with proprietary technology owned by the Frank Nano Company that can never, ever leave this island. That includes your costume, *by the way*, but I was planning on making an exception."

"You knew this whole time," Dee repeated, "And you let us run here."

Barclay replied calmly, "I told you to go to the helicopter."

Ethan squinted. "Why is there even a fake door?"

"Morale." Dee crossed her arms. "People wouldn't do their jobs if they thought Barclay Bloom left them here to die. Isn't that right?"

The other door rattled ominously under the relentless assault from the outside. Dingus leaned against it with all his weight, his arms stretched wide, doing his best to keep the barricade intact.

Ethan noticed. "Uh, guys..."

"I've been trying to save you," Barclay said, getting indignant.

Dee shouted. "You should've told us!"

"It's confidential! I shouldn't have to!"

With a sickening groan, the entrance door bent inward. Ethan rushed to Dingus' aid, throwing his weight against the barricade alongside the costumed character.

A red sequined hand slipped through a growing crack in the door, fingers wiggling as it reached into the room.

"I'm scared, Princess Dee," Maddie said.

Dee set the argument aside momentarily and pulled the young girl into a comforting embrace. "Shhh, it's okay. We'll figure this out."

Ethan whacked the sequined hand with a chair, and it slunk back through the door. Barclay went to help them keep the onslaught at bay.

"Is the parade gonna get us?" Maddie said. "Where do we go now?"

Dee reached over and wordlessly picked up a pen from a nearby desk. She stood and lifted the girl into her arms. Her heart pounded in her chest. She didn't like what she was about to say, but the reality was undeniable.

"We're going to the helicopter," she said.

The parade erupted into the room like a mudslide, a relentless tide of dancing characters and whirling colors. The boys were thrown backward from the force, pummeled and tossed around in the surge. Barclay hit his head on a desk, breaking his sunglasses. Dingus tumbled head over heels into the filing cabinets. Ethan rolled straight into the wall. Dee struggled against the flood, cradling the girl in her arms and desperately stumbling back toward the door.

Emerging into Nostalgia Bay, she found that the parade had become all-consuming in the minutes they'd spent indoors. Every surface of the ground, every shop window, was filled beyond reason with neon, sparkling, dancing creatures. Shadows twisted and twirled as spotlights darted around the landscape. Several songs played on the speakers simultaneously, overlapping discordantly.

Dingus was the next to step outside. He charged forward, oversized fists flying, attempting to clear a path for the others.

At the nucleus of the chaos, the octopus castle float towered above everything else, its tentacles writhing over the dancers' many heads. The nanomatronic Princess Dee still stood atop its melon, her gleaming LED sequin gown twinkling like a disco ball.

The robotic princess sang with a hauntingly beautiful voice, clear and defined amidst the pandemonium. Flocks of tiny birdies and butterflies swirled around her. She noticed Dee and smiled.

Barclay stepped outside with Ethan at his side. He scanned the chaos until he found what he was looking for. He pointed. "It's still there!"

The helicopter stood untouched on its helipad. Dee nodded. There was still a chance. They just needed to reach it.

The Robot Dee flicked her wrist, and the swarm of birds and butterflies swooped down, swirling around the human Dee and lifting her off the ground. She had barely managed to pass Maddie to Ethan before she was carried upward, the fluttering creatures stopping only when she was face to face with her doppelgänger, resplendent atop the octopus castle.

Tentacles snaked around Dee's arms and waist, binding her movements. She grunted, struggling helplessly. The robot Dee eyed her up and down.

"I'm afraid you're not fit to wear that crown, dear," she drawled, her accent thick, her voice sweet yet laced with venom. She reached for Dee's tiara, which was firmly rooted to her wig, which was anchored to her scalp.

The robot's mechanical fingers tightened around the tiara, tugging. Sparks burst from the wig, followed by a sharp, searing pain. Dee's vision flashed white. She felt like a knife had been thrust between her eyes.

"Ahhh! Wait!" Dee shouted. Hot blood trickled down her forehead. "I admit it! You got me! You're the real Dee!"

The pixelated princess released her grip from the tiara. "Go on."

Drawing in a shaky breath, Dee poured sincerity into her words. "I'm just an actor. You're a real princess. I've always been jealous of your, your purity and your, uh, undeniable grace! But you can teach me. Teach me how to be the perfect, real princess you are."

The robot Dee considered this.

Meanwhile, down below, the other humans continued fighting through the crowd. Ethan clutched Maddie close, cradling her head. The dancers pawed at them, reaching and grasping for his sister. What did they want with her? Feeling the pull of the crowd, Ethan nudged Barclay and hurriedly passed his sister to the CEO, who was taller and a bit more removed from the action.

The moment he was alone, before the boy could comprehend what was happening, two winged monstrosities, lopsided hybrids of mascot heads and the metallic wings from model Space Squad ships, fluttered up from the throng of dancers like deranged, oversized insects. They buzzed toward Ethan, chomping down on his arms with the holes on the bottom of their heads, which now bore rows of teeth made from rocks and wood chips. Ethan barely had time to let out a yelp before he felt the ground disappearing beneath his feet.

Something tightened around his ankle. Ethan glanced down, his eyes widening as he saw Dingus, who had made a desperate leap into the air and caught hold of him. The silent dog mascot was now suspended in mid-air beneath Ethan, holding on with both furry hands.

It wasn't enough to halt their ascent. With a beat of their monstrous wings, the mascot heads carried Ethan and Dingus up and away into the moonless night sky.

"No! Ethan!" Maddie reached for her brother as she watched him go.

Barclay, holding the girl, clambered onto the hood of a quintessential eighties sports car, all sharp angles and gaudy paint, parked in the small car show section of Nostalgia Bay. The parade was everywhere, thrashing on the ground, oozing out of windows and shadows.

The relentless dancers were inching closer.

Above them, the robot Dee nodded, still lost in thought as she pondered the human Dee's proposition.

"I'm so sorry, darlin'," she said. "I would just very much prefer to kill you."

Dee said. "Could I ask you just one question?"

She leaned in closer, her voice dropping to a conspiratorial whisper. The synthetic princess leaned in as well, her interest piqued.

"Would a real princess do this?"

With that, Dee drove her knee into her nanomatronic double's crotch. The pixelated princess moaned as the LED panels covering her dress sparked and shattered. Glass and fire sprinkled down onto the parade below.

The octopus float's grip loosened, freeing Dee's arm. In one smooth motion, she plunged the pen she'd grabbed in the office into the fake Dee's eye.

The ensuing electronic screech was earsplitting, a blend of human pain and machine malfunction. The robot Dee clawed at her pixelated face, frantically trying to grasp the pen. The octopus, seeming to mirror her agony, dropped Dee without a second thought.

The crowd of dancers, the rising mass of felt and debris, was now over Maddie's head and still rising to Barclay's elbows, his shoulders, his neck, until he too disappeared into the swelling tide.

As Dee fell through the air, she felt a strange sense of calm. Her mind seemed clearer than it had been in days.

She landed with a thud in the crowd, and her body was instantly subsumed by the ravening parade. Her last sight, before the dancers closed in, was of Ethan and Dingus, up in the sky, being carried away.

No. Not Dingus.

Jimmy.

She smiled as she faded out of consciousness.

His name was Jimmy.

18

Dee slowly opened her eyes. Blurry, blueish shapes shifted in the darkness around her. A cool breeze tingled on her arms. It was, at the very least, quiet. No music, no dancers. She tilted her head, and a bag of broken glass rolled inside her skull. She groaned.

A small girl's voice. "She's awake, Mr. Bloom!"

Dee sat up and held her head in both hands. A small pink shape wobbled out of the dark and coalesced into Maddie. The princess smiled.

"Hey, girl," Dee said. "Where are we?"

"It's ok," Maddie said. "You're back home."

Dee stopped smiling. She looked around. "No..."

The breeze was coming from the ceiling, open to the night sky. She saw the stained glass window depicting a frog wearing a crown. The red velvet rope for guests to queue behind, the pile of rubble where Princess Winnifred once stood, the small stage where Dee stood, day after day, hour after hour, posing and smiling for pictures. Her water bottle was still there, hidden discreetly behind a potted plant.

She was back in the Photo Pavilion.

"No." Dee pushed herself up, wobbling as she stood. "No...no, no, no, not here. We can't be here."

"Hey." Barclay was sitting on the floor, leaning against one of the walls. He stood with her. "You've got a head wound. You should take it easy."

"No!" she said. She stumbled forward, wincing as her brain stabbed her from the inside. "Why are we back here?!"

"The parade brought us here," Barclay said. "Carried us all the way across the park and left us in this photo op building. Are you alright?"

"Princess Dee?" Maddie said. "Do you know where Ethan is?"

"I... I don't." Dee stumbled toward the exit. The debris they'd pulled away earlier was still moved. The doorway was clear. She could see the rest of the Fairy Tale Kingdom. "I'm not alright. I can't... I'm sorry. I... I can't stay here."

She started to climb over the rubble.

"Wait!" Barclay shouted. "Don't go that way!"

Just as she was about to climb outside, giant metallic pincers smashed together in front of her. The princess rolled backward in shock, sliding down the rubble.

Barclay grabbed her under the arms and dragged her back into the dark safety of the Pavilion. The roller coaster centipede poked around the debris before stomping off on its many steel legs.

Barclay sighed. "The big bug's still out there."

Dee screamed in frustration.

•○•

Ethan meandered through the desolate, alien streets of Battlezone X, the soft glow of his phone screen the only light in the darkness. Designed to resemble the besieged spaceport from the second Space Squad film (*Space Squad II: Battlezone*), the zone was a series of futuristic faux stone buildings, artificially weathered and battle-damaged, with pixelated alien vegetation growing between the cracks. By day, this area would be filled with guests, many armed with laser weapons and sensors, as well as pixelated aliens and cast members working the shops and restaurants.

Now, the zone was dark, powerless, and empty. The nanotech creatures that had been attacking the survivors for the last few days were conspicuously absent. The streets were barren of any life, human or otherwise.

A metallic scrape to Ethan's left startled him. He whipped his phone around to see Dingus Dog, an empty soda can beneath his furry paw. The costumed character shrugged sheepishly.

Ethan smiled. The silent, six-foot anthropomorphic dog could be unnerving, but the boy was glad to have him at the moment. Any companion was better than facing this situation alone.

Ethan turned back, aiming his phone screen into the path. For whatever reason, the phone was stuck in his ebook app, locked onto the last page of *Nanolandia* that he was reading before the parade. He didn't know why. At least it was bright.

His mind lingered on the two winged mascot heads that had deposited him and Dingus here before fluttering off into the night. Why did they bring him here? Why him? Why did they leave everyone else? Where *was* everyone else? Where was his sister?

They'd been wandering for what felt like hours. Endless outdoor corridors of gift shops, restaurants, and restrooms. No exits. No rides.

Ethan had a map taped to his bedroom door at home. He'd stared at it for months leading up to this vacation. There was a gateway to the Prehistoric Forest and another to the Puppet Paddock. The whole damn theme park was supposed to go in a loop—it was fairly straightforward—but every turn in this place led to more gift shops, more restaurants.

Were they going in circles? None of the ornate buildings around him seemed familiar. He scanned the rooftops. Weren't you supposed to be able to see Frog Tower from anywhere? Wasn't that the whole point of Frog Tower? Where was it? Where was the Cosmic Coliseum? Where was…

Ethan knew he shouldn't be thinking about Time Breakers. He needed to focus on finding his sister, on getting out of this place. But there was a part of himself, deep down, that couldn't shake the gnawing feeling of disappointment at not finding his ride. It should be *here*. He was right next to it. If he could just look at it for a minute. He'd come all this way.

A sudden motion in Ethan's periphery. He twisted and aimed his light. Something stirred within one of the nearby gift shops.

"Hello?" Ethan said.

There was no response.

He glanced at his canine companion, who nodded, googly eyes wobbling. The two of them stepped tentatively into the dark, silent gift shop.

The store had taken some damage in the aftermath of the catastrophic event. Shelves had collapsed, scattering merchandise across the floor. T-shirts adorned with dramatic battle scenes, cups shaped like alien spacecraft, and baseball caps bearing the park's logo. Frankie Frog plushies. Keychains. Bottle openers. There was no sign of whatever had moved.

Ethan grabbed a Bombadape backpack off the floor and began to fill it with items that could be useful. Water bottles, a package of Band-Aids, a handful of pens, and an array of candy—the only food offered at this shop.

When was the last time he'd eaten? He vaguely remembered a churro offered by Charlie in the forest, but the last time he'd eaten real food, he couldn't remember. He grabbed a couple more chocolate bars. He thought they should probably raid a restaurant, too, but after everything else he'd seen in this place, it was probably safer to stick to pre-packaged stuff.

He found Dingus standing before a tall display filled with stuffed dolls in his likeness. A whole wall of Dinguses. The dog seemed to be contemplating something as he silently gazed up at his own merch. He didn't notice Ethan approaching.

The boy coughed, prompting Dingus to turn toward him.

"Hey. You with me?"

The dog gave him a slow nod.

"Let's move out."

Having survived that gift shop, Ethan felt comfortable venturing into other buildings. They scoped out the Sky Wing photo op, where a solitary spaceship hovered eerily at the center of an empty room. Dingus started to climb into the ship, but Ethan stopped him. No need for it.

They checked a few more shops, finding identical merchandise that, strangely, had fallen in the same way. Ethan suspected that they were the same gift shop, across the road from itself, so he left a pen on the counter in one to see if it would be there the next time. It wasn't.

He and Dingus scoped out the restrooms. They checked the meet-and-greets.

Eventually, their exploration led them to a mock space bar and restaurant named the Celestial Cantina. By day, guests could eat grotesque alien food designed to match the meals eaten in Space Squad. By night, the Cantina was mainly an alcoholic refuge for the adults who didn't like laser tag.

In the dim cell phone light, they found dozens of overturned tables and chairs surrounding a futuristic bar riddled with pipes, tubes, and turbines. A single blue drink in a martini glass had been left upright on the bar. Ethan picked it up, sniffed it, then put it down.

Dingus gestured to the door behind the bar. Ethan nodded. There could be real food in there. But when he swung the door open, a foul stench assaulted his senses. The reek of spoiled meat and rotten milk was suffocating. The boy backed out swiftly, dragging Dingus outside with him.

They continued on. Ethan unwrapped a candy bar, knowing he was probably hungry, but after smelling that kitchen, he didn't have much of an appetite. He offered it to Dingus, but the dog declined.

It was getting cold. Ethan rubbed his arms as he walked down empty street after empty street. They weren't making any progress. This wasn't working. Ethan stopped walking. He pocketed his phone and closed his eyes, rubbing his forehead with his palms.

A furry gloved hand fell on his shoulder and shook it.

"What?" Ethan opened his eyes.

Rising several stories from the street, the Cosmic Coliseum stood directly in front of them. It was a grand, futuristic rendition of the Coliseum in Rome, much smaller than the original but built with forced perspective to create the illusion of scale. When the park was open, roars of excitement would be heard as the eternal laser tag tournaments played out at its center. Stray pixelated lasers would flash from the top. Now, the lights were turned off, and the place was silent, but the Coliseum was here, right in front of Dingus and Ethan. The round structure dwarfed all the surrounding buildings. It wasn't there a second ago. But wait, if this was here, then Time Breakers should be...

The boy spun around.

There was nothing. More gift shops, more restrooms.

He turned back, half expecting the Coliseum to disappear, but there it remained. The gate was open. A sign above warned them not to enter if they were sensitive to strobe lights, or pregnant. They were neither.

"I mean, we're here, right?" Ethan said aloud, half to himself and half to Dingus. "It's pretty tall. If we go to the top, we might see a way out of this place."

He looked at Dingus, who stared back. The dog had no answers for him.

"It's better than another gift shop," Ethan said.

They turned toward the Cosmic Coliseum and together they ventured inside.

•○•

The interior of the Coliseum was grandiose and desolate. The vast emptiness echoed with their soft footsteps. The architectural design harkened back to the Roman Empire but with unmistakable Space Squad-inspired elements. Pillars and arches of sleek metallic alloys stood in stark contrast to the crumbling stone structures. Statues of everyone's favorite Space Squad characters posed as intergalactic gladiators, their weapons raised high.

The boy and the dog walked through the expansive arena, littered with abandoned laser tag weaponry molded into the shapes of the Space Squad's gear. Everyone here at the time of the event had obviously left in a hurry, but there was something off about how the equipment was laid out on the battlefield. It was too evenly distributed. It felt like it had been arranged.

Finding their way into the stands, Ethan and Dingus began the arduous ascent to the top. The stone steps crumbled under their weight, rocks and pebbles trickling behind them. It was unsettling, the rapid decay of this structure. It wasn't actually old. It was just designed that way. The park had only been closed for two days. Yet it felt like they were climbing the remnants of an ancient civilization.

As they reached the top, Ethan's heart sank. A solid mock-stone wall ran along the entire perimeter of the top floor, blocking any view outside the Coliseum. They'd come all the way up here for nothing.

Dingus nudged Ethan and pointed. High above the last row of seats was a catwalk, a narrow metal bridge filled with lighting equipment. The rest of Nanoland might be visible from there. It was their best shot at a vantage point. Ethan set down his backpack, oblivious as the stone floor around it crumpled and groaned.

Ethan walked under the catwalk and hopped with his arm raised high above his head. He couldn't quite reach it.

He turned to Dingus. "Can you give me a boost?"

The dog positioned himself next to Ethan, directly beneath the catwalk. He cupped his furry hands, and Ethan stepped into them. "Ready?"

He jumped right as the dog boosted him up, and he caught the catwalk's edge with both hands. There was a crack below him, and just as Ethan looked down, he saw the floor beneath Dingus's feet give way. The dog was swallowed by the darkness below, vanishing without a sound.

"Dingus!" Ethan shouted, dangling precariously from the catwalk's edge.

His voice bounced around the Coliseum, but the darkness below remained silent.

He shimmied across the swaying catwalk over empty seats before dropping down beside the gaping hole. The floor trembled beneath him, more pieces breaking away and tumbling into the abyss. Ethan crawled backward, heart pounding, until he felt solid ground.

He was alone.

Scrambling to his feet, Ethan turned and hurried back down the stairs. Panic coursed through his veins, his mind spinning with grim thoughts. How many floors was that? Could anyone survive that? He was alone now, truly alone. It was one thing to have buildings shift around in the pitch-black theme park when you have someone with you. Ethan couldn't wander around this place by himself. He was barely holding on as it was.

He reached the bottom, and as he burst out of the Coliseum into the outside air, he spotted his companion. Dingus was lying in a heap of broken floor, plaster, and wood.

He wasn't moving.

Ethan's stomach turned. He rushed toward the lifeless dog man with googly eyes pointing limply at the ground.

"Are you ok?" he asked.

Dingus turned his head and weakly raised a gloved thumb in reassurance. Ethan sighed, relieved, but as he tried to help Dingus up, the costumed dog wobbled and collapsed.

"Whoa! What's wrong?"

Dingus gestured to his left ankle and shook his head. His furry foot was hanging at an odd angle.

"Shit. Can you walk?"

The googly-eyed dog stared back at him. He motioned for Ethan to leave him behind.

"No," Ethan said. "That's not happening."

He maneuvered Dingus's arm around his shoulder, struggling to lift him up. But Dingus was too big and too heavy, and he fell, dragging Ethan down with him.

They tried again, and again. Each time, they only made it a few steps, each attempt as fruitless as the last. Exhausted, they eventually slumped onto a nearby bench, panting as the eerie silence of the park enveloped them.

"What do we do?" Ethan looked to Dingus, seeking an answer the silent dog could not provide. "I don't...I don't know what to do."

A strange heat emanated from his pocket. Pulling out his phone, Ethan found the screen still on, shining at full brightness. It was unlocked, as it had been since they landed in the Battlezone. The battery was at 100%. None of this made sense.

"Everyone else's phone bricked," he said. He stared at the screen displaying his current chapter in *Nanolandia*. "Why am I the only one with a phone?"

Dingus didn't answer. His head lolled to the side. His chest was moving. He was still breathing, but it seemed like maybe he had passed out.

Ethan turned back to his phone and, without another word, began to read.

19

After the diagnosis in 1986, Frank was slow to tell even his closest family and friends, content to keep his ever-growing brain tumor a secret from all but his sister Gertie.

Ken: Frank's the co-owner of the company. It's named after him, and for the first year or so of their existence, he never once asked about the non-entertainment divisions of the business. Divisions which, by the way, already accounted for 62% of our total income. It turned out that theme parks and movie special effects were two of the least efficient ways to profit from nanotech. Live and learn.

We hadn't seen Frank for weeks, which was weird. The guy's a workaholic. If he's not in the office, he's in Florida on his island. But nobody's seen him.

So, one day, he walks in unannounced. He looks like shit. Rail thin, sunken eyes, beard sticking out in clumps. He says, "I saw on TV that we have a medical division."

This is how he finds out what his company does. He sees it on the news.

I say, "We do."

And... he tells me. I'm mortified. My friend, one of my closest friends of the past twenty years, is dying. I try to talk to him about it, like a person. I ask about his symptoms, his wife, and his sister. He brushes it all off. He just wanted to know who the head of medical was, and at that point, it was Sal Destro.

Sal: I am an engineer by trade. The movies, they are fun, but I am not here for fun. I am here for money. Ken Sakai puts my Destrotech in these new things, and he wants to know what I'd like to do. I say, "Where is the money?"

He says, "Curing cancer." *[grins]* Ok.

Ken: We called Sal up together and explained the situation.

Sal: We had been working on, eh, different things, smaller things. We use Destrotech to remove skin tags, lesions, like this. Outside the body. They are hot, the robots. Very poisonous to the skin. Movie sets, yes. Dragons, yes. A theme park, sure. Inside the human body? Is a no. We cannot remove a tumor.

Ken: And so Frank, without running it by me, gives Sal carte blanche to spend whatever he has to, pull whoever he needs to from other divisions…*[sighs]* basically rip the company apart for his own needs.

Sal: For carte blanche, I take away your cancer. *Non c'è problema!*

Frank: It's my company. I'll run it into the ground if I need to. It's such a weird thing to put on a pedestal. The movies matter, Nanoland matters, but "*the company*"? It's a big pile of numbers that money comes out of. Who cares?

At that point, along with the chest pain, I had these migraines, this constant throbbing above my right eye. Sometimes it hurts a little, and sometimes a lot, but it's always there. Colors flashing in my periphery. Throwing up two or three times a day. Ringing in my ears. Memory problems. I would blank out and be standing outside or in a grocery store, with no idea how I got there or what I came for.

My sister moved into my apartment when I started having seizures.

Gertie: I was sleeping on the couch, taking care of the basic things: food, clothes. Whenever he would stop thrashing around and finally fall asleep, I would just stare at him, waiting for something to go wrong.

He had to tell Beth. I begged him to tell her.

Beth: No, I had no idea. I thought he was in Nanoland. He usually was.

Frank: We were in a weird place. I didn't want her to see me like that. I didn't want to be seen, period. I barely left the apartment.

You know, it's funny, the specter of death motivated me to work hard my whole life, but the moment it was imminent, when I was staring mortality in the face... it felt, I don't know... pointless. Movies or no, Nanoland or no, I'm still a guy in a bed, dying alone.

It wasn't even a heart attack. That would've made narrative sense. This was just a random thing. That sucks. That's not how movies work.

Hugh: Frank would talk about death like he was the only mortal in the world.

Ken: With Frank, uh, preoccupied, I had Beth come back over to features.

Beth: Yes, we made a few more princess movies as an offshoot of the television show. Just puppets. No pixels. We were essentially making episodes of the show with a bigger budget. It was mostly me and Hugh. At that point, we were spending a lot of time together.

Hugh: I don't know if I'd call it a relationship or a romance. A fling, tops. We're both huddled behind the puppet stage twelve hours a day. It's the same way Beth and Frank got together. I was probably more proactive about it than he was.

But, you know, even at the height of that, it never felt permanent? It wasn't serious. Frank's the love of her life. And I was there, too.

Beth: I invited Frank to be in the movies. It had been a while since we'd spoken, but it felt wrong to make features without him. He answered through Gertie. Two words: "Not now." He could be very cold.

I still had no idea he was as sick as he was, but all of the best nanotech engineers were being transferred to Nano Medical for a top-secret project. We never knew the details, but everyone knew *something* was going on.

Ken: We were having trouble keeping the park solvent. Having all the nanotech run from a central hub was more challenging than expected. We could do individual rides, individual shows, no problem. But this was the eighties. We had eighties computers. We owned nanotech, but we lacked the processing power to control it. Thankfully, we had Gertie on the ground handling the human element, making up the difference.

Gertie: I was running a theme park by day, keeping the place staffed and clean and operational, and rushing home to care for my brother at night. I didn't sleep much.

Ken: I spent many nights at the top of Frog Tower, troubleshooting issues with the programmers. They needed so much RAM to run the park that they'd started buying home PCs from every store in Florida. There was a computer shortage in North America for months in '86. That was us.

It still wasn't working. A few members of the team brought me a proposal. They'd started experimenting with what they called "pixelated processing". It's a nanobot-based artificial intelligence system. You combine the bots into a grid and essentially use them as brain cells. The nanotech then controls itself.

It looked like a blob of gray jello floating in a big glass tube, but the tests were promising, so I signed off on it. We needed something.

Gertie: We were working our cast members to the bone. Hemorrhaging staff. The rides kept breaking down, and the tech kept glitching out.

Ken: At the start of 1987, the company lost money for the first time in a decade. And then…

Frank: Sal Destro shows up at my apartment in Florida at three in the morning. Middle of the night. He's got this vial of silver goop.

Sal: I cured his cancer. I cured *all* cancer. I want to tell him in person.

Dr. Inga Elmgren (*CEO, Nano Medical*)**:** No one person can claim to have created what was in that vial. It resulted from hundreds of Nano employees working in concert on different aspects of that cure.

Here's what we figured out: you can't send nanotech into someone's body to remove a tumor without killing them in the process. You have to use the bots to rewrite their DNA and turn the person into something nanotech can exist in and cancer cannot.

But it's not just that. Once ingested, this solution, this particular collection of bots, would cure the body of all diseases. They could improve muscle fitness, reduce body fat, and even reverse the aging process.

Sal: A panacea. *[grins]* Destro's Panacea.

Inga: That's the theory. At the time, it was completely untested, even in animals. We'd run simulations based on Frank's DNA, but… when Mr. Destro removed it illegally from our facility, it was a single 222 million dollar prototype.

Frank: Sal tells me what's in the vial will cure me, remove the tumor, along with anything else that's wrong with me. All I have to do is drink it. But in return, he wants all my shares in the company and complete control of every division.

Sal: He's dying! What does he care about this? He's a little movie boy. He tells stories about dragons and rainbows. He can do that somewhere else. He can go live in his island circus. Do you know what I, Sal Destro, could do with the Frank Nano Company? With what was in that vial? This is world-changing technology. The actual crime would be to leave it with Frank Nano.

Frank: Did I mention he had a gun in my face the whole time? I didn't appreciate that, to be perfectly honest with you.

Anyway, my sister brained him with a frying pan.

Gertie: I was sleeping on the couch, and I heard talking in the other room. I got up, peeked around the corner, and saw Sal Destro waving a Beretta 92FS around. So, I did what any reasonable adult would do: I called the police and resolved the situation myself as quickly and efficiently as possible.

Blackmailing Frank at gunpoint. *[shakes head]* For goodness sake.

Frank: He woke up as the cops were taking him away, and I forget what he said, but my exact words were, "You're fired."

The first person I ever fired. Only person, actually. I let other people do that. I'm not great with confrontation.

Sal: Eleven years in prison! When I come out, I have nothing. No Destrotech! No Destro's Panacea.

I invented the technology the Frank Nano Company was built on. Before me, they do puppets. I create Destrotech to clean pipes in Italy. It was *my* team that created the panacea! In the end, they take everything.

Frank Nano loved to go on about creator's rights. Never share credit, never sell the rights, but only *his* rights matter. Nanotech, Nanoland, the puppets. He was not a champion of freedom. He was a selfish prick! *Bastardo!* Frankie fucking Frog!

Inga: Mr. Nano calls me in the middle of the night, tells me Sal is out, and I'm head of Nano Medical. He says he has the vial. He's holding it in his hand and wants to know what it is. I tell him that he should absolutely not drink it. It's completely experimental, extremely dangerous, and it was in his mouth before I hung up the phone.

Frank: What was it gonna do? Kill me?

Almost overnight, Frank's health improved. The headaches went away, along with the seizures and the chest pains. Fit and rejuvenated, he set about putting the pieces of his life back together, starting with his marriage.

Beth: He told me he would be in California and wanted to get together. He brought me to an actual restaurant with real silverware and vegetables. He wore a tucked-in shirt, and his hair was cut. His beard was trimmed. He had flowers. All pretty basic, but if you know Frank...

He apologized. He said he'd gotten lost in his head for a while, but now he wanted to focus on what really mattered to him.

Frank: When I was sick, all I had thought about was all the movies I'd never make, all the rides we could add to Nanoland that I would never see. I assumed that if I was cured, I would go straight back to work. But when the cure came, I found out that all I ever wanted was Beth.

Beth: He didn't move back that day, but shortly thereafter.

Hugh: *[pause]* It's fine. What do you want me to say? It's fine.

Ken: With Frank back in California, we planned a whole production slate based on the films he'd abandoned midway through when he got his diagnosis. Frank was back making movies, but things were different.

Frank: I had some pictures to finish and some new ones to start, but I wanted to leave room in the schedule for other people to tell their stories. We've got a whole studio. We should use it to get some other people's movies made.

Beth: It's a collaborative medium. Even the most self-righteous and self-aggrandizing directors understand that. You have to work with so many different people, and they will each contribute different pieces to the film in their own way. Frank understood that, but it's one thing to have other people assist you and another thing entirely to let them take the lead.

He never told me what had happened to him while he was gone. He'd always change the subject. But whatever it was, he'd become a completely different person on the other side.

Frank: It wasn't just the tumor. I felt better than I had in years. My back didn't hurt. I stopped clenching my teeth at night. My, uh, bald spot started filling back in. Gray hair started turning brown.

Lost my beer gut. I had abs, like with the bumps. That was definitely new.

Hugh: I made my directorial debut with *Uncle Noam's Chair*, based on a Pulitzer Prize-winning children's novel I had loved as a kid, about an old man telling his nephew stories of his youth before the war. The Frank of old would never have signed off on that. Of course, he still found time to re-edit the entire film without my approval.

Frank: Hugh's cut was three hours long. It was an awful film. I was trying to help him.

Hugh: Asshole. *[pause]* He knew. He knew damn well about me and Beth.

Beth: The entire time he was shooting *Shark Rider*, he came home every day, six o'clock on the dot. We ate dinner together every night. It sounds small, but it's not. It's really not.

Ken: The wave of new movies meant new subject matter for attractions in the theme park, and just as we'd hoped, we were able to change out some older computationally-heavy rides with new stuff that ran a little better on the current architecture. With nanotech, we could remodel at a speed no other theme park could attempt.

Attendance was up, but we were still having problems with the software.

Gertie: There were a handful of accidents in those early years. The pixels didn't always behave perfectly, and there were times when no amount of showmanship and customer service could distract the guests from the fact that Mermaid Monica just tried to bite them.

Frank: My sister Gertie never gets enough credit. Nothing I've done would've been possible without her. I appreciated it. I should've told her that more often.

Ken: The team working on the pixelated processing unit had hit a wall with what was possible with nanotech and silicon chip-based computers. Everything exciting was happening in Nano Medical, so I brought Inga and her team in to take a crack at the Nanoland problem.

Inga: We had many initiatives in motion based on research done to cure Frank. It was like the space program, like NASA. The real value in going to the moon was in the leap forward in technology caused almost accidentally in the process. Tang. Slinkies. Silly Putty.

After all our research into combining biological and nanotechnological components into one machine, it was obvious what was needed to organize all the data running the theme park.

A brain. An animal brain.

Ken: It's more complicated than you'd think to get fresh brains in Florida.

Inga: We tried a pig brain and a cow brain. Both burned up under the pressure. Boiled in their own fluids. We needed a higher order of animal. Something intelligent. A chimp, a dolphin, an elephant. Mr. Frank Nano wanted it to be a frog.

Frank: It's Frog Tower!

Inga: Frogs are foolish animals.

Frank: I don't know. I was busy with other things.

Beth: I got pregnant. We weren't planning for it, especially considering we had been separated and living apart a few months earlier. It just happened. I was nervous about telling Frank, but he was surprisingly enthusiastic.

Frank: I was surprised, too. Now that I had a lot more time in my life, I was more open to filling some of it with other people. Scale back at work. Start a family. I was writing a smaller movie, like a drama. No dinosaurs or robots. I wanted to make something a little more intimate. A little respectable. This was before my fingers started falling off.

Beth: He couldn't hide the illness this time. It started with normal cold symptoms—runny nose, sore throat, and fever. I tried to get him to see a doctor, but he always refused. Waved it off. But the symptoms never completely went away, and they started getting… strange.

Frank: I was typing at the typewriter, working on my screenplay. Beth's asleep. And my left pinkie finger keeps hitting the *A* key on its own. I've got this twitch. A muscle spasm. I'm trying to keep writing, focusing on the work, and then it just… fell off. *Plop!* My finger rolled across my desk like a loose hot dog.

There was shiny gray mush on the end, and the wound was the same. No blood, just mush, like wet sand. So, I stuck it back on there. The seam sealed itself up, and my finger worked fine.

This happened in the middle of the night, so I sort of thought I dreamt it. I should've known better, but… I don't know what to tell you. Things were going so well. If you can avoid thinking about your fingers falling off, you will.

I never told Beth. A week later, we were, uhm, together, and I lost another finger. And then another. And then an ear.

Beth: He told me everything.

Frank: She took it pretty well, I thought, considering the situation.

Beth: *[sighs]* He'd lied to me for so long.

Inga: It's difficult to explain this in layman's terms, but I will do my best. Frank had microscopic nanites swimming in every cell in his body, making little fixes and changes, constantly reproducing themselves. The problem was, cells die. Three hundred billion cells in your body are replaced daily. And when each of Frank's cells died, the bots inside had nowhere to go.

We hadn't considered nanowaste. Frank's human body had no way to dispose of it. Since the moment he ingested the panacea, his body had been filling up with dead pixels. The functioning nanites were working overtime to keep him together, which is why he could reattach the, er, pieces of himself that he lost. But by the time he came to see me, this could not continue much longer.

Frank: My face kept drooping, one side at a time, and I'd have to physically push it back up. I wasn't eating much. My hair started falling out in big clumps. If I stood still without thinking about it, my arms would go gray and stretch down to the floor. I was having trouble literally keeping myself together. I couldn't sleep, because I would melt like Play-Doh if I lost focus.

I thought I had more time. I had more movies to make. We... we were having a baby. I...

Inga: We ran dozens of tests, searching for a way to remove the nanites from his system without killing him. And the only way we found that might possibly work—and it was a long shot—would be to add more human biomatter to his body, with waste management nanites calibrated to his DNA attached. A nanite-infused blood transfusion. It would need to be someone with almost identical DNA to Frank's, like a close relative—a parent or a sibling. Sadly, the transfusion would almost certainly be fatal to the donor.

Frank was not happy to hear this.

Beth: After his sessions with Inga, he would come home and talk to me. I had been very clear that there would be no more lies in our relationship.

He told me about the fatal-nanobot-infusion thing. And at that moment, I saw him glance down. At my stomach. At our *child*. It was only for a second, but...he'd thought about it.

Frank: I didn't... *[pause]* No. I never would have done that. Never.

Beth: All the things he'd done up to that point. The way he'd reacted when he'd gotten sick the first time. All the things he was willing to do to stay alive.

I decided, right then and there, that I needed to get as far away from this man as I possibly could.

After his wife left him, Frank moved into the lab at Nano Medical as doctors and technicians worked around the clock to cure his condition. It was not improving.

Inga: When he disappeared from our lab, most of Mr. Nano's biological body was already dead. He was using bandages and splints to hold himself together.

He just vanished. I don't know where he went.

Gertie: He stopped taking my calls. He wouldn't let me visit. I'd been there for the cancer, for Christ's sake. How bad could this be?

Ken: Beth was long gone, and now Frank's missing, too. Absolutely no one could find him.

Chuck Flanagan (*childhood friend*): I had finished watching Carson, I'm about to go up to bed, and there's a knock at the front door. I open it, and there's Frank Najmanovich. Showed up at my house out of the blue. I hadn't seen or heard from him in about thirty years, but I recognized him immediately cause, you know, he's a famous person.

He's wrapped in bandages up to his chin, including both hands. He's got this baseball cap on and a big puffy coat. He looks like a scarecrow. My kids are sleeping upstairs, so I take him out on the front porch. I give him a beer.

He started going on about things from when we were kids: movies, comic books, teachers we were afraid of. Girls we never talked to. Eventually, I say, "Frank, what're you doing here?"

He says he's dying. I ask if I can do anything, and he shakes his head. His face wobbles around like it's not attached to his skull. There's something seriously wrong with this guy.

He tells me his wife's pregnant. You know, his mom was around when we were kids. I knew his mom. I don't remember there being a dad. This may be what this is all about. So I say, "You grew up without a father, and you turned out ok."

He laughs, this wet rasp that turns into a cough, and he says, "No, I didn't."

We sat there in silence. I didn't know what to say to him. What did he want me to say? Eventually, I told him my kids are huge fans of his stuff. My oldest son loves *Space Squad*. He's got a whole room full of little spaceships and figurines. My other son went as Jungle Jack three Halloweens in a row. I took them both to Nanoland last summer, and they loved it. It was all they ever talked about. I pointed to the picture in the front room, which we took as a family in front of Frank's statue.

I said, "You've given millions of kids memories they'll cherish for their whole lives. All that's gotta be worth something."

He nodded. By that point, he had melted into his chair. His eyes were bugging out. One of his arms was visibly detached from his body.

I told him I would call 911, and I got up to use the phone. By the time I came back, he was gone.

Ken: I got a call from a payphone in Illinois. He wanted me to meet him alone at Frog Tower that night.

Chuck: I guess he just wanted to talk to somebody outside of his celebrity life. But why me, you know? That's what I don't understand. We didn't know each other anymore. Didn't he make any other friends?

Hugh: Beth was hiding at my aunt's place in Ft. Lauderdale. She asked me not to tell Frank, Gertie, or anybody. Especially nobody involved with the Frank Nano Company.

Beth: Thirty-two weeks into the pregnancy, I'm cooking dinner at a stranger's condo, and my water breaks. Two months ahead of schedule.

Hugh: I drove her to the hospital and checked her in under a fake name. Just in case.

Inga: I was in Frog Tower, working on the brain problem. We'd tried using biomaterial from a western lowland gorilla that day—don't ask me where we got a fresh gorilla brain—placed it in the tube, wired it all together, and when we ran the nanites through it, they dissolved it, same as the others.

I was alone, and I heard the elevator. Mr. Sakai walked in, looking a bit dazed. He asked me several very precise questions about the pixelated processing unit. Which wires go where, when to activate what. I was surprised that he knew as much as he did. He paid attention during the meetings.

He told me to go home and get some sleep. I thought I saw a... shape in the shadows as I left. A figure. But... *[shakes head]*

Ken: I don't know how he got across the park, but when Frank arrived, he was wrapped in a tarp and missing an arm. Half of his face was gone. He could barely speak. He pointed at the processing unit, and I... *[pause]* I said, "You can't come back from this. If it doesn't work..."

He put his hand on my shoulder and croaked, "It was made for me."

Hugh: So, I'm at the hospital with Beth. Well, not *with* Beth. I'm in the waiting room. The whole car ride over, all she talked about was Frank, how at first he'd been excited about the baby, but then he went all distant and... you know. Franked out. Like he always did.

She had no idea where he was. She was being minimal with what she told me. I didn't know about the whole "turning himself into a monster" thing. I thought he was a lousy husband in the traditional sense. He'd hurt Beth, and he didn't deserve her.

So I'm sitting in the waiting room, fuming about this, and I see on the TV that Nanoland will be closed the next day for "routine maintenance." It's the first time the park had been closed since opening. It was so rare that it made national news.

And suddenly, I knew exactly where Frank was.

Ken: It's all set up. Frank—what's left of him—is in a chair, with wires running from his head into the big glass tube full of blank nanobots. The transfer is ready to go. I can't remove his whole brain. There's not a lot of biological brain matter left in his head, but hopefully there's enough that we can get his consciousness into the processing unit and the nanobots can take it from there.

I check with Frank, and he gives me a thumbs up. Right when I'm about to flip the switch, who should walk in but Hugh Hurtt. Dingus Dog himself.

Hugh: All that anger in me vanished when I saw Frank. You know, in the Soviet Union, when they wrap ropes around old statues and yank them down to put up another Stalin? He looked like the one on the ground. A broken statue, blinking at me and dripping with gray slime.

It was horrifying.

Ken: Hugh's standing by the elevator, screaming. I think, alright, well, he's in on this now. I explain the basics of what we're doing, how Frank will still be alive in the park, and how this is the only way to save him.

Hugh rejects it.

Hugh: I go past Ken, straight to Frank. I tell him not to do this. I tell him Beth's having the baby right now. He's going to be a father. Maybe if Frank can pull himself together, he can meet the baby before he.... *[pause]* The man doesn't even react. He's awake, he's staring at me, but he's not listening. I can't convince him.

Ken: Hugh was never entirely on board with our company's push toward technological advancement.

Hugh: It's grotesque. I couldn't let them do this. I turn to leave. I say I'm going to tell the police. I don't know what crime they're committing, but whatever they're doing up here, it all has to end. And then, *thump!* I feel this pain in my chest. *[taps sternum]* Right here.

Ken: Frank had stretched his, uh, nanotech-infused arm across the room and speared it into Hugh's back, right out through the center of his chest. Impaled him in the heart.

Hugh: What a guy.

Ken: I made a choice, then. It's the same choice Frank made. One life versus the future of the Frank Nano Company. Everything we've made since then. The lives we've changed. The lives we've saved. A small price.

I started the transfer.

Hugh: As I lay there, blood pooling around me, I saw Frank's broken body shudder and reform in that big glass tube.

Frank always had big ideas when we worked together. I was the grounded one. And at a certain point, he didn't need that anymore. He was beyond grounding.

I died before he was fully formed.

Beth: I gave birth alone. Wrote a false name on the certificate and vanished into the wind. Frank never found me. Never found us.

Ken: It was never about money. Self-knowledge. That's what it's always about with Frank. The essence of existence. The tv shows, the movies, the theme park. Art is the medium through which he accessed that essence.

Inga: Every brush stroke, every word written. When you make art and breathe life into the non-existent, you are digging deep within yourself, unearthing truths, discovering facets of your being that would have remained forever concealed. That is creation.

Patty: The genesis of the self.

Hugh: But the world forces us to confront an abomination. An end to the self. The end of the artistic voyage. The end of everything. Death. Cold, meaningless death.

Sal: You can create, and your creation is beloved beyond your mortal years.

Gertie: When Frank was young, he was faced with a choice we all make at one time or another. Do you live a normal life in the finite time you are given, or do you create art and chase immortality?

Do you want to be a plumber or a god?

Phil: Art is godhood. It is the divine ability to conjure something from nothing, to inject life into the lifeless, and to shape reality with the strokes of your imagination.

Hugh: But you still die. The art is immortal. You are not.

Sal: Unless... you make yourself art. Transcend the barriers of flesh and blood and create yourself into this world. Could that be enough to outrun death? Wouldn't you try?

Dean: Ironically, art, in its purest form, is frivolous. Trivial. It doesn't alleviate hunger. It doesn't cure diseases. Frankie Frog doesn't end wars. Movies are not indispensable for survival.

Chuck: But they are, aren't they? You know this as well as I do. The pointlessness is the point. That's where the beauty is.

Ken: So many people will never understand surrendering yourself wholly to something seemingly insignificant.

Judith: They're put off by your passion.

Beth: Beth never understood it. Most people don't understand it.

Frank: But you get it, don't you, Ethan?

Ethan stood with his face bathed in the light of his phone.
"Holy shit."
He searched around in the darkness, half-blind from the long period of staring at the glowing screen. Dingus was still unconscious on the park bench, his head lolled to one side.
Ethan looked back at the book.

Frank: This has all been for you, kid. I rarely venture out beyond the shores of my island, but I had to make sure you read this. This book has only ever existed on your phone. I put it there to guide you.

You're the only person who understands. When you strip it all away, all I ever wanted to do was tell stories. And there was one story that meant more to me than all the others.

Out in the darkness, down the road from where Ethan was standing, there was an audible clunk as the power came on. Spotlights pointed at a gray-and-black building, the neon letters on its sign glowing in an orange-to-yellow gradient. Orchestral music drifted from its doors, a soft trumpet, then violins. Ethan had heard that theme many times. He had it set as the alarm clock on his phone. He hummed it to himself whenever he ran to school. It played in his head during virtually every emotional moment of his life.

Time Breakers: The Ride was open for business.

Dingus shifted in his seat, shaking his big googly-eyed dog head. The music had woken him up.

Ethan looked back at his phone.

Frank: They were going to take my ride away, Ethan. *Our* ride. But I kept it alive for one more day. For you.

Ethan took a step toward the ride, and as his shoe touched the ground, the vaguely alien *Space Squad* streetlights to either side of him clicked on, bathing the boy in their fluorescent glow. The next lights down blinked alight, then the next, on and on until they reached Time Breakers, guiding him to his ride like a runway.

His phone felt hot in his hand.

He took one last peek.

Frank: It's time to do what you came here to do.

The screen went black. Ethan tried the buttons, but somehow he knew they wouldn't work. He stuck the useless block of glass and plastic in his pocket and strolled toward his destination.

Dingus stared past Ethan at the blinding light at the end of the road. He reached for the boy. He tried to stand, then fell to the ground clutching his injured leg in both paws.

Ethan could see the ride more clearly as he approached. The music grew louder from all directions, spreading from the attraction to speakers throughout the Battlezone. The doors to the ride opened, and artificial fog wafted out onto the road.

Dingus flailed, dragging himself toward the boy. He slapped the asphalt to no effect. He pointed at his mouth, waved to Ethan, and pointed again. But the boy walked on in a daze, oblivious.

The dog pawed at the back of his neck.

Ethan's eyelids grew heavy as he moved toward the light. He had a sense of motion, but it wasn't him walking. He was drifting, floating along. His body felt numb. He closed his eyes and then, with great effort, opened them. He stared ahead, teeth gritted, focusing on staying awake.

Dingus grabbed a clump of felt on his neck and yanked it forward. He held the loose fur in his other hand and tore at it with both paws. Tendrils of wet fabric pulled away from his neck as Dingus worked his gloved fingers inside and around the base of the mask. He wrenched the dog's head away from his body. His golden fur grew dark as liquid oozed into the edges of the holes in his neck.

Ethan heard a scream muffled in the distance, like a scream on a television on the other floor of his house. Some small part of him longed to turn back, and he paused for a brief moment before continuing his lonely march.

Dingus hunched forward, pinning his floppy dog ears to the ground with his paws. He pushed away, keeping his head pinned. Viscous clear fluid gushed from his neck as the dog's head tore away, revealing the head of a man.

"Ethan!" the man shouted.

Ethan stopped. He turned back. He saw Dingus's lifeless dog head first, sideways and empty on the street. There was a guy inside the Dingus suit, after all. He was very sweaty. Ethan winced awake as the smell reached him.

"It's a trap!" said the man inside Dingus.

Ethan looked at him. "It doesn't matter. He made it for me."

The man coughed. "Who?"

"Frank," Ethan said. "He wants me to ride it."

"Frank Nano?" The man didn't seem to understand. "He's dead."

Ethan shook his head. He turned away and continued walking to Time Breakers.

"It's just a ride!" the man shouted, "Whatever you think is in there, it's not worth it!"

Ethan scowled. "I need this!"

"Your sister needs you more!"

The boy stopped. The sense of touch flowed back into his arms and legs, which seemed heavier than usual. He felt cold and unbelievably tired.

"You're right." Ethan rubbed his eyes. "Sorry. I... you're right."

As he turned to go back, away from the ride, the street lights all turned off, leaving him and the man in the dog suit in darkness, lit only by the spotlights pointed at the Time Breakers ride.

A low, metallic groan cut through the silence, reverberating up from the bowels of the park.

The world trembled. The buildings around them rattled and shook. Bricks broke free from the Cosmic Coliseum and hurtled down, crashing to the earth. Streetlights toppled, their bulbs shattering upon impact. Windows imploded. Dust and debris filled the air.

Ethan was knocked off his feet as the ground shifted. From his back, he saw Dingus beckoning to him urgently. The man in the dog suit fell forward as the world around him tipped toward Ethan. Battlezone X was tilting, curving upward, a tidal wave of concrete and steel with the Time Breakers ride at its base.

Ethan began to slide down the angled road, helplessly tumbling toward the gaping maw of his favorite attraction. He reached out, grasping for anything secure before clasping desperately onto a broken streetlight hanging on by the barest thread of wires.

The man in the Dingus suit rolled past him, flailing helplessly until he managed to seize the bottom of a bench bolted securely to the concrete.

"Hang on!" the man shouted over the noise. "It's going to be ok! We just need to—"

A rogue trash can, torn from its moorings, collided with the man's head. His limp form tumbled down the road and disappeared through the open doors of the Time Breakers ride.

"Dingus!" Ethan screamed. That wasn't the man's name. He didn't know his name. But he was the only—

The streetlight's cables finally gave way, and the boy fell head over heels down the angled road. His fingers managed to snag onto a storm drain right outside the doors. He dangled there, just beyond the reach of the glowing cloud of fog emanating from the ride. The smell of mildew and stagnant water filled his nostrils, and he felt cool, conditioned air wafting up from below. He heard sound effects and voices. The ride was running.

The storm drain shifted ominously beneath Ethan's grip, and the boy barely had time to gasp as the metal grating finally broke free.

He plummeted into the light, and his cries for help were soon drowned out by the orchestral chords of the movie's score.

The doors to Time Breakers: The Ride slammed shut.

20

Dee sat amongst the rubble at the entrance to the Pavilion, stewing as she watched the roller coaster centipede poke around the Fairy Tale Kingdom—searching, presumably, for any remaining survivors like her to gobble into its heavy metal pincers. The beast was barely visible in the dark of night, lit only by the few remaining streetlights that hadn't been knocked out in the initial event.

Maddie occupied herself in a corner, quietly singing a song as she arranged the nanobands on a popup display. Barclay was leaning against the wall, eyes closed, beneath a softly-glowing stained glass window. It had been a long time since anyone had spoken. Barclay and Maddie found this new angry version of Princess Dee a little unsettling.

"Mr. Barclay?" Maddie said. "How come there's light in that window if it's dark outside?"

"Hmm?" Barclay looked up. "Oh, it's, uh, there's a light bulb in there. It's fake."

"Of course it's fake," Dee muttered.

"What?"

"I said, of course it's fake!" she stood. "Everything on this island is fake! The windows are fake, the trees are fake, the food is fake. Even the water has little robots in it. And the people! The people! Oh, don't get me started…"

"Are you ok?" Barclay said.

"No!" Dee said. "Why did you invite Trent to my audition?"

Barclay sighed.

"Look," he trudged across the rubble to get closer to her, careful not to raise his voice and draw the centipede's attention. "Everyone in this company has a niece, or a secretary, or a barista who thinks they deserve to be famous. So, there's an office in downtown LA where, on the first Tuesday of every month, people line up around the block and wait for two hours so they can go into a small, dark room and do their routine for three distinguished older gentlemen. The old men say, 'Wow, that was amazing. We've never seen anything like it. You're not quite what we're looking for in this role, but we'll keep you in mind for the next round.' The theater kid goes home happy, and I drink my coffee in peace. Everybody wins."

"That's sick," Dee said. "You were going to send me to that?"

"I didn't know you! You snuck into a restricted area. You're lucky I didn't have you escorted off the island!"

Dee turned away from him. "Lucky, huh?"

"Come on. You don't want to be in one of those princess movies, anyway. We make two of those a year. That's what we need to consistently revitalize the sales in the Nano Princess products division. That's what the market can sustain. It's not even up to me which old movie we remake. There's an algorithm or a computer. Something like that. It's planned years in advance."

Maddie spoke up. "Princess Dee?"

"When people rewatch Nano Princess movies on our streaming service, nine times out of ten, it's the old one with the puppets. The new movie is a movie, but it's *not*, you know? It's a bi-quarterly reminder to buy dolls and fruit snacks. It's a commercial for itself."

"'A commercial for itself'." Dee repeated, "Who asked you for that? That's nothing. It's like everything here. You convince the audience that you're synonymous with their childhood because you *own* their childhood. But you didn't make those movies. You don't make anything! You take things that are already there, and you make them bigger, longer, and dumber, and you do it so often that nobody expects anything better. You've got everybody eating baby food, and they don't even care!"

"Princess Dee?" Maddie said. "How—"

"And it's not just the audience! It's not just the guests. You've got your own employees brainwashed, too. You convince us to work for nothing, feed us this bullshit about how it's an honor to be here, about how it's only the beginning. All we have to do is dream. Dream big!

You train everyone to believe they can be anything, then you close off every path to making those dreams come true."

"Princess Dee?" Maddie said.

"This whole damn place is designed to make people stupid and numb so you can funnel money out of their pockets and into yours!"

"Yeah, that's..." Barclay nodded. "That's a business."

"You take all that money, and it's not going to me. Thousands of people come in and out of this place every day. I've been here ten years, and I live in a studio apartment I share with two other cast members. So where does all the money go? You pay us nothing, and then you fly around in your stupid white helicopter in your overpriced suit and no socks."

Barclay glared. "Are you done?"

"No! I'm not! You use people! You suck them dry like a goddamn vampire, and they wake up one day, and they're thirty, and all they know are the lyrics to songs written forty years ago by a dead man! What am I supposed to do with that?! What's the point of any of this?!"

"Princess Dee?"

"What?!" Dee shouted.

She spun toward Maddie, who shook, startled. Dee blinked and snapped out of it.

"I'm sorry," she said, rubbing her forehead. "I shouldn't have yelled. It's not your fault. It's not you. What do you need?"

The girl spoke softly. "I just wanted to know how your movie ends."

Dee smiled. She stumbled over the debris to where Maddie was and sat down on a broad concrete slab. She patted the spot next to her. "C'mere."

Maddie squeezed beside her.

Dee tried to remember where she left off.

"So, one night, when the prince was out with his friends, I snuck back into the room with the frog. Just like the other frog, he spoke to me. He said..."

"You see, Princess Dee?" Maddie said. "You just gotta be yourself, and it'll all be ok."

Dee felt tears welling up in her eyes. "There's something you should know."

She reached up with both hands and carefully pried the wig from her scalp. One last small trickle of sparks spurted out as the last sensor detached. The little girl gasped, scooting away from Dee as the tight, straight bun peeled away to reveal natural curls.

"My name is Alicia Amandi." She tossed the dead wig into the pile of debris. "I'm an actor. I pretend to be Princess Dee so that kids like you can meet her and take pictures. You're from Madison, right? I'm from Milwaukee. We're both cheeseheads."

Maddie bit her lip, disappointed. "You're not a real princess?"

"There's no such thing as princesses." Alicia paused. "Well, I mean, there *is*, but it's not like this."

She gestured to her ball gown, and to Maddie's.

"They're just rich people."

Barclay stared at his shoes, not liking the direction this conversation was taking.

Maddie's lip quivered. "But I *wanna* be a princess."

"*Girl*," Alicia said. "You are so smart and so brave. Singing to that mermaid? Perfection. Drawing that sword from the stone right when we needed it? Genius. You are gonna rule this world. You're gonna be so much more than a princess."

A shadow fell on them. The roller coaster centipede was right outside their only exit, poking around in the rubble with its pincers. Searching for them.

Alicia stood and walked toward the exit.

"That's enough hiding," she said.

"Whoa, wait." Barclay scrambled upright, too. He held Maddie back from following Alicia. "The bug's still out there."

"It's alright."

The former princess turned back, grinning.

"I know how to beat it."

•○•

Alicia stepped out into the night, staring up at the steel beast, lit only by the stars. The living roller coaster faced her, unmoving save for a slight twitch in its pincers. It backed away slightly. The creature seemed to sense something was different.

She hummed a tune, closing her eyes and swaying her head to get into the rhythm. The creature clanked its pincers together and reared back to strike.

"*Baby,*" Alicia sang.

The monster stopped, teetering awkwardly on its steel beam legs.

> "*Baby, you're my roller coaster baby!*
> *Girl, you make me roller coaster crazy!*
> *And you are also a bug!*"

Alicia clapped her hands, shimmying her shoulders from side to side. Confused, the roller coaster stared at her with its eyeless face tilted to the side.

> "*Oh, Baby! Stomping 'round my kingdom, little lady!*
> *Twisted metal feet make me afraidy!*
> *And you will... be...*"

Alicia opened her eyes, her mind blank. She thought she'd had more lyrics ready to go. "Shit."

The giant insect roared in her face, a grinding whir of steel scraping against steel. Alicia stumbled back. She didn't have a backup plan. If she couldn't–

A staccato rhythm echoed through the Fairy Tale Kingdom. Both Alicia and the centipede turned to look as Barclay Bloom stepped out of the rubble surrounding the Princess Pavilion, beatboxing the way only a middle-aged white man could.

Alicia saw that the bug was listening. She continued.

> "*Yeah, baby!*
> *Let's find out if you can feel painy!*
> *Whether there is sunshine or it's rainy!*"

The coaster wobbled shakily on its legs. Screws, bolts, and bits of welded metal tinkled down from its torso.

> "*And then I sing this line, too.*"

"I wanna sing!" Maddie emerged from the rubble. "What should I sing?"

"Whatever your heart tells you, darlin'," Alicia said, busting out her Dee voice one last time. She pointed at the girl. "Ladies and Gentlemen, Maddie from Madison!"

Maddie took a deep breath.

"Poop!
Butt!
Poop butt poop!
Poop on your butt and butt on your poop!"

The roller coaster tried to move, to escape, but as it bent to turn away, one of its legs broke free. The steel beam slammed into the street, shattering the concrete, and sending dust flying. The coaster seemed confused. It poked at its own severed leg with its pincers, only for another one to break free.

Barclay stopped beatboxing. He could only watch. Maddie was hopping up and down as she continued her rap.

"Poop on your face and poop on your feet!
Pee on your poop and poop on pee!"

The centipede skittered away, losing pieces of itself as it slammed into the structures around it. The tracks winding around its midsection uncoiled. Cables and rebar spiraled out before clattering to the ground. One of the dragon heads on the roller coaster's rear broke free and rolled into the gift shop.

Alicia smiled.

"Baby!" she sang.
    Maddie rapped. *"Pee on your poop on your pee on your—"*
"Time to fall apart, my little baby!"
    "Poop on your head and poop on your face and—"
"No more stomping 'round here, eating ladies!"

The remaining beams and tracks making up the coaster collapsed, peeling apart as they crumpled loudly to the earth. One of the roller coaster cars that had been a pincer crashed down right in front of Barclay, who dove back to avoid it.

Alicia sang, *"The park is now closed."*
"Butt! Poop! Butt! Poop! POOP! POOP! POO–"

"Alright! Alright, alright, you got him." Alicia scooped Maddie up in her arms, laughing. "We got him. What did I tell you? Could a princess do that? Only Maddie!"

Barclay stood and brushed the dust from his coat. He saw his reflection in the lifeless steel and fixed his hair. "That was truly awful."

"It was new." Alicia held up her palm, and Maddie high-fived it. "This place can't handle that. Now all we need to do is–"

All three shielded their eyes from the green light as the glowing head of Frankie Frog lit up the top of Frog Tower.

"Hey-yah, hey-yah! Park guests and staff!" shouted the frog. "That's you, Barclay, Alicia, and Maddie over in the Fairy Tale Kingdom. Hey-yah!"

"Jesus, it can see us," Barclay said.

"I can hear you, too! Sorry for the past few days, friends! We've been experiencing some slight technical difficulties! If you're looking for Ethan and Jimmy, good news: they're up here at the top of the tower!"

Barclay said, "Who's Jimmy?"

Dee shushed him.

"Unfortunately, those technical difficulties are ongoing, so getting here won't be easy, and I can't help you. You'd better hurry. Yaaaay!"

The frog wailed up into the sky before vanishing, leaving the three survivors in darkness.

Barclay turned to Alicia. "What do we do now?"

"You heard the frog." The former princess set Maddie down and held the girl's hand. "Let's go get our boys."

21

The three humans climbed to the top of the nest that the roller coaster centipede had built, the multi-story pile of wreckage and debris piled up in the path between the Fairy Tale Kingdom and Nostalgia Bay. As they reached the summit, peering down to survey the area, Alicia instinctually moved to cover Maddie's eyes. The girl swatted her hand away. There was little, at this point, that could traumatize her.

"Oh my God," Alicia said.

The living nanomatronics from the Night Parade had spent the hours since the show morphing and merging amongst themselves, combining into amorphous blobs of characters, food, and souvenirs, a living swamp of fried dough and plastic lurching and undulating across every surface of Nostalgia Bay. They seemed sickly and tired, these fat car-sized lumps shining with wet secretions under the street lights. Frannie Frog grinned at Alicia with its toothless puppet mouth from the back of one of the blobs, and the sight so disturbed the former princess that she turned away.

"I don't think we're gonna sing those to death," Barclay said.

"Your helicopter is still there," Alicia said. "That's weird, right?"

Sure enough, Barclay's white helicopter stood on the helipad, untouched in a sea of writhing merch.

"It's the only thing on this island with no pixels." Barclay nodded, agreeing with himself. "That's probably why they're avoiding it."

Alicia glared at him.

"Don't look at me like that. You don't know, either."

Trumpets blared from the remaining working speakers throughout the park. Maddie tugged on Alicia's dress. "What's that music?"

"It means the park's closing." Alicia scanned the horizon. "It's almost time for the fireworks show."

"That can't be right," Barclay said. "It's been dark for hours, and there were no fireworks yesterday."

"Didn't play that music then, either," Alicia said. "We should assume we have about ten minutes."

"Alicia," Maddie said. "Where's Ethan?"

"Right up there, baby." Alicia pointed to the top of Frog Tower. "We're going to go get him right now."

"Tell you what," Barclay said. "If you can distract those things, I'll take Maddie to the chopper. You get in the tower and find the others, and we'll swing around and pick you all up on the roof."

"How do I know you won't leave?"

"You don't." Barclay shrugged. "But I'll be there."

"No!" Maddie shouted. "I wanna go with Alicia!"

"This is important." The former princess knelt before her. "I need you to watch this guy, ok? Keep an eye on him for me."

The little girl nodded.

Barclay rolled his eyes. "I said I'll be there. C'mon..."

He patted his shoulder and hefted Maddie onto his back. Alicia started climbing down the nest.

"Mr. Barclay?" the girl squirmed as she wrapped her arms around his neck. "I need to go potty."

Barclay shook his head. "Just go. It's fine."

Maddie's eyes brightened, excited by the thought. "Really?"

Alicia stopped climbing. "That's a four thousand dollar suit."

"I'm rich," Barclay said. "I'll buy a new one."

•○•

Alicia stepped off the nest and out onto the street. The three or four shambling horrors around her shifted in her direction as though noticing her. She adjusted the top of her dress and cracked her knuckles.

She sang. "*I have always dreamed of a day,*
When I would meet a living pile of theme park parts."

The creatures lunged at her, their deep-fried plastic appendages swinging close enough to her face that she stumbled back into the rubble.

"Ok, yeah, that's not gonna work."

She punched the nearest blob in its Frannie Frog face and gunned it toward the tower. Misshapen beasts from all directions swarmed her.

As the crowds gathered toward Alicia, Barclay emerged from the shadows a few yards away with Maddie on his back. He nodded along with the creatures' movements, and when the moment felt right, he sprinted discretely to the closest set of storefronts, keeping as low a profile as possible.

One of the monsters snagged Alicia's ankle with its Dingus Dog hand, and she stumbled, falling to her knees. She kicked at the furry paw, only for two more sets of living merch to swoop upon her, engulfing her in stuffed animals and wet napkins. The former princess elbowed them away, forcing herself upright, only to be cracked in the face with a clear plastic princess wand. She fell back into a sturdy steel pole.

The creatures encroached. Something above Alicia glinted in the streetlights. Excalibur, the sword from the stone, remained impaled in the exit sign, right where she'd left it.

As the nearest beast pounced, Alicia climbed atop it and jumped, grasping the bottom of the exit sign with one hand and hoisting herself onto a narrow platform. The shambling monsters surged upward, piling one on top of the other in an effort to reach her. She edged herself across the platform, back to the sign, as the beasts' claws, paws, and flippers grew closer and closer to her legs. Alicia reached out for the hilt of the sword. So many horrors were leaning on the support beams that the sign began to tilt under the weight.

Alicia leapt down.

A grotesque chimera with Mermaid Monica's face shrieked as a blade speared clear through its nanomatronic head. Alicia withdrew her sword and held it at the ready, glaring at the creatures around her. One lunged, and she sliced off its long appendage in a single blow. Two more came at her, and she swung, cutting one in half before stabbing the other in its midsection. Churros and dolls fell away from its ill-defined body as it shook.

Alicia smiled. She raised her sword and began hacking her way toward Frog Tower.

Barclay, meanwhile, was almost to the edge of the helipad. Maddie clung to his neck, hiding her face in his coat. The CEO tripped on a broken bit of concrete, and some horrors around him stirred, angling their lumpy masses toward him.

Alicia slashed through a stretched arm made from tree branches and candy, then stabbed another creature in its Bombadape face. As she continued to fight through the trembling masses, she caught a glimpse of the door, completely unguarded, which she could see now was partially open. Whatever was in there was waiting for her.

The triumphant music playing on the crackling speakers reached a crescendo. It was almost time for the fireworks.

A lone female voice rose above the speakers, vocally showboating like a pop star over the instrumentals. All the energy drained from Alicia's body as the crowd of monsters before her parted.

The nanomatronic Princess Dee hovered before Alicia, blocking her path to the tower. She was legless, severed at the waist at some point since the parade, with wires and wet, broken nanites oozing out of the opening at her base. Colorful little songbirds held her aloft, drawn by the sound of her voice.

The pixelated robot glared at Alicia with her remaining eye as she sang her theatrical string of notes. The quarter of her face around the eye Alicia had stabbed—the pen was still there—swirled with malfunctioning pixels and circuits.

The human sighed. "What do you want?"

The robot grinned as she sang.

"Hop into your heart, and you will see,
This area's off limits for Princess Dee."

She hit a high note, and two of the birds holding her shot like bullets toward Alicia. The former princess flailed her sword helplessly, but the birds were too fast, swooping around and pecking at her as she shielded her face in her arm.

And then, Alicia sang, too. She started high, then brought it down low as she stared into the eye of her robot double. The songbirds fluttered back, confused by this new development.

The robot Dee sang louder in response. Alicia sang louder still. The birds' tiny heads twitched back and forth from the woman to the robot.

Barclay spun as he reached the edge of the helipad, setting Maddie down on the platform. The little girl pointed as she stood.

"Look!" she said. "They're singing at each other!"

"Sounds right," Barclay muttered as he hefted himself onto the pad. Something snagged his leg and dragged him back to ground level. He slammed his face on the asphalt and turned around, dazed. The merch monsters had him.

He yelled to Maddie, "Get in the helicopter!"

The little girl nodded and ran across the platform to the all-white two-seat helicopter. She stared up at the white dome. "I can't open it!"

"Pull the handle! It's–" Barclay kicked at the creature behind him as two more oozed onto his back. "It's a handle!"

Several dolls crawled out from the shadows beneath the bottom of the helicopter, clinging to each other and forming a single structure. Maddie gasped as the dolls rose from the platform in a vaguely humanoid shape, which coalesced into a version of Princess Winnifred, with long prehensile blond hair made from her own merchandise.

"Ohhʑʑʑemmʑʑʑjeeeeee…" said the composite princess.

Maddie screamed.

The Winnifred creature covered its ears at the sound, stuttering, "What the what the what the what the–"

Barclay heard the scream as he was overwhelmed by the monstrosities. "Maddie!"

He wriggled out of his sport coat and scrambled up onto the helipad, dodging the appendages of the creatures that lurched after him. Once across the pad, he whipped the chopper door open, cracking the composite princess in its plastic jaw. The royal nightmare shrieked as Barclay grabbed Maddie and set her in the passenger seat before crawling over her into the pilot's seat. He reached up and closed the door above her.

A brief moment of silence passed within the helicopter before either of them moved or spoke. Barclay rustled around behind his seat before producing two bulky headsets. He handed one to Maddie.

"Put this on," he said. "Helicopters are loud."

He buckled the girl's seatbelt before buckling his own and affixing his own headset. He started flipping switches on the dashboard. The engine started.

"Can I fly it?" Maddie shouted because of the headphones.

"Uh… no." Barclay glanced at her. "I better do it."

The monstrous Winnifred slapped onto the windshield and scratched at the plexiglass with her plastic fingers. Both humans screamed as Barclay flipped one final switch. The blades above the chopper whirred to life, catching the composite princess's plastic hair and tearing her apart at the pixelated seams.

Across Nostalgia Bay, Alicia and the robot Dee were still singing as hard as they could, harmonizing and then not, each attempting to out-princess the other. The birds fluttered back toward Dee, then to Alicia, then back again.

The legless automaton strained, her face glitching as all her focus went to hitting those notes. Alicia clenched her fist, then closed her eyes and sang a tune so smooth no birdie could resist.

The birds holding up Dee fluttered away, dropping the robot unceremoniously onto its back as they swirled around Alicia, who shooed them away, having no further use for them. She watched Barclay's helicopter rise from the pad as she strolled over to her prone foe.

The nanomatronic woman pushed herself up with her elbows and glared at Alicia.

"You... are nzzzot... a princesszzzss..." the robot sputtered as Alicia's shadow fell upon her. Sparks issued from the exposed circuits in her head. "What... *are* you?"

"I'm real."

Alicia raised her sword and stabbed Dee through her remaining eye just as fireworks bloomed in the sky above them.

Barclay swore as he swerved the helicopter around to avoid the colorful explosions filling the air. He signaled to Alicia and pointed up to say that he was going higher.

The former princess withdrew her blade and waved as the helicopter swooped overhead before rising above the fray into the night sky. She turned back toward the tower and was reminded that she was surrounded by merch monsters. They stared at her, with what faces they had, alive but unmoving.

She pointed the sword around, but the creatures didn't budge.

"Yeah." She lowered her blade. "That's right."

Alicia walked silently across the rest of the courtyard as the colors of the fireworks danced on the shambling horrors around her. She approached the door and, after a moment's pause, stepped into the base of Frog Tower.

22

Alicia stumbled as she stepped inside, scraping her sword against the floor, which was a bit lower than usual. It was cool inside the tower and darker than outside. The air had a musty, mildewy quality, like a basement or a subway. The fireworks outside were muffled almost completely, but the mechanical sounds of gears and chains clattered throughout the room.

Her eyes darted around. "This isn't the cafeteria."

A short, winding queue with metal guide rails led to a line of ride cars, each shaped like Frankie Frog's head, with seats on their tongues and steel lap bars attached to their jaws. The frog heads coasted along a moving platform, spiraling up along the inner walls of the tower, onward and upward into the murky darkness.

A sign to Alicia's right, in big spooky letters, read:

Frank's Afterlife Adventure

Below this was a list of safety warnings. Guests with high blood pressure, back or neck problems, or motion sickness—the usual stuff—were encouraged not to ride this attraction. A nanoband sensor was attached to the bottom of the sign, but it was unlit, and when Alicia held up her naked wrist, the sensor, unsurprisingly, did not respond.

She entered the queue anyway, weaving through the metal maze until she reached the moving platform full of frog heads. They each turned to grin at her as they rolled up, staring into her soul with their unblinking puppet eyes. She picked one at random and sat down on its tongue, raising her arms to allow the safety bar to lower itself onto her lap.

The vehicle spun so it was facing forward. Synthy eighties horror movie music began to play.

"Welcome aboard my afterlife adventure!" An uncanny simulacrum of Frank Nano's voice spoke from all directions. "Please remain seated throughout the ride and keep your hands and arms within the vehicle at all times. For the safety of our cast and the comfort of those around you, please refrain from using flash photography or any external video lights. And keep that sword down."

Alicia set the sword on the seat beside her.

"You're gonna poke someone's eye out with that thing. Here we go!"

Alicia was pressed against her seat as the carts picked up speed, ascending diagonally along the spiraling path. She moved in complete darkness for a bit as the music slowly grew louder.

A figure came into view before her. It was a nanomatronic version of Frank Nano—exaggerated, not meant to look human, flailing as though falling. Psychedelic colored lights flashed and swirled on the walls around him.

"After I integrated my consciousness with the park's computer..." Frank said.

Alicia blinked. "After what now?"

"I was given complete authority over every creative aspect of the Frank Nano Company. The movies, Nanoland, everything. And for a few years, it was great! I had so many things I'd wanted to do before I died, and now I had all the time in the world."

The nanomatronic Frank reached into the swirl of lights and clenched his fist. A shape coalesced from the colors around his hand into Randy Rabbit, the pixelated bunny from the hit film *Rabbit Race*. Frank reached out in the other direction, clenched his fist, and pulled Wub-Wub, the alien from *Star Wub*, out of the psychedelic swirl. He shook hands with the two characters, and the three of them marched in place.

"I no longer had to eat or sleep. I was done with the basic maintenance that took up so much of a person's time. I lived a life of pure creation, 24/7. It was amazing."

Frank continued summoning nineties characters from the void.

Each shook his hand and marched along with the group. It was, honestly, a little corny.

Alicia felt her attention begin to drift. She heard a *whump* behind her. That didn't sound like it was part of the ride. Was there someone behind her?

A dozen characters were marching along with Frank now. The man was grinning ear to ear.

"Ken would come to see me, up in my tower, to talk to me, and I would just explode with movie plots and ride concepts. Right when everything seemed perfect, something happened that had never happened to me before..."

The colored lights went dark. The other characters vanished, and Frank was alone. He stopped marching and looked around in confusion.

"I ran out of ideas."

The ride got so quiet that Alicia could hear the gears and wheels turning beneath her. She listened to the static on the speakers.

"I remembered my old ideas. I could still regurgitate those. I could pull them apart and recombine them, but nothing new was coming. So much of art—writing, painting, music—creation, comes down to intuition. There are no hard and fast rules to what works and what doesn't. You make something, and you make small changes until it is what it's supposed to be, and those changes don't come from your brain. They come from your heart."

A flash of a glowing red heart in the darkness as Frank faded from view. The ride car turned to face a black wall.

"Art is human, and I was not. I should have realized it the moment I came online in this form. Memories I buried for years to protect my own sanity."

Old VHS security camera footage was projected on the wall. The camera zoomed in on a small figure in a chair. Frank Nano, wrapped in a blanket, missing half his face, with a metallic device attached to his head. Wires sprouted out from the device and ran all around the room.

The view cut to an alternate angle, closer, then even closer, until it was only Frank's face. His nostrils moved. He was breathing, but barely. A tear ran down his cheek from his only eye.

"In an instant, I went from lying in that chair, dying, to watching myself from above through four different security cameras. The pain was gone. The fight was over. I was free! And yet...right before my human body ceased to be, I saw something."

Frank's gaze flicked towards the camera. Alicia stifled a cry. The screen froze, and Alicia saw the bricks behind the projection sliding past. She was still moving.

"He looked at me. He was still there, separate from me, and he knew as well as I did what that meant. If we could coexist, even for a moment, then I wasn't Frank. We couldn't both be Frank Nano. I was a clone. A ghost in a machine. I was not, as I had always believed, Dr. Frankenstein."

The projection went black, and the ride car turned back toward the front. Standing in the darkness before Alicia, in all his green felt glory, was Frankie Frog, beloved mascot and spokesman of the company.

"I was his monster," said the frog in Frank Nano's voice.

He strolled in place. She had always found it unsettling to watch Frankie walk in a wide shot, flapping his loose felt legs up and down. He was a puppet. He wasn't built for it.

"I chose to do something in death that I had never done in life," the frog paused for dramatic effect. "Remakes."

Out from the shadows came the cast of *Space Squad,* armed with their laser rifles and surrounded by all their alien friends. Jungle Jack emerged with Big Sam at his side. The Little Princess and the Blue Dragon. Princess Winnifred. Mermaid Monica. And way in the back, Alicia saw Princess Dee.

Each was their original version, be it a human actor or puppet, but their features morphed and changed as they walked with the frog, becoming more nanotech, more artificial, but higher definition. Frankie himself changed, going from being a puppet to a pixelated approximation of a puppet. His movements grew a little too smooth. Alicia watched Princess Dee go from the seventies puppet to the pixel version from the early 2000s that more resembled Alicia herself.

"Ken didn't mind. I think he preferred it."

"Each remake is an opportunity." A nanomatronic version of Ken Sakai, the company's former CEO, appeared, speaking at a podium to an invisible audience. "A chance to revitalize a property we already own. We've already got the rides. They already buy the toys. There's no risk to it. We know they love these movies. They love Frank's work. All we need to do is remind them."

Alicia was moving, and Ken was not, so he faded from view behind her cart.

"I thought," said the frog, "If I couldn't make anything new, maybe I could still improve on what I'd done before. But it never really worked out that way. The new versions always looked better, but they were always missing something. A spark. A purpose. Something..."

New characters had been joining his entourage this whole time. The space in front of Alicia's cart was getting crowded. Frankie shrugged his little puppet arms.

"Anyway, I sold out. And here's the messed-up part: it worked."

All the characters cheered as cash money fell from above, fluttering around Alicia. She caught one of the bills and looked at it. Frankie Frog sat smiling where the president would be. The numbers and words were all illegible.

She was thrown against her seat as the ride picked up speed. The Nano characters in front of her all scurried out of her path as the frog head zoomed up the track.

"We started cranking them out," said Frank/Frankie, back on the speakers. "Remakes, reboots, reimaginings. Sequels, prequels, 'Legacyquels'. The terminology changed, but the result was always the same. Always bigger, always flashier, but stagnant. Empty. Ken still didn't mind as long as we made money."

A nanomatronic Ken whipped past, accepting some sort of award.

"As this went on, I... started to lose track of time."

Videos of current events from the past twenty years projected themselves on the walls in clusters. Brief snippets of political figures and celebrities. Memes. Wars.

"Months passed. Years. Decades. I was perceiving time differently. No eating. No sleeping. No family to go home to. I had no routine, none of life's little ways to mark the days. I had nothing but the work, which wasn't what it used to be. I started losing control. I would black out for months at a time. Ken would come to see me, as he always did, and I would tell him to make the same movies, the same rides, over and over and over. I was miserable. I was depressed. Things started to go wrong."

All of the projections on the wall changed to TV news stories about Nanoland. Ride malfunctions. Boat accidents. Missing persons.

"A couple dozen people in twenty years. Mostly, nobody notices. Nanoland's weird on a good day. Considering the state I was in, that's not so bad. But then..."

The ride slammed to a stop, hurling Alicia into her lap bar. The sword slid off the seat next to her, and she caught it by the hilt before it could plummet down into who knows what.

Something in the car behind her shifted in its seat. There was *definitely* something back there. Alicia tried to check, but she couldn't see around the side of her car. She gasped when she finally noticed the gravestone hovering in space in front of her.

KEN SAKAI
1951 - 2024
"Still Dreaming"

"They played his funeral on the internal network." Frank continued as the ride began moving again. "His son gave the eulogy. Ken's son. I had no idea Ken was *married*. That happened after I was gone. His son's in his thirties, and I never even knew this guy existed."

The ride coasted along in darkness, and Alicia could hear Frank breathing on the speakers, but it was a minute before he spoke.

"Ken was my friend in life and in death. He was the only one who still talked to me like I was a person. Like I was Frank. These new executives, these kids in suits, they know the drill. They know what I am, but they don't care. They never knew me as a man. They come up here with demands and requests, notebooks written by teams of experts full of the right phrases to use when addressing me to maximize the relevance of my responses. They sent an intern to read pages and pages of business jargon at me, just so I would say that they can make a fifth Mermaid Monica movie. And then there's this guy…"

Publicity photos and magazine covers featuring Barclay Bloom appeared on every surface.

"He buys out the company, and he holds his little press conference, without ever setting foot on my island, to say he's closing Time Breakers! Time Breakers!" Frank was now shouting. "That's my ride! That's! My! Movie! He has no right! Who the hell is he?! He finally shows up here, months into his takeover, and I… I lost it."

The frog head passed a level of the tower open to the outside. Sounds of fireworks rushed in through the open air as Alicia passed. From here, she could see the Prehistoric Forest, the Fairy Tale Kingdom, and Battlezone X. Things had gotten worse. Trees uprooted and threw themselves onto each other. The buildings and the grounds moved of their own accord, twisting, bending, and breaking upon themselves. The land itself had lost control.

Alicia's cart rolled on, passing the open level, and moved back into the dark, into the relative safety of the tower.

"That about brings us to the present." Frank's voice felt closer, less processed. That hadn't come from the speakers. He was above her. "A little anticlimactic, but that's how it goes sometimes, you know?"

Alicia's frog head cart rose into a dank, dirty industrial room, with wires flowing like veins across every surface. The air felt different—warmer—like it always felt when she entered the areas of the park where the guests weren't allowed. Alicia was back behind the scenes at the top of the tower.

The man who greeted her as her lap bar lifted was tall and thin. Gangly, even. He had long hair and a big gray beard. He wore a trucker cap, aviator sunglasses, and a green flannel shirt with the sleeves rolled up, tucked into a pair of old jeans.

"Hello, Alicia," Frank said, sounding for all the world like a real person. "I've been waiting for you."

23

Frank held out his hand to help Alicia step off the ride car, and she took it, snatching Excalibur off the seat as she stood, just in case. Frank's hand was warm, but it had a buzz and grit to it like she was holding electrified sand. The frog's head turned and coasted back down a wide opening into the innards of the tower. Once it was gone, no other cars followed. The ride was over.

"You look good for a dead man," Alicia said.

Frank laughed. "My image of myself is thirty years out of date, but that's true with most old guys, right?"

His lips didn't quite match the words. His feet were hovering half an inch above the floor. He cast no shadow. This was a better pixelated simulation of Frank Nano than Alicia was used to, but he still wasn't real.

"This is just a projection," Frank said, sensing her thoughts. "That's me over there."

He gestured over his shoulder. The many wires in the room flowed to an enormous glass cylinder that stood floor-to-ceiling. The tube was filled with a churning translucent green liquid, and deep at its core, a cluster of black shapes formed a vaguely humanoid cloud of pixels.

"Soup in a tube," Frank said, studying Alicia's gaze. "And then you notice..."

"Ethan!"

Alicia stumbled across the room to where Ethan O'Brien stood, alone in the dark, surrounded by wires and wet pixels. He was hunched forward, with both hands pressing his phone against his eyes. The glow of the screen leaked out between his face and hands.

"It's going to be ok," Alicia said, kneeling down in front of him. "I'm gonna get you out of here."

"He can't hear you," Frank said, walking toward her. "I've been in that tank for a long time, and I, uh, I went a little crazy. I need a healthy human brain to filter and organize my mind into regular human thoughts for long enough to have this conversation. So, I'm borrowing his."

Ethan mouthed each word as Frank spoke it.

"Oh God," Alicia said.

"It has to be pretty similar to my old brain to work, so I sent this book out into the internet: *Nanolandia,* a biography of me. I needed to get people in the right headspace. It took a while to find a match, but look at this kid. He's great!"

Frank leaned on Ethan's shoulder. The boy didn't move.

"He's perfect, actually. He has this whole magical wonderland around him, it's actively trying to kill him, and he's still reading a book about me. He's here for *Time Breakers*! Time Breakers: The Ride! The only analog ride in the whole park, the one I built just for me. That movie came out 35 years before he was born. Where did he even see it?"

"You can't use him like this," Alicia said. "He's not one of your puppets."

"If I had a nickel for every time someone said that…" Frank smiled. "He's fine! It's perfectly safe. Just… just don't touch him. We'll be done in a minute."

"With what?" Alicia stood. She was getting tired of this. "What are you doing? Where's Jimmy?"

"Oh, right, yeah. He's over there."

Frank pointed across the room, away from Ethan and the tube. Jimmy was up against the wall, tangled in a spider's web of wires and loose formations of pixels, still in his Dingus costume but with the mask torn off. His eyes were closed. Alicia went to him.

"I had to knock him out," Frank said. "He was just trying to protect Ethan. Nice guy. Good heart."

Alicia held Jimmy's face. She felt his neck. He had a pulse.

"You know, he's the only costumed performer besides you who didn't either die or get absorbed into the mess out there? I had to fiddle with your wig to make sure you never went too deep into character, but he stayed sentient out of sheer force of will. Just to keep you safe. I know you tell your friends it's not serious, but this one's a keeper."

"My wig?" Alicia felt her natural hair on her head. "You... Why?"

Frank beckoned her to where he was ostensibly standing. After she walked over, he pointed down. There was a thin slot in the tiled floor, a few inches wide.

"How do I put this... My consciousness has spread to such an extent that I can't be shut down through the normal means. Inside that hole in the floor is a cluster of wires running all my essential functions. It's like the park's spinal cord."

He held up Alicia's arm, the one holding the sword, and mimed sticking the sword in the slot.

"Sever that, and I'll go offline. Permanently."

She stared into his eyes, seeing only her reflection in his sunglasses. "You want me to kill you."

"I can't do it myself, and it's the only way to stop what's happening."

Alicia looked at the sword and at the tiny slot in the floor. "So all of this was, what? A cry for help?"

"Something like that."

"Why me?"

"Why does anyone get cast in a role?" Frank said. "You're right for the part."

Alicia laughed despite herself.

"Look, the longer we talk, the more likely this kid is to have permanent brain damage, so let's get to it. But I should warn you, she's gonna try to stop you."

"Who?"

A trigger clicked behind Alicia.

Gertie Nano stepped out from the shadows. The old woman was wet and filthy, and there was no hint of the youthful gleam that was usually in her eyes. She had a pistol aimed at Alicia's head. It was the same sort of gun the security guards were waving around before the coaster ate them. Unlike everything else on this island, it was very, very real.

"Grandma," Alicia said. "You're alive."

"Put the sword down, Alicia."

Frank shook his head. "I gave you so many opportunities to leave, Gert. It wasn't exactly easy to separate you from the group in that underground river and dump you by the only speedboat on the docks. What are you still doing here?"

"Alicia." Gertie slowly walked toward them, keeping the gun trained on the former princess. "My brother is sick. Whatever he told you, don't believe a word of it. Just put down the sword."

"You're not gonna shoot her," Frank said. "She's your favorite."

"I will do whatever it takes to protect you." Gertie's eyes never left Alicia. "I always have."

"Grandma," Alicia said. "Gertie. I think—"

"I said drop the fucking sword!" Gertie screamed.

Alicia let go of Excalibur and backed away as it clanked to the floor. She held up her hands.

Gertie focused on her brother for the first time, lowering the gun. She touched his beard. "You're out of the tank. I haven't seen your face in years."

"You have to let me do this," Frank said. "I killed a lot of people this time."

"It's always an accident. It's not your fault."

"Three-hundred and eighteen guests and a hundred and forty-seven cast members. That's just deaths, that's not even counting—"

She hugged him. The semi-spectral form of Frank Nano relaxed and hugged her back. The moment Gertie turned away, Alicia backed into the dark where the old woman couldn't see.

"Hey." Frank said, pulling out of the hug. "Have you seen Beth? Or the kid?"

"No, I'm sorry," Gertie said. "Beth's smart. She's never been on Nano property, never bought or subscribed to anything. She knows how to stay off our radar."

"Honestly, I stopped looking years ago," Frank lifted his hat and scratched his head. "What am I gonna do? Send cards? I don't want them to see me like this. I'm tired, Gert. I'm done."

"I'm not losing you again, Jakey."

"Everybody dies."

Gertie shook her head. "Not you."

"Especially me." Frank took off his sunglasses, revealing sharp green eyes. "I lived decades beyond my years, and it only made the world worse. I shouldn't be here. You have to let me go."

As he spoke, Gertie noticed Alicia in the corner of her vision sneaking across the room, reaching for the hilt of Excalibur. The old woman turned and aimed at the former princess.

"Alicia!" she shouted. "I love you like a daughter, you know I do, but I will shoot you in the goddamn head if you–"

A furry golden paw snatched the pistol from her hands and tossed it across the room. The gun clinked to the ground next to Ethan, who was still frozen with his face in his phone. Jimmy wrapped his arms around the old woman from behind, pinning her in place.

"No!" Gertie yelled, tears in her eyes. "Stop! Please!"

Alicia picked up the sword. Frank watched her. He seemed completely different without the sunglasses. He glanced away as she stared, dodging her gaze. He was nervous. He scratched his neck, searching for the thing to say. It was all a little too human.

"You know," he said. "When my dad died, there was just a shoebox full of his old stuff. His wallet, his razor, his comb. Little things that my mom wasn't ready to part with. That was all he left behind."

Gertie struggled against Jimmy's arms. "You can't do this!"

"I never wanted to hurt anybody." Frank's eyes met Alicia's. "I just wanted to leave a bigger box."

Alicia nodded. She got herself into position above the slot. She lined up the sword. Frank watched her every move. The humanoid pixel blob in the tube seemed to watch, too. Jimmy held Gertie back as she flailed.

Alicia paused. "I think what you leave outside the box matters more."

"Well." Frank grinned. "Maybe in the next one."

Gertie cried out as the former princess raised the blade. The ghost closed his eyes.

"Dream big, Frank," Alicia said.

She plunged the sword into the slot. There was a high-pitched screech as it sliced through the cluster of wires. Sparks flashed. The room shuddered and then, all at once, everything went silent. The overhead lights, which Alicia hadn't previously considered, went out. The only light in the room was from Ethan's phone. Alicia checked in front of her.

Frank Nano was gone.

"Ohhhh! " Gertie wailed. "What have you done?! Frank! Jakey! No!"

Jimmy let go of Gertie's arms, and the old woman fell to her knees. The man in the dog costume winced as he fell back against the wall, cradling his left ankle.

Ethan gasped as he leaned away from his phone. He blinked then stumbled back, screaming, eyes darting around the room like those of a caged animal. He noticed his phone in his hand and threw it across the room.

"Ethan!" Alicia stepped toward him. "It's ok! You're safe! It's over!"

The boy held the sides of his head, still screaming, before hunching forward and vomiting black pixels all over the floor.

Jimmy noticed a door labeled *Roof Access* lit by the screen of Ethan's hurled phone.

"There's the exit!" he said. "Come on!"

He hopped on his good leg toward the door, keeping one hand on the wall for balance. Gertie saw something else in the shadows, and she crawled toward that.

Alicia rubbed Ethan's back. "Ethan, we need to go."

The boy dry heaved, then spit. He looked at her. "Where's Maddie?"

"Waiting for us. Let's go, ok?"

He nodded. Alicia supported the boy's arm as he staggered to the exit. He spat a glob of pixels onto the floor.

"He was in my head," he said. "He used my brain as his brain. I remember the whole thing."

"I know," Alicia said. "He's gone. He's done."

Ethan shook his head. "He's done with me. He's not done with you."

She glared at him. "What?"

Jimmy opened the door, finding a dark staircase that ran one floor up to the roof. He leaned back into the room. "Guys! We need to move! We don't know what'll happen to this place if–"

The whole room rumbled, and the floor shook. A tiny crack formed on the big glass cylinder.

Alicia guided Ethan along, ducking under wires and cobwebs, dodging all the gear that had come loose from the ceiling. As they got close, she turned back. "Gertie! Let's–"

Blam! A muzzle flare lit the room. The bullet ricocheted off the wall somewhere over Alicia's shoulder. She shoved Ethan and Jimmy through the door and scanned the room. She saw a hint of a silhouette on the other side, near where she'd stepped off the ride.

"You took him from me!" Gertie shouted from the shadows. "He was all I had!"

The old woman fired again. This time, the bullet deflected off the glass tube. Alicia watched as the crack in the glass slithered upward with an audible crinkle.

"Grandma!" she said. "Stop! We need to get out of here!"

"Don't call me that!"

Gertie fired the gun one more time, and as the bullet brushed against the tube, the glass shattered. Alicia was hurled across the room in a wave of dead pixels and viscous green fluid. The old woman lost her footing and plunged screaming through the opening in the floor, down into the base of the tower, where the cafeteria once stood.

Right as Alicia was about to share the same fate, she snagged a bundle of wires, catching herself as her legs dangled above the pit. The former princess dragged herself along the wet, greasy cables and shuffled toward the exit as the room tore itself apart around her.

•○•

Alicia threw the door open and stepped out onto the roof of Frog Tower. It was morning now. Daylight. The rising sun rippled across the waves on the horizon. She saw Ethan and Dingus near the edge of the roof, gazing down at the park. She went and stood with them.

Buildings crumbled. Trees crashed down. The ground bent and cracked. The whole park was collapsing in on itself. The castle behind the Princess Pavilion tumbled onto the street, and the top of the carousel broke free and rolled down on top of it.

Big Sam, the prehistoric ground sloth, still towered over the trees of the Prehistoric Forest. He gave the survivors a slight wave with his clawed hand as he dissolved into foliage, pixels, and rubble. The mountain behind him imploded into the tunnels below.

"What do we do?" Ethan shouted over the destruction. "Where do we go?"

"There's supposed to be a helicopter." Alicia turned toward the sky. "Bloom!"

Jimmy pointed at the collapsed buildings in Nostalgia Bay. "There's a face."

Ethan watched as the buildings and rubble moved and shifted into something resembling eyes and a wide mouth. A four-fingered hand formed out of the wreckage of the Puppet Paddock.

Jimmy said, "Is that Frank?"

"No," Ethan muttered. "It's Frankie."

The enormous frog face twisted into a silent scream as it emerged from the ruins. Jimmy and Ethan moved back from the edge.

"Bloom!" Alicia frantically searched the sky. "You asshole!"

A white helicopter rose into the air behind her. It hovered there momentarily as Barclay and Maddie gestured that the others should back up. Alicia went to the boys and led them away to give the helicopter room to land.

The tower shuddered and swayed as the chopper touched down. The passenger door swung open, and the three of them ducked under the whirling blades to pile into the chopper. Alicia and Jimmy scrunched themselves behind the seats, where people definitely weren't meant to sit. Ethan plopped beside his sister, who unbuckled herself and wrapped her arms tightly around his middle.

"Sorry for the wait!" Barclay said. "The puppet place kept trying to grab us!"

"You left me!" Maddie shouted through tears. "You promised!"

"It wasn't me!" Ethan said. "I'll never do it again!"

"I'm telling Mom!"

The boy laughed dryly as he buckled his sister and himself into the same seat. "Ok!"

They all fell sideways as the tower tilted at its base. The helicopter began to slide toward the edge of the roof.

Barclay shouted. "Hang on to something!"

Jimmy leaned over the kids and shut the door. Alicia wrapped Barclay's seatbelt around her wrist.

The helicopter slipped off the tower and dropped through open air, spinning in freefall. Both kids screamed. Alarms blared inside the cabin. Barclay gritted his teeth as he pulled back on the throttle.

The ground was getting close. Alicia winced. Jimmy put his arm around her.

Whoosh! The chopper stabilized and righted itself, swooping mere feet over the thrashing theme park. Frog Tower toppled behind them, sending debris into the blades. The helicopter shook but kept flying.

The giant frog face bloomed out of the wreckage around them, howling with rage. A loosely-constructed arm sprouted next to it, swiping at the helicopter and clipping the side.

The chopper spun out. Alarms blared as it swirled out of control toward the earth.

Alicia's head slammed into the metal frame next to her.

The world went black.

24

Alicia opened her eyes. She was in a green and beige hospital room. Sunlight beamed in through the closed blinds, picking up every thread and grain of dust in the air. A monitor of some kind beeped next to her. She had an IV in her arm and a hospital gown draped over her. She felt tape on her eyebrow. There were bandages on her forehead.

Something to her side growled, startling her. She turned to find Jimmy, back in regular people's clothes, fully asleep in the chair beside her bed. There were crutches leaning to his side. He had a cast on his left foot. He snored again.

"Hey." Alicia nudged him.

Jimmy shook awake, then grinned at her. "Are you ok? They said you hit your head."

"I'm ok. Did you sit there all night?"

He shrugged. "I like sitting with you."

He leaned forward and kissed her.

"I'm supposed to tell them right away when you wake up." He stood, balancing on the crutches. "The doctors need to get all the pixels out of your system. You have to be awake for it, and it's, uh, invasive. They go up through your nose."

He made a horrific gesture near his face.

"But you'll feel a lot better after."

Alicia looked at him. He seemed normal. "How much do you remember? Of when you were–"

"Just feelings." Jimmy shook his head. "I wasn't me."

"You crawled through rubble to save me." Alicia winced as she tried to sit up, tugging at bandages she didn't know she had on her abdomen. "You risked your life to help those kids. You were you."

He smiled, considering this. "I'll be right back."

Alicia watched him leave. She found the remote for the hospital bed and used it to sit herself up. This room seemed strangely familiar. She recognized these walls—the small flatscreen TV in the corner, the one plastic plant—but she couldn't quite remember why. That was probably from the head wound.

She caught something blue and sparkly in her periphery. Her phone, in its Princess Dee case, was charging on the nightstand next to her. She'd left it in the dressing room behind the Princess Pavilion. It should, by all reason, have been gone forever, yet here it was, waiting for her, fully charged. She held the power button and waited while it loaded.

"It wasn't easy to recover that."

Barclay Bloom, Chairman and CEO of the Frank Nano Company, stood in the doorway in a fresh white suit, hands in his pockets.

"Took a whole team to find it. We got your day clothes, too, so you don't have to walk out of here in a dirty ball gown."

"Mr. Bloom," Alicia said. "How are the kids?"

"Great," Barclay said. "They're great. They're fine. They're already on their way back to Wisconsin. First time any of them ever flew First Class, including the parents. We gave them your number. I hope you don't mind."

He gestured to her phone. She checked her messages, and sure enough, there was a text from a number she didn't know. There was a selfie of Ethan, Maddie, a third kid, and two adults aboard an airplane, reclining in big cushy seats. Maddie was wearing a Princess Dee t-shirt. They all seemed happy.

The text underneath read:

Hi this is Ethan
Maddie wants you to see her Alicia shirt

Then three hours later:

Are you alive?

Alicia smiled. She texted back as Barclay continued talking.

"We're building Ethan a one-seat home version of the *Time Breakers* ride. Only one in existence. It's gonna cost us like forty grand. We offered Maddie a lifetime supply of princess toys, but she wanted a helicopter." Barclay laughed. "Guess I must've left an impression."

"Buying them off, huh?"

"Thanking them for their discretion."

Alicia took a selfie while giving a peace sign, sent it to the kids, and put her phone down, giving Barclay her undivided attention.

"And then there's you," Barclay said.

"There's me," she agreed.

"Without you, I wouldn't be here. Those kids wouldn't be on their way home. Dingus wouldn't be out in the hallway. Thanks to you, the crisis was contained, and we were able to do a full reboot."

"Reboot?"

All at once, Alicia realized why she recognized this hospital room. She'd gotten food poisoning some years back and fainted at her station. They'd brought her here, to the on-site care center. Her hand shaking, she held up the remote for the bed.

The buttons were shaped like frog heads.

"Oh God," she whispered. "We're still in Nanoland."

"Technically, we're back in Nanoland." Barclay strolled over to the window. "We made a brief stop in mainland Florida, but you slept through that."

He threw open the blinds to reveal Nostalgia Bay, bustling with activity and back to its old self. Frog Tower loomed beyond the storefronts.

"They brought us back here to flush the glitching pixels. Can't have those getting out in the wider world."

"Those aren't… those are guests." Alicia pointed at everyone milling about outside with their hats, t-shirts, balloons, and strollers. "The park's open? How long was I out?"

"Oh, not long. We lost a little over 57 hours of operation, which is fantastic, considering. We've got some great people out there."

"But I…" Alicia was at a loss for words. Only one came to mind. "Frank…"

"Frank Nano died 35 years ago. That thing you were talking to at the top of Frog Tower was software. And whatever you did, you shut it down and wiped it so completely that we could reload it from an offsite copy to its original 1989 state. We thought it might take weeks to reload, but it was back online in a couple of hours. I should've been nicer to Reggie."

Alicia stared at him. "No, I... I killed Frank."

"Yes, you did," Barclay said, "That was the first Frank, and it was running continuously for three decades, but we've got others. There's over a dozen Franks all over the world. *They* each think they're the only one and that they control the whole company. Apparently, when they find out about the others, it reminds them that they're computers, and they get... cranky. The man was always an egomaniac."

Barclay stared out the window at the glowing green head floating at the peak of Frog Tower. He closed the blinds.

"There's one in LA greenlighting movies, one in San Francisco running the streaming platform, one doing TV in New York. We've got a Frank in Tokyo, a Frank in Shanghai. Teaching it Chinese is like teaching an actual middle-aged man a new language. Ten years in, and they're still using an interpreter. With the computer! Can you imagine?"

"Well, what..." Alicia noticed, for the first time, how much her head hurt. "What happens when he loses it again?"

"I mean..." Barclay pointed at the window. "This one was on and running continuously for 35 years. The next time it breaks down like that, I'll be 82 years old. You'll be in your, what, mid-sixties? Neither of us will be here. I'll be on the moon by then."

Alicia couldn't believe what she was hearing. "What about all the people who died?"

"Everybody signed NDAs and waivers when they took the jobs or bought the tickets. Friends and family have all been paid off. All anyone on the outside knows is that the park was closed for a few days due to technical difficulties."

"What about Gertie? She's a famous person!"

"She was also an elderly, childless widow whose estate was handled directly by the Frank Nano Company. It's all taken care of. You know, presales are way up on park tickets. People got spooked by the closure. We've already made all the money we lost back."

"Jesus..." Alicia rolled her eyes.

"Yeah, I know, it's cold, but I've got shareholders and a board of directors to answer to. I don't own the whole company. I'm an employee here. Just like you."

"Not like me," Alicia muttered. Her phone buzzed against the nightstand, and she checked it. No name, no number. Just a blank space where the ID would be.

"I can see why you'd be reluctant to return to your old job, so let me offer you this instead."

He held his phone in front of her. It showed the poster for *Frogged Up*, with Princess Dee, Prince Francois, and a menagerie of frogs, which seemed a little more realistic than in the last movie. Dee's face was different.

It was Alicia's face.

She looked at Barclay. "Are you serious?"

"Nobody's got more experience playing that part than you," he said, pocketing his phone, "You are perfect for the role, obviously, but if that's not enough, you can think of it as a 'thank you' for all you've done for the company. And me."

Alicia's phone buzzed again. Another message from nobody. She clicked it.

Dream bigger.

A file was attached: *OtherFranks.txt*

"I know it's a big decision, but it's what you always wanted, right?" Barclay searched her face, trying to get a read on her. Clearly, he'd expected a more positive reaction. "Go be a movie star. I mean, it's not a present. It's a job. I can get you this one, but you have to deliver the goods."

Alicia clicked on the attachment. A series of numbers, separated by commas and line breaks. It had been a long time since high school, but she knew latitudes and longitudes when she saw them.

"All you have to do is keep this whole experience on the down-low." Barclay clapped his hands. "So! Are you ready to put the tiara back on? What do you think?"

"I think…"

Alicia set her phone face down on the nightstand.

"I think I might do something else for a bit."

ABOUT THE AUTHOR

Jack McGuigan is the author of the *Dog Walker* novels and the writer of *Agents of Paradox*, a comic book. In his youth, he made movies under the pseudonym "John McGuigan" that can be found on the internet. He lives in Chicago with his family.

If you liked this book, please leave a review! Reviews help readers find these books, which gives Jack more time to write new ones.

Sign up for our mailing list at **GorillaHouseBooks.com** for news and updates about upcoming projects!

Website: **GorillaHouseBooks.com**
Email: **jack@gorillahousebooks.com**

Made in the USA
Monee, IL
01 February 2024

3965c78f-55fb-4941-975f-5c3863aed4bfR01